MIDNIGHT IN NEW CALIFORNIA

By Lisa Renée Julien

MIDNIGHT IN NEW CALIFORNIA
Lisa Renée Julien
© 2020
Interior Formatting: C.E. Higgins (carlyhiggins on Fiverr)

Contents

CHAPTER 1

I tilt my head and use my teeth to filter the last watery drops of my Manhattan through the ice. From across the room, the server meets my eyes. I lift the glass, place my index finger on the rim, and mouth *another*.

I don't know how many I've had. I counted everyone else's but lost track of my own. My chief technology officer is on number three and a faint slur further emphasizes the mellow drawl of his southern California accent. Across the glimmering San Francisco Bay, a heavy fog slices the Transamerica Pyramid into a trapezoid.

I sip my drink, rest my elbow on the table and worry about the etiquette. Is it only impolite before dinner? I only think of etiquette on rare occasions when I am with people more powerful than me. Perhaps because the chairman is such a well-groomed, well-mannered man. He even usually wears a suit. He could easily be cast as a stock photo model—handsome and well dressed. Whisked up an escalator with a briefcase and a faint determined smile.

The server returns with my Manhattan. Her screen juts out of the elasticized pockets of her jeans-but-not-jeans pants.

Multiple pieces of tape cover the microphone piece. A faint sadness trickles through me at the thought that some people can't even afford the cute metal covers that most people use. Which reminds me—I need a new one. Though, I don't believe the conspiracy theory that the government is listening in on our conversations. Sadly, I don't think anyone is even *interested* in my conversations. I'm not anyone. Even the chairman, this mild-mannered man who no one could possibly love or hate, isn't anyone. He's just another guy in Silicon Valley worth eight figures. And my net worth is only in the mid to high sevens.

I glance at the rest of our group, their eyes pulled toward the window. I spin around. Two New California government cars lurk in front of the restaurant. We continue our conversations but steal glances. I crane my neck when the car door opens. The chairman, filing his screen in his jacket pocket, does the same.

He raises his eyebrows and glances back at me. "Looks like Josh Winston," he says. "And his wife."

"Wow," I say.

I catch a glimpse of Josh Winston's familiar perfectly trimmed brown hair and broad shoulders as he steps back while his wife emerges from the car. A government protection officer swoops in and ushers him into a back entrance, blocking my view.

The chairman turns back toward me. "Guess this is the place to be. You'd think they would have more security for him."

"Yeah I guess so," I reply.

"Have you ever met him?"

"Josh Winston? No, I haven't."

He smiles and shakes his head. "Great guy."

Outside, young government protection officers with semi-automatic tranquilizer guns patrol the area.

The chairman drinks the last of his beer and sets the glass down hard.

He pivots toward me. "Cora, the potential investor I

mentioned—we'll have a call with him next week. Look for the invite."

"Sure," I say. "I look forward to it."

The chairman stands and pats the pockets of his black suit pants. I nod goodbye and meet his brown eyes, flanked with tan skin weathered from too much time at his beach house. His large frame, paired with his mild-mannered personality, is a complete waste on him.

Rather than join my co-executives at the adjacent table, I stay and work on my drink. A wave of excited hushed tones and turned heads point me to where Josh Winston has reappeared. A few meters away, he scans the restaurant before he sits. He's taller than I would have guessed and somehow softer-looking, *fleshy*, like apparently I thought he'd be made of the cold glass of the screens I see him on. A government protection officer steps in to shield him from view. His arms crossed, his tranquilizer gun around his shoulders swings until it settles, pointing at a petite stylish woman obscenely sucking a sauce-covered chicken wing like she has no idea our Minister of Technology is seated at the next table.

I wonder what it's like to have that kind of power. That opulent importance. Even as the CEO of a small organization, no one acts like that when I walk in. There's no hush of excitement. No one sitting up taller in their seats, trying to look engaged.

Until recently, I always barreled forward towards my next accomplishment with a wholesome enthusiasm that now makes me cringe. Yet, whenever I achieved something, I was already over it, and onto the next thing. It worked for me, though, and made my day-to-day life abuzz with a kind of glow.

I leave and wait outside for my UberLone among a sea of vapers young enough to be my children. I wave away the sickeningly sweet cherry vanilla cloud lazily drifting toward me. I'd almost rather smell cigarettes. I avoid interaction, but in my peripheral vision I detect a purple-haired woman drifting toward me.

"Are you from New York?" she asks.

I make eye contact for a millisecond only. "No."

"Where are you from, then?"

"Michigan. And then Chicago. But, yeah, I did live in New York for several years," I say.

Proud of herself, she nods. "Right on." She smiles and stares into my eyes.

I regard her blankly. Her eyes linger on mine while she wraps her lips around the vaporizer and sucks in hard, mangling her face while she holds the fumes in her lungs. She exhales with a slight cough. The smoky fog reaches my nose and I realize it is not an e-cigarette, but marijuana through a vaporizer.

"Want a hit?" she asks.

"No."

Is she flirting or being a friendly New Californian? How would anyone ever know? I look her over once more. Young, short, splotchy eyeliner. Smells of dirty hair. Definitely not my type.

My UberLone arrives and I climb in. The car crawls along until we reach the autonomous-only lane.

Why do so many people ask me if I'm from New York? The first few times, I was proud I hadn't erased the grit of New York. Now, ten years after California seceded and I moved here, I wonder if I will ever belong among these relaxed, casual-chic Californians. Sometimes, to assimilate, I consider purchasing non-black clothing, but once I try them on I look like my mother. Far too wholesome and middle-aged—and decidedly un-Californian.

My UberLone rolls by blocks of modern glass and steel apartment buildings which house recent college grads for free while they work entry-level professional-class jobs. They wear stylish clothes and strut around the Shipyards neighborhood, speckled with tech gadgetry. Rolling by, I marvel at their arrogance.

The jobber colonies are markedly different. While jobbers also receive free housing and pay zero income and sales tax, they're destined to a life of service jobs and it shows in their look, their walk, and their resigned attitude. Of course, you can't generalize. Not out loud, anyway.

I settle into the plush seat. I don't take UberAir unless my blood alcohol level is high enough to overcome my claustrophobia. I like the friction of the road.

Back in the United States of America, everyone always said you could do whatever you wanted, and you could, it was true—but it was hard. Anyway, this isn't the United States of America, this is New California—the U.S. v2.0. No poverty, no guns, but all the freedom and ostentatiousness.

I chuckle, reach into my purse, and fish out a small bottle of port. My racing thoughts call for another drink. I uncap it, throw my head back, and let the medicinal sweetness burn through my body. I just want to lay back, listen to French Electro Swing, and watch the lights on the metal pylons flick by above the dark seductive boil of the water below.

Just a few hours ago, the sober reality of Monday swirled through me. The mild discomfort of my own skin occasionally detonating into a deep thud of existential dread. With just a few drinks, I was put back together. The part of me that is usually asleep—the shark, appeased by alcohol, finally relaxed rather than circling.

Then Tuesday comes and it's gone. The dread, the shark, everything. Like it was a dream, and I'm always numb, like after a good cry. Then, Wednesday and Thursday—sometimes I don't even drink, and the drive comes back and I float through the days on the high of using my mind and doing it well. Then Friday, drinks, because, really, they complement time with my wife and kids so well. Then Saturday, Sunday, the same.

Then the cycle starts again.

Right now, though, everything feels just right. The orange glow of sunset matches the lights of San Francisco below. A low fog lingers between the harsh wind and the sun-warmed air.

I need somewhere for my mind to go when other thoughts spoil. A quick jolt to ride out the mundanity. Are other people really content with normal things, like a decent enough spouse, some kids, and a job? I want the best job, the most money, the prettiest wife, smart interesting kids. Like, three girlfriends, for people on the street to recognize me—but only sometimes. Limousines, hotel rooms with stairs, vacation houses in foreign locales. But if I had all that, I'd be bored already and discontent once again.

A wave of exhaustion overcomes me. My thoughts settle and I walk through tomorrow's schedule. Work, then a talk for kids at the jobber colony. The novelty of money and success wear off, so I try to be a good person and do positive things. I need a purpose. I dread going because the last time I went, one of the parents was rude to me. She said something about brainwashing the children to be power-hungry and greedy, while regarding me with complete, withering disgust. After I left, the initial hurt and shock mutated into anger. My greed and appetite for power earn the money I pay in taxes, which in turn pays for her housing and supplemental income. And she had the nerve to insult me!

With a fresh burst of electric car might, the car leaps up the last steep hill, cementing me to the seat back. I marvel at the narrow Victorian houses, sigh, and rest my head. Once at my own narrow but imposing Victorian house, I emerge from the car, trot up the steps, and scan my screen to let myself in.

*****

Perhaps not entirely by accident, the following day, I arrive at the jobber school late. When my UberLone concludes my ride there, I am tired and unmotivated. I drag myself out of the car. The school is stylish and modern, but cheaply built, as if purchased from Ikea.

I arrive in the classroom which is abuzz with the sounds of children talking among themselves. Many crane their necks—presumably told to stay at their desks—attempting to communicate across the room. Fewer parents are present than the last time.

I smile and mumble apologies to the teacher while she guides me to the front of the room. The children continue to chatter while I plug in my screen. I scan my audience for the rude woman from last time. She's not there. Instead, there is a skinny, well-dressed guy who I presume to be a stay-at-home dad, an overweight woman with an endearing smile, and an attractive woman who makes me skip a breath.

Her legs crossed, she leans heavily on the armrest of her chair and converses with the smiley woman. She half listens, twirls her messy but sexy blonde hair, and nods. She wears a stylish blue and white striped dress and red lipstick. Her full, pouty lips form a secretive smirk in the shadow of her high cheekbones. She turns to me. Her eyes are brown and not the blue or green I expected. I smile, mouth closed, and let my eyes linger on hers before I turn away. Every time I glance back, her smile grows.

I picture her hands on me and my hands around her waist, her face close to mine, and what sorts of words her pretty lips might form. An intoxicating wave of emotions blooms within me, like the onset of hallucinogens. A line in my life. A before and an after. Without any explanation I think: *this, is one of those lines.*

Fortified by her seductive gaze, I am confident and excited

to speak. The teacher introduces me and explains I'm part of New California's Share the Knowledge program. A program in which rich assholes tell jobber children how they came to be rich assholes.

I tell them about my career. How I earned my MBA in Chicago, then moved to New York, then finally San Francisco, where I ran various tech start-ups and walked away with a payout.

With the right motivation and energy, I can be quite charming—which exhausts me, so normally I don't bother. But now, I can do anything under the spell of this woman's gaze.

Once I'm done, a few of the children run up to tell me my talk was funny and interesting, and to ask me questions.

A boy with dark brown hair and navy blue eyes approaches. "You're my *favorite* share the knowledge talker, most of them are so *boring!*" he says.

I smile. "Thank you."

I peer over the children's heads for the woman with pouty lips. She saunters toward me. She approaches the boy with the large glasses, places her hand on his head, and whispers something into his ear, causing him to nod and run away.

"Nice to meet you, Cora. I enjoyed the talk," she says.

She isn't as tall as I thought, about four centimeters shorter than me. She's very curvy, but with a slim waist that my arm feels magnetically drawn towards. Her strong yet feminine hand holds her screen which I'm surprised is not government-issued. She types something into her screen, somehow unhandicapped by her talon-like, manicured fingernails. Her perfume smells of black cherries and USD. Transfixed by the warm texture in the deep brown of her eyes, I stare at her, smiling stupidly.

"Nice to meet you…"

"Ashley."

"Ashley. Nice to meet you, Ashley."

Her eyes meet mine through her thick, dark eyelashes. I

attempt to gaze back in the same seductive way but she throws her head back and laughs. I turn away, embarrassed. I jump in surprised delight when she grabs my forearm and guides me to the side of the room. Her hip touches mine. We stop. Her eyes dart around the room then refocus on me. She clutches my bicep, sending waves of excitement through my body.

My ear tingles from her warm breath as she whispers conspiratorially: "Listen, there's this party tomorrow night in Oakland—Shipyards neighborhood. Come. I'll send you the details." She gestures with her screen. "My screen is open, send me your info."

Before I can respond, she gives my arm a final squeeze and disappears. I scramble to retrieve my screen from my back pocket. Ashley. I find her account and share my info. She accepts and I have her saved. Ashley Doral.

*****

Once I return to work, my excitement and lust morphs into suspicion and second guessing. Up until this moment, I've been absolutely certain that she was flirting with me, but could there be some other motivation for her inviting me to this party? Like, maybe she wants to talk to me about a pyramid scheme, Jesus, or some fucked up new cult? I decide to message her. I struggle with what to say. I write and delete rambling, awkward messages. Next I go for flirtatious, then brusque and professional, but delete those too. Finally, my thumbs compose a final draft and I press send.

Nice to meet you Ashley! Tell me more about this party.

I fidget in my chair. Panic rises and I second guess what I sent. Screen in hand, I pace around my office. I check if she's writing back. She's not. I tear myself away, sit down, and refocus my attention on my work screens, but find it impossible.

My screen buzzes. Anticipation surges through me. It reads "Ashley Doral." I like how her name looks on my screen. I open the message:

Hello Cora darling, it was nice to meet you too… Party is at Middle Harbor and Seventh. Would you like to pick me up?

I smile involuntarily, my eyes dart toward the door to my office to make sure no one sees. I picture her heavily lined sultry brown eyes boring into mine. I imagine kissing her red lips, placing my hands on each side of her waist and pulling her to me. I respond.

Sounds great, I'm looking forward to it! I will pick you up in an UberAir. Let me know where/when.

The message app indicates she is typing. I shakily hold my screen directly in front of my face in anticipation.

7:45 Vallarta colonies #33. Don't be late baby. We'll have fun.

CHAPTER 2

When I arrive home from work, bass notes of dance music thump through the floor from the den. When my wife Jane and I purchased our four bedroom Victorian house, we thought we would use the den for storage, but our daughter Simone actually likes to hang out there. I open the door to find her. The perfect hardwood floors and original architectural details of the rest of the house give way to cheap wallboard and carpeting. Simone lowers the volume and turns her head to me. Her eyes are wild as she focuses, like she is transporting herself back to reality from wherever she goes in her head. I examine her face, unsure if she will act like the adorable child, or nouveau angst-ridden Simone.

I flash a silly smile. "Hi Simone," I say.

She sighs. "Hi."

I lean my arm against the banister. "Where is your other mother?"

She shrugs. Her eyes squint as she glares at me. "Probably upstairs."

"How about Drake?"

"I don't know."

I nod, smile, and meet her murderous eyes. "Nice glare," I

say. "You know you inherited it from me, right? Drake doesn't have it."

She betrays herself and smiles. "Yes." She turns around and dismisses me.

Contented by my positive interaction, I turn around and ascend the stairs. I made her smile and I don't think I smiled at all the entire time I was eleven.

I re-emerge on the main floor. My fifteen-year-old son Drake descends the staircase carrying a paper bag just delivered to our roof by a food delivery drone. He greets me with the same easy grin he's had since he was a baby.

He opens the door to the den. "Simone," he shouts, "food's here."

I turn around to find Jane behind me. She hugs me and I kiss her cheek. I roam to our wet bar and prepare a bourbon Manhattan. While I'm up, I sneak a glance at my screen and check for messages. Nothing from Ashley.

I lean against the bar and sip my cocktail while my family unloads the food. They identify each dish and shift it from the delivery container to plates and bowls. Simone spoons curry onto her plate, and uses the opportunity to lap up several bites with the serving spoon. I smirk, amused Jane and Drake don't notice. Simone proceeds to sample a few other dishes before making her way to the table. Once everyone is settled, I serve myself.

"How's the food?" I ask.

"Good," Jane says.

Drake nods in agreement.

"How's yours, Simone?" I ask.

She opens her mouth full of chewed food. Her voice drips with sarcasm. "How does it look, Mom?"

"Delicious," I say.

She smiles.

"Drake!" I say. "Tell me the most interesting thing that

happened at school today."

"Nothing," he mumbles without putting any thought into it.

"If you had to pick something."

He looks upward in contemplation while Jane and I stare at him, rapt with attention.

He slaps the table. "Oh! there was something."

Jane and I lean forward and nod, urging him to continue.

"Some kids at school are planning on doing a protest," he says.

"A protest? For what?"

He's just taken another bite of his food. I wait, but already a deep thud of anxiety detonates in my chest. They're so young, kids Drake's age. As a teenager, I was already bitter and jaded; chain-smoking, drinking, and committing petty crimes. Drake's generation seems so wholesome, content, coddled by loving parents who want to do better for their kids. Parents whose own childhoods were rife with bitter divorces, and the toxic combination of too many rules but complete emotional neglect. These kids live in a country that takes care of its people, while not over-legislating personal freedom. A country that hangs onto the old American promise of rewarding those who work hard, while completely discarding the racist, classist prerequisites for that actually being true at any scale. What are they *protesting*?

"The U.S. The secretary of state is coming," he says.

My immediate reaction is that they're too young to remember California seceding ten years ago, but of course that's not true. Drake remembers.

Simone giggles. "That's not good hospitality!" she says.

I chuckle at her unexpected humor. "Yeah, well, it's okay to be rude to politicians for some reason."

Drake is not amused. "They eliminated freedom of the *press*, Simone. And there are rumors that the Dictator is going to even shut down the internet. He's anti-technology. People go to jail sometimes if they say things the government doesn't like. Haven't you ever heard of the Truth Laws?"

"I thought it was called the Sanctity of Truth Act," Simone retorts.

"Everyone calls it the Truth Laws," Jane says. "Simone, the right to protest is very important for any democracy. It gives power to people instead of letting the government have all the power. The Truth Laws oftentimes prevent people from protesting in the U.S. so it's important that people in other places protest."

I nod, only somewhat sarcastically, at her professorial tone.

Drake—at this moment so clearly Jane's biological child—chimes in: "Without freedom of speech the government has too much power, and someone could easily do really terrible things. Communication and freedom are some of the most important facets of democracy."

I nod, impressed at my fifteen-year-old son's passion for democracy which I was unaware of until five minutes ago.

"But the government here has too much control," Simone says.

Her words strike me with surprise. A confusing mix of emotions stirs in my chest, the strongest of which is annoyance.

"What do you mean, Simone?" I ask.

"They spy on us," she says. "The government protection officers are spies. They listen to people's conversations and stuff. Then when they don't like people, they shoot them with tranq guns and take them to *facilities*."

"The government protection officers are highly trained and trying to help people. They're trying to focus on real crimes, not like in the U.S. where they have real guns and arrest people for petty crimes."

"Cora," Jane interrupts, "she has a point. Let her have her own opinion."

"Of course she can have her own opinion." I turn to

Simone. "I want you to have your own opinion. I appreciate your rebellious nature. But, I just want to make sure you're not saying that out of nowhere."

"It's not out of nowhere!" Simone yells. "Everybody thinks everything is so great just because the government lets people take drugs and say whatever they want, but it's not so perfect."

"Nothing is perfect." I pause, before smiling. "Except my children and my wife!"

"Three out of four is pretty good," Jane says.

"That's like a C," I shoot back.

Simone throws her head back in a fit of unfettered laughter. Drake smiles at her.

"I think you're perfect too," she says to me.

"Aw, I love you my baby Simone."

"I love you too," she says.

"*You're* all arrogant," Drake says with a smile.

We eat in amused silence. Jane and I exchange a glance, congratulating ourselves for successfully engaging our kids in conversation at the dinner table.

"Guess who was at the restaurant I was at last night?" I ask.

Three sets of eyes regard me with mild interest.

Drake breaks the silence. "Who?"

"Josh Winston," I say.

Drake and Simone perk up in unison, truly dazzled.

"Did you talk to him?" Simone asks.

"No."

"Why not?"

"Because that would be obnoxious," I respond. Simone throws her hands in the air. I take a long sip of my cocktail, reveling in my children's full attention.

"At restaurants, it's rude to talk to people at other tables, Simone," Drake scolds.

Simone rolls her eyes at Drake then reengages with me. "Is

he going to be the prime minister?"

"Hopefully," Jane says.

"Probably," I say.

Simone gesticulates with her fork. "Then you should have talked to him and said it was because you wanted to know whether or not to vote for him." She turns to me for validation.

"Yeah, I guess I should have."

Drake suppresses a laugh.

"He was just eating there?" Jane asks.

"Presumably," I say.

"I mean—it wasn't an official appearance?"

"No, he was there with his wife."

"Did he have a bodyguard or something?" Drake asks.

"Yeah, there were officers with tranq guns, but they stayed outside by his car," I say. I stand and clear Simone's plate.

"Cool," he responds.

After depositing Simone's plate in the dishwasher, I sneak over to my screen to press the button one more time. Nothing.

After dinner, Jane follows me to our rooftop deck. A strong, warm wind snakes through the city. We sit close on the outdoor couch and gaze at our panoramic view of the dark void of the bay and Golden Gate Bridge. I wonder how many cameras can see me right now. Probably no one is actually looking, a thought both comforting and deeply depressing.

Jane nudges me. "What are you thinking about?"

I shrug and lean over to kiss her. "I love you, wife."

"I love you too."

I turn to her. "So."

She raises her eyebrows.

I continue: "So you know I had that thing at the jobber school today?"

She nods.

"Well, I actually met a woman there."

"You met a woman? Like, a woman you're going to fuck?"

"Well, maybe, I'm not entirely sure, but she was flirty and invited me to come to a party with her in the Shipyards."

"Is she a jobber?"

"Yeah she was a mom of a kid at the school."

"A jobber invited you to a party in the Shipyards? Something seems off there."

"I mean—I don't know—isn't that kind of... awful? Are you insinuating that jobbers can't be friends with the upper classes?"

"No, not at all, it just seems odd that you just met her today and she invited you to a party. Like, maybe she chose you because you're not a jobber."

I shrug. "Well, maybe she's trying to bring herself up."

"By fucking you?"

"There are worse ways."

She glares at me.

"At least I'm nice and I treat people well."

She sips her wine and cocks her head. "So you found her attractive? I'm confused. Jobbers are not your type at all."

"I know, that's exactly what I thought. But there was something about her, she doesn't seem like a jobber, something about the way she carries herself. She has an odd sort of confidence that I don't even have."

She turns away. I wait, and attempt to take her hand in mine. I retract my hand casually, like I never meant to hold her hand in the first place.

"Okay, well, sure. It's fine with me if you go to that party."

"Thank you," I say.

Jane lets me take her hand. I study her face and sense she has more to say.

"Just be careful, Cora. I don't want to make assumptions, but she could be after money or opportunities or something, and I don't want you to get hurt."

"I'll be level-headed about it."

She takes my hand. "I know you will be. You know, I have seen you notice different types of women lately, so maybe I shouldn't be surprised by this."

"Oh, really? Like when specifically have you seen me noticing women?"

Jane laughs. "Remember that restaurant we went to last weekend? When the chef came out to talk to us?"

I nod, recalling the woman's pretty smile and emerald green eyes.

Jane continues. "You chatted with her for like five minutes! And you didn't take your eyes off her the whole time! You only ever talk to strangers that long if you want something from them, or if it's a woman you find attractive."

I laugh. "Maybe I was trying to get her to comp our meal!"

Jane smiles. "That's definitely not what you were doing."

I take a deep breath and smile at her. "Well, I love you more than all of them."

"All of who?"

"All of the women," I say.

"All of them?" she repeats with sarcasm.

"Yes." I put my arm around her shoulder and pull her close. I kiss her cheek. "So, it's okay with you that I go to this party? And that I possibly get involved with this woman?"

"The chef?" Jane asks.

"No! The jobber woman who invited me to the party!"

"Yeah, sure, I mean—you don't even necessarily know that is what she wants. Don't get your hopes up."

"Yeah, okay, I won't," I say.

"And be careful. Involved can mean a lot of things. Especially with a jobber."

"Yeah, I know."

I pull her closer and kiss the dimple on her cheek. The darkness of the bay pulls my eyes toward it. I stare into the void, as if for answers. Already, after exchanging only a few words with Ashley, I feel pulled toward her by some force I can't control. It's hard to believe that this morning, I didn't know she existed. *Ashley Doral.* I turn her name over in my mind, picturing her dark sensuous eyes, her curves, her lips. *What does Ashley Doral want from me?*

CHAPTER 3

Propelled by my excitement about my plans with Ashley, I walk to work faster than usual. The air is crisp and my forearms welcome the soft thin leather of my coat. At a stop light, I fasten the highest clip. I shiver and trudge past UberLones, some empty, some with passengers.

My thoughts are interrupted by a group of American tourists blocking most of the sidewalk while they crowd around a screen trying to hail an UberAir. The loudest of the bunch gestures upward in frustration at one flying above. I glance up at the now familiar sight of the self-driving helicopter. The large propeller on top blurs into a distorted gray circle, while the small propellers below attached to landing pads modulate their speed to steer the vessel.

For my entire life, Midwestern tourists have dressed the same. Under my breath, I snicker at their high-waisted khaki shorts with New Balance tennis shoes and college football sweatshirts. The only thing differentiating the women from the men are their knockoff Coach handbags.

While rushing by I catch my reflection in the freshly cleaned window of a cafe—leather wrap coat hooked on the side.

Sleek boots, dark eye makeup—as I strut past the Midwesterners. They do not stop me. Moments later they stop a different woman.

I turn a corner and clop down a hill, the last and steepest of my commute. I try my best to walk smooth and cool despite the awkward angle. At the end of the street, an unfamiliar sight flusters me. Police tape blocks my path and a capsule ambulance idles nearby. Curious, I walk toward it. I discern the outline of a person on the ground surrounded by tranquilizer paramedics checking vitals. Awkward young government protection officers stare and whisper among themselves. Tranq paramedics hoist the person onto the stretcher and insert him into a slot in the back of the ambulance. Anxiety brews deep within my stomach at the sight of the eleven unoccupied slots. People yet to be shot.

I slow my pace and study the scene for evidence of why they shot the person. Nothing seems amiss. An officer glares at me with his hands on his hips and I reflexively stop.

A man at the edge of the alley appears in my peripheral vision, startling me. "You see that?" he asks.

"No, what happened?" His municipal worker uniform hangs surprisingly stylishly off his muscular limbs.

"So, this guy there, the one they shot with the tranq gun, he was yelling some things. Nothing too crazy, just, you know, stuff like—the government controls your mind, yadda, yadda, you know. He one of them guys. Then, you see, this motherfucker right here, he—"

"Which motherfucker?"

He gestures towards the officer staring at me. "This one right here, this officer. So, this motherfucker shot him, just like that, doesn't say anything first, just shoots."

"Wow that's crazy." I slip into the alley, away from the officers. I don't want to fill another one of those slots.

He shakes his head. "Sure was."

I meet his eyes and nod meaningfully. "Yeah."

"You be careful now," he says.

"You too."

Capsule ambulances and tranquilizer guns never fail to unsettle me. When I merge onto the sidewalk at the next street a block away, I jump when a government vehicle slinks by. I try to distract myself; thinking of work, Ashley, my kids, and my wife. Maybe the guy I talked to was wrong. There is always more to a story.

*****

At work, three young guys squeeze into the narrow stainless steel elevator joking about exceeding the 200 kg weight limit. They summon me to join them, and I nearly recoil at the thought as I rush past them to the stairs. The elevator at work, barely larger than a casket, always strikes terror in me. I picture it arriving at the designated floor, waiting for the door to open, and then—nothing. Is there a button to press when that happens? Would my screen work inside the tiny metal box? Would I slowly breathe all of the oxygen until none was left? I would panic immediately and thrash like a rabid animal in a cage. I shudder and tear my eyes away. I only take elevators if I absolutely have to, and never those tiny metal ones.

I ascend the stairs, up, up, up. I need to overcome this elevator phobia because a nine-floor climb is kind of ridiculous. At least in these converted warehouse buildings huge windows separate every floor. The total opposite of the spooky, echoing cement staircases in modern buildings. At each window, the perspective changes and the cars and people on the street become smaller and more anonymous.

With my current company, I don't feel the same level of excitement and motivation I did in some of my previous positions. I'm amazed at the extent to which my personal enjoyment and satisfaction with life are linked to my career. Since

I started this job, my focus drifts toward women and alcohol and away from work.

Today, however, I am miraculously motivated. I host a company-wide meeting which leads to a productive discussion. An ambitious but shy girl approaches me afterward to talk further and gather career advice. Throughout the office, there's excitement in the air. Like when people set the table and pick out wines for Christmas Eve dinner. I love to manage and motivate people, but the whole driving-the-ship thing with this company is the problem. I don't know where to go with this product. The trash, perhaps. Now, though, calmness sweeps through me and I am clear-headed, resolute, and certain the answer will come to me.

My screen dings. I peer at it on the windowsill and tell myself it will probably only be Jane. But when I approach, I can tell by the equally sized first and last names that it most definitely does not say Jane Broussard. I lean in close enough to read the name—Ashley Doral. I stare at the screen in awe, followed by fear of what this message might contain. What if she cancels? I open the message.

Hello Cora darling. Looking forward to seeing you tonight.

Her message soothes and resolves something deep within me. I turn toward the window, to the slice of San Francisco in my view, and clutch the phone to my chest. I respond:

I'm looking forward to it as well! Can't wait! I will see you at 7:45.

I try to shift my focus back to work but find myself typing her name into my work screen search bar. I slog through pages of people that share her name. I search images and find three that are actually of her. In a web browser, I open them up in separate tabs and study them, exhilarated that tonight I will have new material beyond these occasional texts and low-res pictures.

I check my screen for a notification, but don't find one. I pull up our messages and gasp in delight at the animated gray dots that indicate she is writing back. I wait, breathless with anticipation, until the message comes through:

You're adorable.

My heart beats out of my chest. I'm not sure how to respond.

Thanks, I like it that you think that.

She responds with a smile emoji. Smug and pleased, I set my screen down.

I head home feeling buoyant. I listen to music—something anthemic with horns and a strong woman's voice, dissonant notes, and syncopated rhythms. The sun turns gold and begins to sink. The air is cool where the shadows of buildings create the illusion of darkness, but when I am ready to take off my sunglasses, bam. I round a corner and golden stripes of light shower me. Basking in the warmth of the light, I squint under my sunglasses and trek into its blinding uncertainty. I smirk and barrel down the hill. Everything turns out easier than it appears, simpler than it seems.

At home, I greet Jane and remind her of my plans with Ashley. Grim, dramatic music courses through the floor from the den.

I make a champagne cocktail to sip while I get ready for my evening and hike up the two floors to the master suite. On my speaker, I select a gypsy jazz station. Other than the recording quality, I can't tell this music is one-hundred years old.

While I rummage through my clothes I pace the room and sip my drink. I am pleased to find all my favorite options are available. I climb into my burgundy breeches, high boots, a black silk scoop neck shirt, and my leather wrap coat. I stand in front of the mirror and reach down to touch the leather of my pants. These aren't cheap knock-offs. They're from Spain, handmade from denim spun with silk and the softest leather from some sort of premium cow.

I fix my makeup, add more eyeliner, and add some green eye shadow to the gold. I reapply my perfume, step into my boots, put my coat on and fasten the bottom two clips. I clutch the thin, soft leather sheath which swoops down and frames my neckline. I admire myself and walk toward the mirror. The coat parts and my tight pants highlight my strong legs. My boots meet my knees and lace up in the back. The solid heel is square, and about five centimeters high.

I head downstairs. Drake scrolls through his screen browsing restaurant options for dinner. I'm reminded I don't know what kind of party this is or to what extent food will be served. *Fuck.* I stuff a handful of almonds in my mouth and reach for another.

Once the UberAir lands to pick me up, a man across the street stops and gapes at it. Made self-conscious, I brusquely enter. I shoot up into the sky. My house becomes smaller below, and only moments later the bay is below me. Time races. I panic and fear I'm not ready to meet with Ashley. I close my eyes and try to relax. When I open them, I recognize the distinctive, repetitive architecture of the colonies. A gray splotch at the edge of colorful Oakland. While descending, the grayness spreads until it fills my view entirely. People freeze in place and turn their heads upward while the UberAir gently glides onto a patch of level grass near a block of townhome-style apartments. Once I land, I open the door to ease my claustrophobia and locate the idle button on the small operating screen. I peer out and do not see Ashley. Some curious kids with a smiley man saunter toward me. I retrieve my screen and do not acknowledge them. The man is chubby, and dressed in clothes so casual I wouldn't wear them around the house.

I fidget self-consciously, conspicuous standing next to a flying taxi dressed in dark leather clothing. I double check the address on the Air's screen. I message Ashley I am here and receive a reply almost instantly:

Almost ready baby.

The corners of my mouth form a smile. My stomach flutters and churns.

The man with the kids slowly approaches with a friendly smile plastered across his face. I keep my eyes on my screen and feign oblivion.

"Hey there, do you mind if my kids take a look? They just want to see what the inside looks like."

"Sure, of course," I respond. "Make sure not to touch the screen though, I already programmed my next destination."

The three kids swarm the small space, barely big enough for two adults, and—following my instructions—take great care not to touch the operating screen.

Confident the children will not hijack my UberAir, I turn toward Ashley's building just in time to see her emerge. I inhale sharply. She's more attractive than I remember. She wears heavy makeup, a stylish tight red dress, and sandals with heels. She could stand next to Jane or me and no one could tell who was from what class.

"Ah, I should have guessed you're here to pick up Ashley," the man says collecting his children. "She's always blastin' off to fancy places." He laughs at his own joke.

I smile and murmur in agreement. He smiles back, cocks his head, and wanders away.

Ashley approaches the UberAir with the same secretive half smirk she wore when she met me, like she is in on a joke no one else understands. We sit down and seal ourselves inside. Her arm rests against mine and we turn to each other and smile. Our gazes linger until our attention is redirected toward the windows when the whir of the propellers ramps up and a blast of electric power rockets us into the air. The colonies below shrink and the people become indistinguishable. She rests her hand on the denim over my knee and squeezes.

"I like this," she says.

I'm not sure if she means my pants, the Air, or me. Unsure of how to react, I let my hand wander to her leg. I can't think of anything to say because it strikes me that I do not know this woman at all. Her strong, purposeful fingers begin to stroke my thigh as she leers at me through her long eyelashes. I smile shyly and cast my eyes downward.

"Am I making you uncomfortable?" she asks. She grins, suggesting she hopes she is.

"Not in a bad way."

She laughs and her hand travels higher on my leg. I meet her eyes and consider kissing her. Instead, I place my hand over hers. We stare into each other's dark brown eyes. The whir of the UberAir changes tone when we begin to descend.

"We're almost there," I say. I wonder what would happen next if we had more time.

Her hands clutch me tighter and she kisses me on my cheek. "Yeah," she says.

I smile once again, replacing her kiss on my cheek with a dimple. Her hand rests comfortably on my thigh. I crane my neck for the familiar sights of Oakland's Shipyards neighborhood— mostly recent construction or converted single-story warehouses that contain all the charm of a parking garage.

"So, whose party is it that we're going to?" I ask.

"A friend's. Someone I actually don't know very well. He used to throw warehouse parties until the government cracked down. So now he tries to recreate them in his townhouse and it's just not the same."

"I went to one of those warehouse parties once and it just made me feel old and all the people were annoying."

She gasps with surprise. "Really, sweetie? I always loved warehouse parties. Why did it make you feel old?"

I shrug, worried that I've made her reconsider her affection toward me.

"I don't know, maybe I just went with the wrong people. Or left too early."

She nods. "Hmm, yeah. You have to go late and stay all night. And get access to a VIP room. You'd be surprised who you see at those things."

I'm surprised to find myself intimidated by her, yet thrilled by the possibility of future adventures with this attractive, apparently well-connected woman.

We land on the sidewalk. The door unlatches and we disembark. She leads the way and doesn't hesitate at all. I follow her at a slight distance, transfixed by her slow, confident stroll.

We walk in the direction of the bay and approach a new construction town home. She retrieves her screen from her purse, points it to the reader, and the door unlocks.

Inside, there are about twenty-five people. Mostly men descended from countries east and south of the Bosphorus. Everyone appears over thirty, but Ashley and I are in the minority being closer to fifty. A handsome man with a Cheshire cat grin recognizes Ashley and approaches her with his long arms outstretched.

"Ashley! Glad you made it. Is Josh coming or is he still in

D.C.?"

"He's coming back tonight," she says.

I study her face, curious who Josh is and why he went to D.C. of all places. Not much of a tourist spot these days.

She continues. "He gets in late. He'll probably just go home and see his wife."

Oh?

He shows us over to where a bartender serves drinks. "Yeah, well that's too bad—I miss that guy."

I ask Ashley what she wants and order a double Manhattan for myself.

Once I have a drink in each hand, Ashley squeezes my shoulder and leads me to the sliding glass door. The large wrought iron deck features a view of the bay with only a few obstructions. We sit on the remarkably clean patio furniture and sip our drinks. She takes my hand and gently caresses my fingers. For the first time, her face is less playful and seductive. Instead, she gazes at the bay with a thoughtful, contemplative expression. I squeeze her hand and move closer so our shoulders touch. The sun has set, but the sky remains aglow. I contemplate whether I should ask her who Josh is, but my thoughts are interrupted when a low-flying drone descends and hovers in front of us. She instinctively drops my hand and lurches away from me. Once it gets close enough to read the logo, we realize it's only food delivery.

"Is someone after you or something?" I half-joke.

She smiles. "No, not quite."

"Not quite?"

She squeezes my hand and turns her head. Not to be distracted, I lean forward to meet her gaze.

"Wait until you meet Josh, then you'll understand," she says coyly.

"Who's Josh?"

She studies me. Her mysterious smirk returns, emphasizing

the perfect bone structure of her face. She turns toward the black void of the bay and the glow from the streetlight frames her profile and dark heavy eyelashes.

"He's my co-conspirator." She turns to me and gauges my reaction. "And we're fucking."

I laugh. "Oh," is all I say. I squeeze her hand.

"He has a wife but so do I," she says.

"I have a wife, too."

She clinks her glass to mine. "To wives."

I laugh. "To wives. All of them."

"You're so funny. Funny and adorable."

I turn away to hide my dopey smile. "Thanks," I say. I caress her hand with my thumb.

When I turn back, she's studying my face and smiling. She laughs and looks down. "You're making me all shy," she says. "That's so unlike me."

"You're not acting shy," I say.

She shrugs. "Well baby, you should see how I normally behave." She caresses my knee. "You'd love it."

"Yeah I'm sure I would." I place my hand on hers, still on my knee, and smile at her mischievously.

"You have such a sexy look, what are you doing to me?"

I laugh. "Thank you. You have all sorts of sexy looks. That's like one of the first things I noticed about you, is like, this sort of sly sexy look. Like a resting sexy face."

She throws her head back and laughs. "A resting sexy face, hmm? Wow, thanks."

Her drink is almost gone and I instinctively pick up the pace to finish mine. Rarely does a woman out-drink me. I'm impressed, but it also triggers my competitive spirit. I take a swig and a rush of leathery bourbon slides down my throat, making my body warm and my breath likely flammable.

Ashley finishes her drink first. "Let's get more, baby," she says. With an outstretched hand, she pulls me toward the bartender inside.

I leap to my feet, glass in hand, careful not to spill the last few watered down drops. We approach the jobber at the bar and Ashley takes great delight in ordering a customized cocktail with a distant, patronizing friendliness. I order mine with my usual reserved politeness and we head back outside.

We approach the ledge and study the dark bay. I breathe in her scent, the perfume I noticed when I met her. *Black cherries and USD.* Was it Tuesday? And now barely forty-eight hours later I feel changed. Re-wired. Ashley picks up my hand and places it around her shoulder. She fits just right. I squeeze her bare shoulder and crave more of her skin against mine. I want all of me touching all of her. Her arm slinks around my waist. Her breath quickens, as does mine. She pivots toward me and slips her arms around my neck. My hands are pulled to her waist like magnets. I stare down into her desirous, vulnerable dark brown eyes. I taste her breath. We connect and gasp at the intensity. I caress her cheek, close my eyes, and gently kiss her red lips. She grasps me tighter, slowly, like a snake constricting its prey. I kiss her again and melt into her, hungrily tasting her mouth. She moans and pulls me closer. I lose myself. I lose time, I lose place. I don't want anything more. Just this mouth on mine, and everything will always be okay. She pushes me down on a chair, climbs on my lap, and I arch my neck to kiss her. A few times we stop, sip our drinks, continue to touch, and speak only with our eyes. My hands trace her wide hips, her soft stomach, her arms, and her breasts. She playfully slaps me across my cheek. A rush of emotions courses through me and I giggle involuntarily.

"You're hot to trot," she says.

"Hot to trot?!"

She pulls me to my feet and I follow her.

The next bit of time is a blur of witty conversation blurbs

and the woozy bliss of a new woman. We make the rounds and chat with various people, several of whom ask her about Josh. These splices of conversation give me the distinct impression Ashley's adventures out of the colonies always involve Josh instead of her wife.

Many drinks in, we're entwined in each other's arms on a couch giggling and bantering. I tell her we should make sure to drink water, and she throws her head back and laughs like I said the funniest thing ever. We talk, joke and tease—punctuated with kisses—and everything is hilarious. We're in the state of drunkenness where we cease to be aware that other people can see and hear us. I ask where she's from—Pittsburgh. I ask about her kids and what they're like. She speaks about them with pride. I ask about her wife. Her mood deflates and she nods slowly while she thinks.

"We've grown apart."

"Yeah? In what way?"

She pauses and contemplates my question. "She's changed. I've changed. And not in complimentary ways. When I met her, she was this fun, strong feminist. She had charisma and people were drawn to her. I felt like if I had her I didn't need anything else."

"Then what happened?"

"She got angrier, I got less angry. I felt like maybe I wanted things that didn't used to matter to me—money, men, other women. Things like that. But she hasn't changed. She's just become even more stubborn. But now we have all these kids so things just are what they are. I'm happy with the status quo, but everything just makes her angrier and angrier."

I hold her close and kiss her forehead. "Everything will be okay."

She half smiles, wary and amused. "How do you know?"

"I don't, I'm full of shit." We laugh.

"What about your wife?" she asks.

I shrug. "What about her? What do you want to know?"

"All the things, baby, just tell me about her. Is she as pretty as you?"

"I don't know about prettiness quantity, but she's pretty in a different way I guess. Like a different type."

"Like what type? Like super femme?"

"Kind of. She's definitely more feminine than me. But in some ways, I'm more femme. I definitely wear more makeup and worry more about my appearance."

"So then how is she more femme?"

"She wears like dresses and stuff. Like cute vintage-y dresses, you know? And I don't know, there is just like nothing masculine about her."

"Do you think there's something masculine about you?" she asks.

"Yeah, a little, but it's hard to articulate. It's like—"

"Your swagger?" she interrupts.

I shrug, full of swagger, and flash an arrogant half-smile. She erupts into laughter and pulls me on top of her. I laugh and kiss her, spreading her legs around my hips. I reach a hand under her to the small of her back and pull her closer to me.

"You seem super masculine right now," she says.

"Yeah? Do you like it?"

She answers by kissing me intensely. Conversations in our immediate vicinity stop or slide into curious lilts. Self-conscious, I disentangle myself and stand up, extending a hand to her. She pulls my hand hard, impressing me with her strength, and I fall to my knees in a fit of giggles.

She leaps up and drags me back outside to the deck and we roam to the ledge. She pulls me to her, kisses me, and rubs my cheek with her thumb. Her arm slinks further around my waist as she moans into my mouth. My eyes close. I melt into her.

Distracted by Ashley, I don't notice the figure of a man standing in the doorway.

"Ashley," he states.

I jump away from her and gasp, but keep a protective arm around her waist. His presence dominates the space, but is not threatening.

"Josh!" She reflexively lurches toward him but stops herself.

He prances toward us with a warm, friendly smile. He possesses a simple, effortless charisma. Even in the dark light, something about him is familiar. I look closer, and it all comes together—he was in D.C., the drone, his weird politician-like charisma—because he is a politician.

He extends his hand. "Josh Winston," he says. He smiles, evidently not bothered or surprised to find his girlfriend in my arms.

"Cora Broussard." I match his firm handshake and we nod hello. His hand is soft but strong.

He turns to Ashley. "I only have a few minutes, I just wanted to stop by."

She unravels herself from me and he takes her hand.

Josh Winston, Minister of Technology. I never understood how he managed to arrive at his place in society. He possesses a distinctly American wholesomeness which is not what this country is about.

I excuse myself and step inside. The unexpected appearance of Josh Winston has erased the effects of my past few drinks. While I wait at the bar, I watch Josh and Ashley's silhouettes. His tall, slim figure looms over her. With both hands on her drink, Ashley tilts her head toward him and nods. I rush back with a Manhattan in each hand and a third balanced between them.

Josh opens the door for me and chuckles good-naturedly.

"Is one of those for me, or are you two thirsty?"

I raise the trio of glasses toward him. He takes the middle one and sips it.

He asks about me and my work. He acts impressed and asks interesting questions. I tell him about the company I co-founded that created email fingerprinting which reduced fraud. I tell him about the acquisition. I tell him about my subsequent positions at various companies. I set my drink down because I realize I am sips away from a much less coherent state.

Ashley listens and holds my hand. Her other hand rests on Josh's knee. Josh and I continue to talk and I'm surprised how earnest and trustworthy I find him. I confide in him I am not excited about my current employer. He nods and hesitates, trying to decide whether to say something.

"Well, if you want to make a change, there will be something open soon at the Ministry of Tech. We're working on a project to combat jobber tax fraud. You know how it works, someone in a high sales tax bracket—say 25%, probably like yourself—colludes with a jobber and sends them money, which they use to make a purchase, leaving the jobber with, say—a 10% commission."

"Yeah, I'm aware of how that works."

"I'm sure it sounds like it might not be very interesting, but the position is to manage the whole project and the whole team, to identify use cases, like when money should change hands. Also public outreach campaigns to explain why this isn't good for society. Stuff like that. We already audit jobbers who spend more than they make, but honestly—between you and me—that's all we currently do. And all it does is move the fraud to black market USD."

"That does actually sound interesting—but working for the government does not," I say.

He nods and glances at his watch. "I understand, it's

definitely much different than tech, even at the Ministry of Tech!"
He chuckles and stands up. "It's getting late. I have to go." He
kisses Ashley on the cheek, holds both of her hands in his, and
stares into her eyes. "I hope I wasn't intruding."

"No, you definitely weren't," I say, but instantly regret
answering his question because it wasn't directed at me.

"It was nice to meet you, Cora," he says. "I'm sure we'll
see each other again. Get my details from Ashley, we should have
each other's info."

He opens the slider door and goes inside. He charms his
way through the space—waving, shaking hands, and bro-hugging.
I take Ashley's hand. I'm surprised to find I like Josh and that it is
not awkward to hang out with my new girlfriend's boyfriend.

His timing is fortunate, because I am in the state of
drunkenness where I may soon make up political opinions on the
spot. Or the point where I talk about something I've had on my
mind 'lately,' when 'lately' only means the past forty-five
seconds. Ashley meets my eyes, like she wants to ask me a
question, but remains silent.

I shake my head. "Josh Winston, hmm?" I say.

She grasps my arm and we return to the ledge of the deck.
"It's been going on over a year," she says. "It's not just an affair."

"What is it, then?" I ask.

She regards me slyly. "Don't worry about it, baby. I don't
know what it is." She kisses me again, closing the topic. "Come
on, I want to dance! Let's have them play something we know
and show these kids how to move."

I let her lead me back inside. She requests a cheesy rap song
I recall from high school and we laugh until we can't catch our
breath and tumble around the room, dancing in a euphoric
cyclone of drunken lust. She shakes her alluring hips. I grab them
in my hands, and pull her to me. With a stupid smile plastered on
my face, I hold her like she's mine. We request songs older than

our children, sing along, dance, grind and laugh while thirty-something guys stare, eyebrows raised, and sip their mocktails.

CHAPTER 4

I lurch awake. My head pounds to the rhythm of my racing heart. Dizzy and weak, I manage to sit up and open my eyes. Stripes of morning light seep through the curtains. Relieved that I made it home, I reach for a glass of water on my bedside. As the tepid liquid reconstitutes my alcohol-ravaged body, I register that I am still wearing my clothes from last night. I set down my nearly empty glass and peel off my clammy wrinkled breeches. Gaining strength, I pedal my legs through the cool, cloudlike sheets.

Jane is not with me. She probably went to sleep in another room because it appears I passed out in the shape of an X diagonally on the bed. It takes me a minute to piece together what day it is, if I need to go to work, and what I did last night.

It all comes back to me. *Ashley.* I reach for my screen—no message from her. I lay back and let the sweet memories swirl through my mind. Her hand on my thigh in the Air. That first delicious kiss. Her mouth on mine, her dark eyes, ringed with makeup, looking up at me. All those whiskey drinks. *Josh.* Josh Winston was there. How did the night end? The end is where it gets fuzzy. Where blank pools of time slice my memories into islands without context. Ashley wanted to take an Air back but I wanted to take a Lone, because even in my drunken state, I tried to scheme to get more alone time with her. "It's past midnight," she said. "I'll see you again soon, baby, and we can spend lots of time alone," she said. We took an Air. We kissed in it. We made plans—but what were they? "Tomorrow," we said. I will carefully craft a text this morning to follow up.

It was late when I dropped her off at the colony. When she got out, she caressed my cheek and kissed my lips. "I'm excited about this," she said. "You're so much more than I thought."

My mood and emotions shot up into space faster than the UberAir as I ascended into the dark fog above the bay. Now, several hours later, hungover, I am not sure what she meant.

I drag myself through my morning routine and head to work. The sun is low, but I wear sunglasses anyway. Propelled by music in my earbuds, I pivot between elation and anxiety-spiked malaise. My brain is fuzzy, like it's filled with cotton balls, but I am high on the thrill of a new woman. Minutes pass before I am aware of a smug smile plastered on my face.

More memories come back. I didn't black out. Not really. I remember arriving home and it doesn't seem like a large gap of time is unaccounted for. And yet the events and conversations I remember would have taken much less time than the length of time that actually elapsed.

At one point, we were intertwined on the couch as we laughed, flirted, talked and drank. She let me sip her drink because one of my arms was around her shoulder while the other one was down her dress. Jesus, did I do that in front of all those people? What if someone posts pictures? There were a lot of people, but no one seemed particularly gossipy or exploitative. In any case, I'm not in politics, no one cares. These people are apparently aware of Ashley's relationship with Josh Winston and the general public is not aware of that.

My stomach growls and I dream of what kind of food I will have delivered when I get to work. I am ravenous when hungover. Any kind of food can be delivered in San Francisco twenty-four hours a day. I think of capitalism and smile. Survival of the fittest. But, in New California, those unfit or unwilling can still live a dignified life—and have affairs with politicians and CEO's apparently.

Perhaps I'm still not quite sober. I'm in a surprisingly good mood. Another memory surfaces—did Ashley say her son is named Johnald? It was one of those moments of clarity in drunkenness in which I thought—*who* is *this person*? She said Johnald was the oldest, seventeen, so not the young one I met at the jobber school. But, seventeen years ago, Ashley named a child Johnald. I laugh and worry I appear crazy. I ask myself again—am I not sober, or just happy because of Ashley? I like her so much despite everything. Despite the fact she named a child Johnald, despite Josh Winston, despite a trace of anxiety and doubt that I can't quite place.

As soon as I arrive at work I order overpriced Thai food. Twenty dollars NCD for an entrée at a place with bad reviews and low sustainability ratings, but I don't care. I don't know why I even came in to work. I won't accomplish much. I shuffle through the screens. In addition to the usual assortment of emails, I find a message from the chairman of the board about a meeting in New York with the potential investors he mentioned previously. He asks when this week would be good for the two of us to talk. Monday, I tell him.

My screen vibrates; Ashley Doral.

Good morning my adorable darling woman. You're hilarious and I can't wait to see you again. Are we still on for a picnic lunch today?

Crisis averted! No carefully crafted text needed. I respond:

I can't wait to see you again too! Yes, lunch works. What time? I can get an Air and bring all of the picnic stuff.

We make plan. I decide I will leave for the day after lunch to maximize my time with Ashley.

I get back to work. This time, I accomplish things and make progress. I'm always amazed that whatever time is allocated for work is sucked up and put to use. Less time equals faster work and more time equals the same work done slower.

Suddenly inspired to motivate the team, I step into a product management meeting. At my sudden unexpected presence, Jaden, a young, inexperienced product manager trips over his words and stares at me, frozen with awkwardness. I motion for him to continue. He sputters out, and his mentor, an older more experienced woman named Kim, jumps in to summarize what he said and ask a clarifying question. I nod in approval.

"Good insight," I say to Jaden. He strains his face to conceal a smile.

"I have more research I can show you," he responds. "I'm planning on writing a whitepaper about it."

"I'd love to read it once it's finished," I say.

"Thanks, Cora," says Kim, touching my arm. The conversation continues and I smile at her, distant and professional. She's someone I know I would be attracted to if I wasn't her boss' boss' boss, and I'm perpetually asking myself if she's flirting with me, or just a nice person.

My thoughts are interrupted by a low digital groan from a simultaneous notification on everyone's screens. Raised eyebrows and gasps take over as everyone ingests the notification. I dive for my own screen.

OFFICIAL NEW CALIFORNIA ALERT: *Mobile and individual internet service appears to be down throughout the United States of America. New California intelligence is unable to confirm if this outage is intentional as part of U.S. de-digitization efforts or if it is related to some other circumstance. Expect communication with the U.S. to be difficult.*

We exchange glances. The cloud of tense silence erupts into a flurry of fast-paced chatter. Mobile and individual? It must be intentional.

I glance at Kim. She grabs my hands and holds it, under the table, and looks at me meaningfully, like we are two people consoling each other. I unravel my fingers from hers and look past her, at her mentee, Jaden. Despite his large meaty frame, he looks like a scared little boy. A surge of maternal protectiveness brings me to his side. I brush past Kim and put my hand on his shoulder.

"You okay, Jaden?"

"Yeah," he responds, too quickly. He attempts to look relaxed, but his face betrays him. He places his screen face down. "My cousins are still there. One of them is a business analyst in New York, and all the companies he works for keep getting shut down." His lip quivers.

I sit down next to him and rub his arm. "My sisters and parents are still back there. My sister lost her job, she used to work for a software company. Were you born there? Like, not in California?"

"Yes," he says. "I grew up in Long Island."

Kim stands up, behind him and rubs his shoulders. She hugs him, her breasts pushed against the back of his head. *My god*, I think, *I'll need to watch this woman.*

"Good thing you have all these pretty women here to take

42

care of you," she says, glancing up at me.

I raise my eyebrows at her and look at Jaden with horror, ready to intervene, but he's smiling and giggling. Entirely soothed by her.

The room hisses like a nest of snakes. I block them out, uninterested in the technical details of how the Dictator of my home country built a kill switch for the internet. The noise fades into an incoherent din. I take a deep breath and let it out slowly. A flimsy calmness settles in.

When I was young, in school, I was told I was lucky to be American. That we had the most freedom and stability in the world. And it was true, until I was seventeen and foreign terrorists hijacked commercial airplanes and flew them into the World Trade Center. But things went back to normal, kind of. Until a president became a dictator when he cancelled a presidential election and redefined freedom of speech.

My eyes burn and I take a deep breath, fighting back tears. It's not often I mourn my former country. Normally I'm thankful that I landed where I did, in a country that takes care of its people and freedom is complete. It's not a popular thing to say, but what we have in New California is superior to the U.S. It's like the U.S. but with all the problems solved and deadweight regulations sliced and trimmed down to the perfect utopia which pleases both the socialists and libertarians.

My thoughts are interrupted by the scent of perfume and pretty feminine hands on my shoulders. Kim.

"Cora, where are you always going in your head?"

I stand up and face her. She smiles and regards me with her pretty green eyes. In her heels, she's as tall as me.

"Nowhere," I respond.

She dismisses me with a friendly smile and reengages Jaden.

The mostly young, mostly male, team continue their

speculation. The loudest, a recent college grad in cutoff shorts and flip-flops, explains step by step how a government could manage to shut down the entire internet. The oldest person on the team—still many years younger than I—stands up and walks to the window. I ignore the chatter and observe him. Tall, broad shoulders, expensive leather oxford shoes. Hands on his hips, he scans the streets of San Francisco below. I approach and stand by his side.

"Hey," I say.

He turns to me, meets my eyes, and nods.

"Are you okay?" I ask.

"Yes, I'm fine."

"Yeah?" I ask.

"Yes. It's just—" He shakes his head. On the street below, figures gape at screens and huddle in makeshift support groups. He continues. "It's just, I don't understand. Why would they do this? Why would the U.S. president want to shut down the internet?" He turns to me, as if for answers.

"For control," I say. "To reduce the spread of information."

"But why? The U.S. was a great country! You are from there, correct? You are not Canadian?"

"Yes, I am from there. From Michigan."

"Do you understand why?" he asks.

I turn to him. His eyes plead with me. "Honestly, no. No, I don't understand. Sometimes I think I do but—" My voice shakes and I feel fragile. I gather my strength. "The Dictator just wants to maintain control. He does things like this when he thinks it's slipping from him."

He nods. "Maybe it's as simple as that."

I shrug. "Maybe." I pat his shoulder and turn to leave.

Many of my employees are so young, they were born post-Facebook. I think about my experience of the world before the internet. Everyone had to meet people at specific places at specific times. I would wait for phone calls, at home. When I called a friend, I had to ask for them because the entire family shared one phone number.

Back at my desk I try to read more about the U.S. outage online, but there isn't much besides speculation. I navigate to the contacts in my screen to find my parents' landline number. I call them but it rings several times and goes to voicemail, which plays an error message about a disconnection. An uncomfortable sense of dread spreads through me. Crippling a nation is much easier than making positive changes. Altruistic presidents accomplished nothing in eight-year blocks, but in just a few years the Dictator crumbled democracy.

My screen dings. A message from my dad:

Internet back. Hope everyone is OK.

I check my work screens for more news. The outage lasted fifteen minutes, but there are already anecdotes about the terrible things that happened as a result. Self-driving cars crashed, payments systems went down, many people are still stuck in elevators. Every article and post speculates the outage was caused by the U.S. government testing their internet kill switch. The U.S. de-digitization program is no secret.

My dad, sisters and I write back and forth on the thread about their plans in case de-digitization becomes long-term. It was a minor event, but the implied threat is not. One more thing that slowly starts to creep into life until it becomes the new normal. Deeply unsettled, I click out of the articles and settle back in to work.

*****

At the upscale market around the corner, I buy everything I

need for my picnic with Ashley. Chocolates, many different cheeses, vehicles for cheese consumption, cured meats, raspberries, champagne, port, cocktails to go, sandwiches, little salads packed in exquisite jars, and sparkling water.

Once in an UberAir, I blast off toward the colonies. The sky is entirely void of fog and the crystal clear glow of the city annoys me. I put on my sunglasses and dream of the pop of the champagne bottle. The crisp sting of that first glass with bubbles dancing on my tongue. I survey the city through my sunglasses and stretch out my legs, thinking about the fact that the windows don't open, that I can't stand. I breathe through several uncomfortable moments of claustrophobia. Mesmerized by the outline of Oakland, the hills beyond, and the momentum of forward movement, I find a thin, euphoric peace.

The now familiar identical modern gray buildings grow larger in the curved glass windshield. The rotor blades change course, stopping their forward movement. I hear the bottom propellers pick up speed while they control the descent to the ground. A gust of wind causes a slight lurch, but the vessel quickly corrects course.

I look down. Ashley calmly monitors the landing through her large sunglasses while she sips from a government issue water bottle. She wears stylish sweatpants and a tight black sweater. When I open the door, her full red lips form a grin, forcing her sunglasses to rise.

"Hi. There's not a lot of room left after this giant picnic bag I bought," I say.

"It's okay, baby, we can sit close."

She holds my arm in one hand and places the other one on my thigh. I lean forward and program in our destination; Golden Gate Park. The door latches and the rotor blade roars back to life.

"How do you feel today?" she asks.

I stretch out my legs and groan. "Well, great now that I'm

with you."

She grabs my face and kisses me on my lips.

"How do you feel?" I ask.

"The same—good now that I'm with you. Luckily I was able to sleep in a bit because Misty got the kids ready, which reminds me—I need to be back home by four thirty."

"That works out perfectly. I'm not going back to work, but I need to get home by what would be a normal time had I been at work."

She snickers "I know what that's like."

We gaze out the window in comfortable, peaceful silence, at the turquoise bay and hills of San Francisco. She mindlessly caresses my leg. Despite my delight at her presence, I'm impatient to be on the ground drinking champagne. We descend and the landscaped greenery of Golden Gate Park grows larger below us.

Once we land, we get right to work determining the best spot to place the blanket and set up the food so it is accessible yet doesn't inhibit our access to one another. Once seated, our first glasses of champagne disappear within minutes.

"This is a nice spot," Ashley says. She takes a long sip of her second glass. She turns to me. "Do you bring all your women here?"

I pause before I answer. "I don't 'have' women, really. There's my wife, and there's another woman I was involved with for several years who I split up with about a year ago. There have been a few others who have come and gone over the years, but that's all."

"That's all, huh?"

I shrug. "What about you? Is it just Josh, your wife, and hopefully me?"

"Yes, just you and Josh. So, tell me about the woman you were involved with for several years."

I try to decide where to start. "I met her when I was in my late twenties, but then—"

"Whoa! So you were together for like, what, twenty years?"

"No, not that entire time. There was like a six-year period in there where I didn't see her at all. Even when we were together, it was a little bit on and off—which was one of the problems. She would want to see me all the time, and then she would be entirely sick of me and I wouldn't see her for months. I would always just be pining for her."

Ashley caresses my face. "Aww, baby, I'm sorry. I would never do that to you. I'm not hot and cold like that."

"Like a faucet?" I say.

"What? Oh! Hot and cold, yeah, baby I'm just like a faucet that's hot all the time."

She grabs my face and kisses me. I giggle and let her tongue slide into my mouth. I lose myself in her kiss. She pauses and caresses my chin.

"I won't ever hurt you like that, baby," she says.

I kiss her hungrily. She pulls me down onto the blanket. We lay on our sides and stare into each other's eyes.

"So are you sure that she's gone for good now?"

"Yes. It felt pretty final. I used to be like her little pet. I was very submissive to her and she was kind of a mentor to me. But as I got older, I just couldn't be that to her—or anyone, for that matter. When it ended, she found someone new, someone younger."

"Ugh! How obnoxious. I won't do that either. I like watching my lovers age." She taps her manicured fingernail on my nose. "Except, no gray hair, that's my only rule. Except for guys, guys can have gray hair."

"Yeah, gray hair does look cool on guys."

"I don't know what her problem was anyway, you look great. You're, what, forty-six?"

"Forty-seven—forty-eight in May."

Ashley smiles. "I'm also forty-seven and will be forty-eight in July."

"No way!"

"Yes way." She picks up her glass. "Cheers to 1984."

I pick up my glass and clink hers. "Cheers to 1984." We drink. I grab the bottle and refill our glasses. "You look great too. Way younger than forty-seven."

"Thank you," she says.

We stare intensely at each other. Her eyes are bigger and darker than mine. If the eyes are the window to someone's soul, Ashley's are the opposite. I want desperately to go deeper and get lost in them, but they're like an armed guard. A cannon guarding a fortress that I desperately want to enter as I wonder what lies behind those walls.

"So how did you and your ex meet?" Ashley asks.

"Pshh! How does everybody meet?"

"I don't know, maybe in a classroom at a school for poor kids?"

I laugh, nearly choking on my champagne. "Good point! That's right, you and I didn't meet on the internet."

"I've never met anyone on the internet."

"Really?"

"Really. I mean, not for sex or dating or anything like that," she says. "I've just never had a problem meeting people in real life, and you just never know from a picture and a profile if you'll like someone off the screen."

"Intersting. I feel like I've always been right about a picture and profile. So where have you met people that you've been involved with?"

She waves her hand dismissively. "Wherever. If I see someone I like, I go talk to them."

"I could never pull that off."

She laughs. "You're absolutely adorable. I bet you could totally pull it off."

I shrug. "Well, I'm glad you came up and talked to me."

"Me too," she says.

"Yeah?"

"Yeah. There's something special about you, baby. Like, already I feel like this is going to be so special. I mean—maybe it's too soon to say, or make predictions, but hearing you talk about your ex, like right away, I was thinking that I hope that *we're* together for that long. Or even longer."

I squeeze her hand. Her words penetrate something deep within me, some sort of ossified hardness, and my emotions bleed out over my body. "Me too, I was thinking that too," is all I say.

She holds my hand, lays down on her side, grabs a cracker and adds a large glob of cheese to it. She puts the whole thing in her mouth and devours it without breaking eye contact, washing it down with a large sip of champagne. I smile at her adoringly.

She laughs. "What?"

"I love a woman who enjoys her food and can drink as much as I do," I say. We laugh and proceed to devour several bites of food.

"So how long have you been in New California?" she asks.

"I came right after the tech tax was announced in the U.S. A few months after that. It was literally right after secession happened, around when all the flights were cancelled and so we had to drive all the way from New York."

She nods. "Did the tech tax affect you?"

"Yeah, the company I was working for shut down. It was a start-up. I was the head of product, so once the tech tax was announced, the venture capital guys just ran. Even if they stayed in business, the personal tax increase would have hurt me. What about you, when did you come?"

"Not too long after you did. Misty worked at this upscale

coffee shop in Pittsburgh, and then all the people with money left, so that place went out of business. She kept getting jobs at other places, but each place was worse. We would have come sooner, but we wanted to make sure the jobber class thing would actually work out and all that. At the beginning it was so vague, you know they were all like 'no taxes and free housing for the lower to middle class' and we wanted to make sure it actually worked and that it would apply to us."

I nod. "Yeah I remember that. It was totally vague at first. Also it was hard to find accurate news."

Ashley laughs. "Yeah, remember when the U.S. government went on the deep web and posted all that shit that was supposedly from Kevin King?"

"That's right, I forgot about that! It was so obvious," I say.

"I know, it was ridiculous, it was basically like 'never mind everything I ever said, here is some completely new shit'—"

"—'and now my screenname is different'!" I finish.

We laugh so hard we can't talk. Ashley sits up and uses a cracker to balance the rest of the now gooey brie cheese atop.

"So are you happy with how things turned out? With the jobber class status?" I ask.

She studies my face and takes a deep breath.

"Yeah, honestly, overall I am. I'm just, not sure it's for me, do you know what I mean?"

"I think so, but how so? How is it not for you in particular?" I respond.

She meets my eyes. "I just want something more. I don't know what. I definitely don't want a career, but I want something. You know?"

I nod slowly. "Yeah, totally. I know. I felt that way when I decided to move to New California. Even if I found a job in New York—because people did, hence the massive wealth disparity—I just wanted something bigger."

"I know, baby, I think we feel the same way." Ashley takes a long swig of her drink. "Man, moving to New C, that was a crazy time," she says.

"For sure."

"I never really followed the news or anything, and I thought I could ignore it, but it just became impossible," she says.

"Yeah I knew we were fucked when the presidential election was cancelled," I say.

"Yeah baby, that's when I started paying attention."

"Yeah that was probably the point where no one could ignore it. At the beginning I kind of felt like, whatever, checks and balances are working, let's just make sure not to get into a nuclear war, but once 'fake news' was outlawed, that's when I actually felt scared."

She caresses my cheek. "Aww, you were scared baby?"

I laugh but can't help but smile at her nurturing gesture. "Yeah I was scared."

She scoots towards me and holds me close. "Let's not talk about politics anymore."

I melt into her and close my eyes. "Okay."

"These are pretty heavy topics, and it's only our second date."

"Yeah, I feel like I've known you longer. I like you a lot, Ashley, I really do. There's something very unique about you that I can't resist."

She smiles, the same smirk as usual, but less guarded, more vulnerable and almost bashful. She looks away and lets her hair fall over her face to hide it.

"Did your wife know about the other woman? Or did you live a lie for all those years?" she asks.

"Yes, she knew about her."

"And she was okay with it?"

"Yes."

Ashley reaches over and caresses my arm. "Will you tell her about me?"

"I already did."

She laughs and stares at me through furrowed brows. "When did you tell her? We just met a few days ago!"

"When I got home the day I met you."

"But nothing had even happened yet!"

"I'm supposed to tell her about people in advance, and, I knew I liked you right away so I wanted to get you preapproved."

She bursts out laughing. "Preapproved, hmm?"

"Yeah."

"I wish it were that easy for me. I rarely tell Misty anything."

I lay down to face her. We're a few feet away because the food is between us. We hold hands and gaze into each other's eyes. The champagne brings a sense of well-being, winning the battle with hangover-induced anxiety.

"Did you get the alert about the outage in the U.S.?" I ask.

"Yeah, I got it."

"It's scary, it was clearly intentional. It's like they're testing the waters to see what they can get away with."

"That's exactly what Josh said."

I sit up, alarmed. "You talked to him? This morning? About the outage?"

"No," she says. She sits up and turns away. "A while ago, about the potential of something like this happening." She crosses her arms.

"Did he know it was going to happen? Did the Ministry of Technology? What about the Ministry of Catastrophe Anticipation? What else did he say?"

"No, he didn't—I don't know if he knew it was going to happen. He doesn't talk to me about stuff like that, it was just something he said once during a normal conversation about the

U.S. Chill out, okay?"

"I'm sorry," I say. "I was surprised, I didn't—I thought maybe you had some inside information and I was curious. Sorry. I'll let it go."

I touch her shoulder and she doesn't react at all. She reaches into her purse, locates her screen and fires out a message. She scans the park, inhales sharply, and focuses on something. I follow her gaze to a government protection officer, about fifty meters away, leaning against a tree holding some type of electronic object. Ashley adjusts her position, laying on her stomach like a sniper, resting on her forearms, the officer in her crosshairs. I follow her gaze once again and try to deduce the significance. There are officers all over, all the time, especially in public places like parks and sidewalks. Why is she fixated on this one? I look around and count at least four others in the vicinity. Most patrol slowly and casually, chatting with one another or enjoying the early spring mid-day sun, but there is something unusual about the officer Ashley is staring at. He is stiff and laser-focused on the device in his hand, as if it's something that requires great concentration to operate. Involuntarily, I shiver and will myself to think of something—anything—else.

"Everything okay?" I ask Ashley.

"Mm hmm," she mumbles. She sits up, and faces away from the officer by the tree.

I scoot closer to her, put my arm around her waist, and rest my head against her neck, "I'm sorry, Ashley."

She spins around, kisses me, and seizes my champagne glass. "Chill out, it's no big deal. Have another drink, baby. Jesus, no wonder you drink." She fills my glass and hands it to me.

The impenetrable, but flirty, coy look returns. Feeling guarded, I study her, amazed this is the same woman who moments ago, opened up and smiled bashfully before moaning into my mouth through kisses.

We drink, eat, flirt, and slip back into the comfortable world we were in before like nothing ever happened. I forget the government protection officer, and her apparent fixation on him. She's probably just worried since she is having an affair with Josh Winston. Her hands on my skin fuse us together, like I am finally complete. She seems real now, like she has come to life, and every movement of hers is interesting. It's like my brain is rewired. When I'm with her, everything is fine and she brings me to a wonderful new world; one I am beginning to need.

*****

I arrive home at my usual time. The effects of the half bottle of champagne course through me like a guilty secret. Jane smiles at me from where she sits on the couch.

"I feel like we haven't talked in days," she says.

"We really haven't."

She sets her book down and turns to me. "How was your night last night? You got home late."

"It was good," I say.

She examines me. "Anything you need to tell me?"

"No, not really. Nothing much happened. We drank a lot, we kissed a lot. That's it."

"Did you have fun?" she asks.

I pause and smile. "Yes, a lot of fun."

She smiles and places her hand on my leg. "Good! I'm glad you had lots of fun."

I squeeze her hand. "I'm going to go make dinner." I leap up and walk to the kitchen where Drake stares aimlessly into the refrigerator. I recruit him to help cook. He took a recent interest in cooking, which I perceive to be related to his recent interest in girls. I make myself a cocktail and comb through the refrigerator and cupboards for the food we need. I direct Drake to boil pasta for Jane, while I cut up pork tenderloin for him, his sister, and me. Once the water is covered and about to boil, I instruct him to slice an onion.

"You've never cried around onions the way your other mother does. Even when you were a baby," I say.

He grins, exposing his perfect teeth below his thin lips. "I guess that means my eyes are pretty tough."

I admire his handsome face and recently cut short hair. Previously, he had a curly man bun, then a fauxhawk, and now a more grown-up man haircut.

The sperm donor we used for both of the children described himself as "extremely outgoing." Drake definitely inherited this from him. Simone did not. Drake possesses an easy smile and an infectious happiness. He loves to charm people and make them like him, which they always do immediately.

He presents the sliced onion to me with a proud smile. He is always impressed with himself for simple tasks.

"It's perfect, thanks Drake," I say.

"Can I be the one to actually cook the stuff and you can tell me what to do?"

"Sure—start with some butter in the pan and put it on medium."

I proceed to guide him through the steps. He sautés the onions, adds the mushrooms, balsamic vinegar, other spices at my whim, and finally the heavy cream, while I stand next to him and sauté the pork in butter. I drink my whiskey to keep my hangover at bay. The food smells delicious.

Simone stalks in like a wolf to oversee the dinner preparation. She stands behind me and peers over my shoulder to watch the pork turn from pink to brown in the sizzling butter. I meet her gaze and smile. She glares and stalks away. She is beautiful, and unaware of this. She hasn't reached the point in womanhood where you need to understand what you are, harness that power, and fucking own it. Growing into attractiveness is so much simpler for men. Everything was always easy for Drake. He is handsome, smart, charming, privileged, and universally well liked. Simone is exquisite and complex. People on the street avert their eyes when she walks by, like they saw something tender and exposed. I went through an awkward phase between the ages of ten and thirty and I hope it doesn't last that long for Simone.

We sit at the table. I serve glasses of wine to Jane and me. The food is delicious—creamy, sweet, and savory. The wine is dry, oaky, and pairs perfectly. Simone covers her mouth trying to suppress laughter.

"Simone, what's so funny?" Jane asks.

Simone throws her head back in a fit of giggles. "Nothing," she says, "I just thought of something funny, it's hard to explain."

I continue to observe her and try to figure it out. She smirks, while managing to suppress her laughter for the moment.

"Now I'm really curious. Will you please tell me, Simone?"

She bursts into another fit of giggles. "The sauce is the same color as the wall."

We each examine the wall and politely acknowledge that yes, the sauce is in fact the exact same color as the wall.

"I'm pretending to eat paint, but it's delicious," she says.

"Thank you." Drake and I accept the compliment in unison.

She reminds me so much of myself when I was her age: odd, wise beyond her years, but not yet void of the innocence and joy of childhood. I examine her as she inhales large bites of food. An amused smile brightens her face, something that is becoming less common as she ages.

From atop the counter, my screen vibrates and dings. I don't get up to check it because I can't break my own rule of no screens at the dinner table.

"Is it my turn to do the dishes?" Simone asks.

"Yes, I did them yesterday," says Drake.

"Ugh!" Simone drags herself and her bowl into the kitchen. With my head cocked and fork frozen in the air, I watch her wince while she slowly opens the dishwasher and deposits the plate, as if the task requires great physical effort.

"Great job, Simone, keep it up! It will be over very quick!" I say.

I bring my bowl to the sink, discreetly checking my screen on the way. Ashley. A jolt of exhilaration strikes me when I open the message to find pictures of her. I smile smugly and set my screen down, excited to study the pictures later.

Simone comically drags herself through the task of placing each dish in the dishwasher, as if each one is extremely heavy. Upon completing the task, she promptly runs away and descends into the den while Jane wipes down the counters. Drake and I sit on opposite ends of the couch with our screens.

The first of the two pictures is a sultry selfie captioned: "this is just for you," with moody lighting and lots of cleavage. In the second picture, with her children in the jobber colony park, a wholesome smile lights up her face and she wears less makeup. Her oldest son, the seventeen-year-old—who I recall is named Johnald—towers over her and drapes his arm around her shoulders. Her arms are wrapped around the younger two. I study her children and try to determine which ones are hers and which are Misty's. It occurs to me I don't know what Misty looks like. I add Ashley on social media and receive a notification that she accepts moments later.

Time floats by serenely swiping through picture upon picture of her captivating face. Her dark eyes, which give away nothing, her cheekbones, and her sly smile. I make sure not to like any but the most recent photos.

I find a photo of Ashley with Misty. Misty's eyes are brown and her hair is wavy and graying. Pale, leathery skin drapes around a permanent scowl. She's not unattractive. In fact, she distinctly looks like someone who *used* to be attractive.

I zoom in on her face and a sickening anxiety surges through me. I match her features to that of a woman from a bad memory. *I met her.* I recall her cold eyes piercing mine while her thin lips spewed vitriol. Misty is the rude woman from the first time I visited the jobber colony, the reason I dreaded going back the day I met Ashley. It wasn't so much what she said, but the attitude behind it. I took time out of my day to volunteer, and she approached me with such hostility. I felt wounded, hurt and confused.

I think this all through. The rude woman is Ashley's wife. Ashley told me they had grown apart, partially because Misty had become so angry. Something about it doesn't sit right with me. Again plagued with anxiety, I pour a tiny amount of bourbon over ice and sit down with it in the living room. I place my screen face down and do nothing but drink, letting the whiskey roll down my throat to soothe me. I close my eyes and recall her soft lips on mine, the taste of her mouth, her smell. The look of constant amusement in her dark impenetrable eyes. I forget about Misty, about Josh, about Ashley's sudden distance at the park, and slip back into the euphoria that can only come from a relationship with a new woman.

CHAPTER 5

I contemplate my relationship with Ashley—the anxiety about when I will see her again, how often I should message her, whether she craves me the way I crave her. Our meeting, now a clear demarcation in time, created a before and an after. I am both impatient to see her as soon as possible and worried she might want to see me too much. My worries are alleviated when I receive a message from her Saturday afternoon.

Hi sweetheart, can't stop thinking about you. Any fun plans for the weekend? I'm just relaxing with my kids and wife. I imagine you're doing something much more fascinating. I really want to see you again soon, does Tuesday work for you? I feel like I need to kiss you again NOW! But unfortunately Tuesday is the soonest.

I respond:

No, nothing special planned for the weekend. Yes! Tuesday

works out great. Did you have anything in particular in mind? Do you want me to make dinner reservations somewhere? I also feel like I need to kiss you again as soon as possible. Tuesday sounds SO far away!

The scrolling gray dots indicate she's typing. I stare at my screen and await her response. Then:

I know, baby, it does sound far away. I miss you already. Yes, please make dinner reservations somewhere.

Armed with plans with Ashley, I am jubilant and uncharacteristically content. I wrangle my family and suggest we go to the park to play croquet. Drake, my good-natured boy, is always up for any sort of competitive game. Simone, predictably unpredictable, is wildly excited.

We set out for the park. The air is warm and a thin veil of fog covers the bay, but up here in Pacific Heights, the sapphire sky is clear. I take pictures of my family parading down the street, with the bay and the bridge intertwined with fog behind us. I take one while Drake chatters in mid-sentence. One of Jane who smiles and looks hot and retro in her cat-eye sunglasses. Another of my girl Simone with her expression of distant wonder. I post a few to social media and imagine Ashley enlarging them on her screen.

I am struck with a jolt of pride for who I am, who I married, and the children we produced. We strut forward, but yield to others on the sidewalk and shuffle the order in which we walk. I'm next to Simone, Drake, then Jane. Simone skips back to be by me and I put my hand on her shoulder and rub her back.

We arrive at the park and I delegate the setup of the game to Drake, who uses his screen to figure out the exact length which must go between the croquet arches. To the south, a few kilometers away, several large news drones hover above the buildings. Below them, a thick swarm of personal drones darken the space.

"What's going on over there?" Simone asks. Drake obliviously continues to setup the game while Jane seeks answers from her screen.

"It's a protest," Jane says.

"Of what?" I ask.

She scrolls through her screen. "The Truth Laws in the U.S. The U.S. Secretary of State is here today."

"Is this the protest Drake was talking about a few days ago?" I ask.

Jane shrugs. "I suppose."

Drake trots up to us with his arms full of croquet mallets. "Are we ready to play?"

Simone and Jane shrug.

"I'm ready, Drake!" I say. "Come on everyone, let's play."

Simone and Jane reluctantly tear their eyes away from the drone swarm and pick out mallets from Drake's arms.

I choose the black mallet and go first. I nearly make it through the entire course in one go. Drake goes next. He walks first to the exact point he wants the ball to land and takes a deep breath before each stroke.

Simone and Jane stand next to each other. At eleven years old, Simone is already taller than her non-biological mother and will likely surpass my 1.74 meters. She crosses her arms and leans moodily to one side. Jane's attention vacillates between the croquet game in front of her, and the drones still parked in the air a few kilometers behind her.

Drake misses a shot a few strokes behind me and stalks off in frustration. Simone, now absorbed in her screen, misses her opportunity to go next. Jane goes and only gets the ball through the first two stakes.

My attention is ripped away when the usual buzz of the city takes on an ominous tone in the direction of the drones. A roar akin to an independence day finale crescendos into a citywide gasp of terror. A moment of near silence is followed by the howl of sirens in all directions. My stomach drops and I gasp like a death rattle when a low-flying capsule ambulance drone flies overhead. I run toward Jane, and place my shaking arm around her shoulder. Simone and Drake huddle with us.

I get behind Drake and rub his arms. Inexplicably, a memory of him as a child floats into my head. Drake, age two or three, in my arms. Sitting on my right arm, my left arm around him. His arms around my neck. We'd walk and talk, his head at my same level. I'd make him laugh, too charmed to worry about the strain in my arms. Him now, his arms, his ears, and neck. If I had skipped through time and fast forwarded to now, I would know my son immediately.

The memory is swept away in the chaos. I look up from Drake's shoulders. The air traffic system grounds the personal drones. All at once they scatter, sharpening the focus of the buildings they just obscured. The news drones rise further into the air and the capsule ambulance drones swoop in and disappear below the buildings as they head toward the ground.

Simone and Jane crowd around their screens and exchange info. Drake stares at the sky, in front of me, arms hanging limply at his sides. I examine his dark gray-green eyes and try to read his expression. I hug him and he buries his face in my shoulder, shaking.

Simone holds her screen up. "They're shooting people!" she exclaims.

"With tranq guns," Jane adds.

I gasp, wanting to un-know, to suspend my disbelief, but over Simone's shoulder, I read the headline: *Government Protection Officer's Open Fire on Protesters.*

In my deep fear and sadness, I resort to logistics. "Where? Why? Like, a lot of people?" I ask.

"You saw all the ambulances," Jane says.

"Tons of people," Simone says. "They're just doing it to everyone, all of the protestors. Like in the U.S. when people go in places and shoot everyone."

Jane is shaking with anger and nearly crying. Her voice shakes. "It was the government. The New California government. They just opened fire on all those protestors."

Drake unravels himself from my grip and begins collecting the croquet arches and mallets. He takes large steps and roughly places everything in a pile. I place my arm around Jane's waist and hold her. The ambulance drones have landed and police helicopters now hover just high enough for us to see. Jane leans against me and I kiss the top of her head. I tighten my grip and feel her relax in my arms.

Drake slings the large sack of croquet equipment over his shoulder and we solemnly follow him toward home. Capsule ambulances, now full of people, begin to exit the drone swarm and fly with sirens blaring toward hospitals and medical facilities. Several grounded UberAirs distribute themselves on empty patches of sidewalk, road, and parks. A high pitched screech blares from my screen and emanates throughout the city.

OFFICIAL NEW CALIFORNIA ALERT: SAN FRANCISCO: *All personal and commercial aircraft including, but not limited to, self-driving helicoptors, personal drones, and delivery drones are grounded until further notice in the city limits of San Francisco. All non-government workers within one kilometer of Civic Center may not go outside until further notice. Please check newcalifornia.nc for updates.*

Jane, Drake, Simone, and I read the alert, put our screens

away, and solemnly continue down the street.

At home, I fix myself a bourbon Manhattan, sit on the rooftop deck, and watch the chaos continue. I scroll the news to piece together what happened. What was different about this protest that made the government protection officers open fire? I check Prime Minister Kevin King's blog. There is only a vague statement that they are looking into the situation. I scroll through social media and find a link to a blog from a guy who was there when they started shooting. I read it hungrily. According to him, there was a coordinated attack from a group of teenagers who tried to storm the Capital Building. He saw a girl throw a brick at a government protection officer at the exact second that another girl did the same. Moments later, a group of teenagers tried to storm past the wall of officers. They were successfully wrestled back, but then another group of teenagers stormed through— that's when they opened fire.

I find a video and click on it. A young girl with curly chestnut hair who resembles Simone screams into a megaphone: "I WILL CONFRONT THE TRAITORS OF THE COUNTRY OF MY BIRTH! LET ME CONFRONT THE TRAITORS OF THE COUNTRY OF MY BIR—" She is shot with a tranquilizer gun and faints. A government protection officer gently catches her. He picks her up like a baby, protecting her head, and carries her toward a capsule ambulance.

Her emotional intensity, the immediate smothering of it, and the graceful way she melts into the officer's strong gentle arms, weakens every bit of ego I have. I try my hardest to fight back tears, but they leak out. I sob silently into my palms and then manage to pull myself together. I walk to the ledge of the deck and lean my arms over it. Whiskey in hand, I look at the spot where the events on the video took place. News drones illuminate the surrounding buildings.

My thoughts are interrupted by a notification on my screen.

Jane Broussard.

Come downstairs.

Alarmed, I jump up, run toward the narrow staircase, and trot down the steps. On the top floor, I fling myself down the familiar wooden stairs. On the ground floor, Drake is on the couch holding his head in his hands. Jane rubs his back. Simone stands by the window, her hands on her hips.

I sit down next to Drake and put my arm around him. "What happened?" I ask.

Jane takes a deep breath. "Nothing is certain yet," she says, "but Drake saw a post about a girl he knows, a friend of a friend, who was shot."

Drake gestures with his screen. "She *died*, they shot her with the tranq gun and she *died*."

"What?" I ask. "How could that happen? Weren't there tranq paramedics?"

Drake rubs his face with his hands. He stares at the wall, his large, expressive eyes, crazed with emotion. Simone turns toward me and I motion for her to sit down with us. She sits next to me and I place my other hand on her shoulder.

Jane meets my eyes. "They think she had an allergic reaction, and that the tranq paramedics didn't get to her on time."

"Who was she?" I ask.

"Her name is Emma Lopez. Drake met her a few times through his friend Noah."

"Oh my god. I'm sorry Drake." I pat his back. "Is it in the news yet? Is it for sure?"

"Noah messaged me," Drake says. "He heard from Emma's sister."

I hold Drake close and run my hands through his hair. He

calms down and leans back on the couch. Jane finds an article on her phone and announces that the death is confirmed.

Simone stands up and paces around the room, her brow furled. "Why would they shoot a kid? Was she Drake's age?"

Jane responds. "She was fifteen like Drake. When they shoot people with tranquilizer guns, they don't expect them to die or become permanently injured."

"Yeah," I say, "that's why they have tranquilizer paramedics that rush over every time someone gets shot."

Simone throws up her hands in frustration. "But why couldn't they save her!"

"I don't know Simone," I say. "It's very unusual, there have only been a few people that have died from tranquilizer guns for the entire time New California has existed."

Jane turns on the projector with her screen. "The Prime Minister is making a statement."

Suit-clad commentators speak into microphones at the scene of the shooting. They review what we know so far. A picture of Emma Lopez fills the screen. I look at her young smooth skin, brown curly hair, brown eyes, and wide rebellious smile. A sick feeling washes over me. She is the girl from the video I saw earlier. Her words come back to me: *let me confront the traitors of the country of my birth.*

Prime Minister Kevin King walks towards a podium. Normally flanked by officers with tranq guns, he is conspicuous without them. Walking just behind him is Josh Winston on one side, and the Minister of Security on the other. Once at the podium, the camera zooms in on Kev King. His broad shoulders fill the screen while the batman-like jawlines of the two taller men flank him. I examine Josh's mouth and recall his full pink lips forming my name when I met him. The camera pans out, revealing Josh's face. He stands stoically. Kevin King, known for starting speeches with long dramatic pauses, scans his audience with his serious brown eyes. He turns to each man beside him. Josh smiles and pats his back. Kevin King leans forward.

"Today, at approximately 3:45 p.m. a protest took place at the New California Government Plaza building against the visiting U.S. Secretary of State. Most protesters were peacefully exercising their right to free speech. A small group, however, were not peaceful. A small group launched a coordinated attack to attempt to break past the government protection officers and gain entry into the building where the U.S. Secretary of State meeting was taking place. As a result, the government protection officers were forced to fire tranquilizer guns on those protesters. Due to the close proximity of the protesters, some of those that were hit were not among the group targeted. One of the protesters hit was a fifteen-year-old girl named Emma Lopez."

He pauses dramatically. Josh places a hand on his shoulder.

"Despite the best efforts of the responding tranquilizer paramedics, Emma did not survive."

A gasp rings out among the audience. I glance at Drake and Simone on either side of me on the couch. They stare at the screen with their full attention. It occurs to me that I haven't mentioned to any of them yet that I met Josh Winston just two days ago. Now is definitely not an appropriate time.

Kevin King continues. *"I am deeply, deeply sorry to the family and friends of Emma Lopez. I'm told she was an intelligent, spirited, and promising young woman. Her loss will be felt by many."* He wipes away a tear. Behind him, Josh strains his face fighting back tears.

"We are conducting a full investigation into the situation. So far, we have matched the tranquilizer dart to the government protection officer who shot her. We know that the firing of the dart successfully provided GPS coordinates to a capsule ambulance, along with an urgent call for help. Despite rumors to the contrary, we also know that the tranquilizer ambulance responded, arrived,

and attended to Ms. Lopez within the required timeframe.

"There are still many unknowns. We will investigate this until we have every piece of the puzzle put together and we will be fully transparent to the public throughout that investigation.

"Additionally, I will work with the two men standing behind me to assemble a tranquilizer gun task force. The three of us will personally work with that task force to improve the policies surrounding when tranquilizer guns should be fired, what we have in those guns, and how we can utilize technology to optimize response time and identify those individuals who are likely to have a potentially fatal response to a tranquilizer dart. We will do our best to ensure that this never, ever, happens again." He pauses and scans his rapt audience. He grips each side of the podium with his muscular arms.

"It's worth pointing out that in the U.S., the police fatally shoot thousands of people each year. Here, in New California, in ten years only thirteen people have been killed by tranquilizer guns. We wish that number was zero, and we vow to do everything in our power to ensure that no one ever dies again at the hands of a New California government protection officer.

"Again, I want to express my sincere remorse to all of the people who were lucky enough to know young Emma Lopez. I am deeply sorry for your loss."

Kevin King turns to leave. Armed government protection officers appear behind him but Josh shoos them away and Kevin King walks away unprotected.

I scan the faces of my family members on the couch. They continue to stare at the screen. Jane turns off the screen.

"Well," Jane says, "he said all the right things."

I nod. "How are you feeling, Drake?" I ask.

He shrugs. "I don't know. I mean, I only met Emma two times. I really didn't know her very well."

"How well did Noah know her?" I ask.

"They were dating for about a week but then they were just friends."

I rub his shoulders. "I know it's still upsetting, Drake. It's always disturbing when someone you know dies, especially when they are young."

He nods and lets me hug him.

I turn to Simone. "Simone, how are you feeling?"

She shrugs. "I'm okay."

We slink away to opposite corners of the house. I can't stop thinking about how young Emma Lopez was, that Drake knew her, that she looked like Simone. I sip bourbon on the roof in silence, hugging a cardigan tight around my torso. The city is cold and quieter than usual, weighed down by the gravity of what happened today. My arms begin to feel numb from the alcohol in my bloodstream. I drag myself down the stairs and into the master bathroom. I stare at my face in the mirror—grim, and malleable from drink. Too tired to return all the way to the kitchen, I hide my empty glass under the sink. I crawl into bed where Jane's slim figure rests. I wrap my arms and legs around her and draw comfort from her familiar shape.

CHAPTER 6

Still fragile from the previous day's events, Jane and I hold hands in the UberAir on our way to a restaurant in Oakland. The vessel glides smoothly through fog aglow from the last trace of sunset.

"Did I tell you I met Josh Winston?" I ask.

"You mean when you went out for work and he was at the restaurant?"

"No. A different time, and I actually met him and hung out with him."

"What? Really? When?" Jane says.

"At the party I went to with Ashley."

She looks at me, confused. I turn toward her, excited for a chance to talk about Ashley.

"He actually was there to see Ashley. They're sleeping together, I guess," I say. I examine Jane's face, moonlit in the UberAir.

Jane appears both intrigued and disgusted. "What? Is she just fucking any professional class person who will have her?"

71

"No, it's just me and him. Please don't tell anyone about Josh, it's supposed to be top secret, I think."

The UberAir starts to descend but pauses mid-air to allow other Drones to pass underneath.

"Besides," I continue, "isn't it kind of cool that your wife's girlfriend's boyfriend is Josh Winston, possible future prime minister of New California?"

She glares at me, but barely suppresses her laughter.

We land in Oakland Shipyards, close to the location of the party I went to with Ashley. The restaurant is obscenely modern, clean, and sterile. Like an upscale medical facility. The host, a very young man with clear blue eyes and slicked-back hair, greets us with a snooty smile. He seats us at a table in the back corner, while a group of women half my age decorates a table by the front window. A young server, who could be the identical twin of the host, takes our drink orders. An old fashioned for me and a bee's knees for Jane.

"Drinks from the old country!" he says.

I wonder, horrified, if young people now view classic cocktails the way I saw martinis that look like cleaning solutions when I was their age.

"I feel like you and I haven't been out together alone in a while," I say.

"Yeah, but it's fun to bring the kids out with us sometimes," she says.

"At a place like this though, kids look out of place, even when they're tall and well-behaved like Drake and Simone," I respond.

We sip our drinks, enjoying the orderliness after the chaos of the weekend. I note with relief that other than the women sitting by the window, most of the patrons are around our age or older.

I meet Jane's eyes. "How do you think Drake's doing?"

She takes a deep breath. "I think he's handling it okay. He seems level-headed about it."

"Yeah," I say. "He's not being dramatic about it."

"And he's talking about it. I think that's good," she says.

"Definitely. I think we need to keep the conversation going. With Simone too. She has a lot of questions."

"I agree. Sometimes with things like this, the negative feelings and anxiety keep coming back."

The server approaches, produces a sleek tablet from his stylish apron, and takes our order.

"It's just so tragic," I say.

"The shooting?"

I nod. "She looked like Simone." My voice breaks unexpectedly. I collect myself and take a long sip of my drink.

Jane reaches across the narrow table and places her hand on mine. "She did look like Simone, and she was Drake's age."

"I don't even know what to say about it. I mean, sure, yeah, barely anyone has died from tranq guns, but that doesn't make it okay."

Jane leans forward. "Well, like I've always said, why do so many officers need guns at all? They are way too quick to use them. They shoot people fifty times more often than in the U.S.—"

"But almost all of the people are totally fine," I interrupt. "They literally go home within twelve hours. If they're not arrested."

"But why shoot innocent people in the first place?"

"Yeah, I guess there's that..."

Jane raises her glass to mine and laughs. "Guess we agree now on tranq gun usage!"

I smile and retract my glass. "No! Your opinion is still much more liberal than mine on this topic."

"My standpoint is liberal and you think they should shoot

people with tranq guns liberally."

"Correct," I say.

We laugh. I pick up my glass and toast to that.

An awkward jobber in a chef hat delivers our first course and scurries away. Our server approaches, clasps his hands, and explains the food in detail while making direct eye contact with me the entire time. I nod and alternate my gaze between him, Jane, and the food.

Once the server leaves, Jane regards me with an unreadable expression. "I want to talk about Ashley," she says.

This provokes both a sense of worry and excitement. I would love to gush about Ashley, but guess Jane would prefer a more serious conversation.

"Okay, what specifically?" I ask.

"I thought about it a lot, and it makes me uneasy. I haven't said anything yet because I was trying to figure out what was causing these feelings."

"So did you figure it out? Why do you think you're concerned?"

"I think I just need to understand what it is you see in her. I'm not against it, but we haven't had a chance to talk about it. From what you told me about her, she doesn't sound like your type at all. And the thing with Josh Winston, that's just weird. Something is off—I feel like I'm missing something."

Jane's words evoke something I've been largely ignoring— a deep, resonant doubt. *Something is off.* A montage of Ashley's strange behavior plays in my mind: the way she looked at the officer in the park, how she reacted to the drone. *Josh Winston.* But just as quickly, I dismiss the thoughts and replace them with more pleasant ones. Ashley opening up to me, laughing, kissing me deeply. The bottomless contentment and relaxation her presence elicits, like the moment just before falling asleep. Her smell, her voice, the way her physical presence in my life is both unfathomable and as solid as a marble statue.

I pause and calculate my response to Jane. "I agree that she's not my type, at least my usual type, anyway. I think what I like about her is pretty simple. She has this sultry seductiveness about her and she is extremely attractive. There is also something kind of secretive about her that makes her intriguing." I contemplate what else it is about her. "She's also confident and well spoken. You would think she's from the professional class, just by the way she dresses, talks, and carries herself."

Jane wants to see a picture. I pull up her profile on social media to show her. Jane agrees she is attractive, which is unusual. We rarely agree on women.

"How does she know Josh Winston?" Jane asks.

"I don't know. I haven't had a chance to ask her. We've only seen each other a few times."

"Okay, well, let me know if you find out, I'm really curious. I think I just have a lot of anxiety right now. Not just about this, but the outage on Friday really bothered me. That the Dictator can do that. Then of course, the shooting."

"I know, it's fucked up."

"Whenever I hear about problems in the U.S., I'm thankful that we don't live there anymore. But now with this shooting, it's making me wonder about everything. What if there's an internet outage here? What if it happens and we can't access our money?"

I shrug. "It scares me too, but unlike the U.S., in addition to individual and mobile internet, we also have satellite redundancy."

"But any of that could go down. In the U.S. it was all at once. Individual and mobile. They just shut it off. We're so reliant on the internet."

"I know. I worry about it too."

"We're the only country in the world that doesn't print currency," she says.

"I know," I say. "Maybe we should consider getting some black market USD, or just bringing some USD back next time we go."

"That just seems so paranoid, but I thought the same thing. Maybe not black market USD, but we could bring some back. I like that idea."

"We could just bring the maximum amount back each time we go and then hoard it. Regardless of what we're doing it for, it's so low in value right now that we could probably get a really good exchange rate."

"Yeah, it's probably a good investment. Too bad we don't have plans to go."

"Oh!" I say. I lean forward and hit the table. "I actually might have to go to New York soon, to meet with some potential investors."

"Investors? Do you think there might be an acquisition?"

"Yes, there's the possibility of an acquisition, in which case I will of course get a payout and leave."

"How likely do you think that is at this point?"

"I have no idea. I don't know anything about these investors yet. I just know I'm probably going to see them in New York. I'll make sure to bring back USD when I go."

Jane nods. "What about more pesos? Realistically Mexico is where we would go," Jane says.

I consider this. "I think it's a good idea for us to have lots of cash on hand in pesos too, but also Canadian dollars and Euros. The last time we exchanged money, it was years ago, when our financial situation was different. We can spare way more now."

"Yes, I like that idea."

"Remember," I say, "do not tell anyone. An interesting anecdote about the state of the economy or political situation can quickly become someone else's robbery scheme, especially if things do become desperate."

She shakes her head. "That's extremely upsetting."

"I know, but not telling anyone includes the kids. We've set ourselves up to be okay, no matter what happens."

We enjoy our next course in quiet contemplation: USD for security, possible new job. The server seats a man and a woman at the table next to us. I observe them, solemnly studying the menus, and try to guess their situation. Awkward first date? Planning an intervention for a shared loved one? At the window, the roar of laughter from the table of young women ceases when the loudest disappears into the bathroom, and the others whisper, staring at the door she just went through. Beyond them, outside, an orange streetlight washes the streetscape in a still fiery glow, like an oven. The empty space on the street in front of the restaurant disappears when a large black government car prowls in and stops. An irrational wave of panic washes over me. Jane whips her head around to see what I'm looking at. A government protection officer steps out of the car with a tranquilizer gun over his shoulder. He checks something on his tablet, looks at the sign of the restaurant, then walks down the sidewalk out of view.

My breath quickens. We exchange uneasy glances. The long, shiny body of the government car lurks like an animal of prey next to the small electric cars around it.

"It's different now, seeing government protection officers," Jane says.

I nod. "Yeah I guess that's all it is. It just feels more ominous."

Jane cocks her head. "Did you think it was something more?"

I study the government car: the utilitarian but classically sleek design, the high-performance tires ready for a chase. "No, no, it's fine."

*****

When I stand up to leave, I feel afloat and unbalanced from my drinks. I place my hand on Jane's back while we exit and nod politely to the jobbers working there. Upon opening the door, I am brought back down to a state of mild anxiety by the presence of the government car still parked outside. The streetlights cast a yellow glow over its shiny curves. In this edge of Oakland, the sidewalks are mostly empty, but a lone pair of heavy footsteps rings through the night air behind us. The distinctive sound of steel-toed boots on concrete transports me back to my old life in Chicago and New York. Once at the UberAir pickup point, we stop and turn to identify the sound. It's the government protection officer. The streetlight silhouettes his tranquilizer rifle and wide imposing frame. We stand still and look down. I glance up. He turns his head and stares directly into my eyes as he walks by. He continues, enters something into his tablet, and turns the corner.

CHAPTER 7

Monday after work, I arrive home to find Simone moodily staring out the window, like she is waiting for me. She pretends not to spot me when I come in. She sits, curled up on the chair with a blanket over her.

"Are you okay, Simone?" I ask.

She shrugs. "I'm okay. Just thinking about serious stuff."

I sit down next to her. "What sort of serious stuff?"

She shrugs and lets out a deep breath. "Just all the stuff. With the countries. And the shooting."

I try to put my hand on her shoulder but she shakes it off. "With the U.S. and New California?"

She nods and turns away. "We learned more about it today in school," she says. She avoids my eyes and plays with her nails. "I can't believe I was born in New York. I could've been a poor American."

"But Simone, we weren't poor in New York and we're not poor here in New California. Plus, there aren't any poor people in New California because of how the government takes care of jobbers."

"There were a lot of people that used to have good jobs who became poor!" she counters, armed with what she learned earlier this afternoon. "Isn't that why we came here? Money? Because your job fired you?"

"My job didn't fire me, the whole company shut down because of laws that made things hard for technology companies. We had plenty of money saved up. We came here because we always liked it here. We could have stayed there like your grandparents did."

"Yeah," she says.

I try again to place my hand on her shoulder to soothe her. This time she lets me.

"Was it scary?" she asks.

"Yes," I say.

I am distracted by footsteps and turn to find Drake. When he discerns what we are discussing, he scampers away. He hates talking about New California partition.

"Was I scared?" she asks.

As the memories sharpen, I'm struck with a lurch of emotion.

"Yes," I say. I collect myself and hold her closer. "You were only nine months old, but you picked up on the tension. When we were on our way, in the car, we were stuck in traffic and we heard about how they were stopping people heading to New California. Drake was just old enough to understand and started crying and you started screaming like I never heard before."

I pause and lean forward to check on her. She stares forward, eyes wide.

"You screamed until your throat was raw," I continue. "We kept trying to comfort you, but we couldn't. Drake kept saying that he wanted to go home, but we couldn't do that, either. We didn't live there anymore." My voice breaks and she lets me hold her.

"I'm sorry," she says.

"For what?"

"For crying and being annoying."

I laugh. "You were only nine months old, there's no reason to be sorry. All nine month olds cry and are annoying."

"Does Drake still remember?"

"Yes. Does he ever talk to you about it?"

"No," she says. "He sometimes says random things, but if I ask him about it he won't say anything."

"It was an awful time."

"I wish I remembered it."

I lean forward to study her distant, sad brown eyes. "Why?"

She shrugs. "Because it was important. I miss all the important stuff. Did we drive all the way here from New York?"

"Yes, we did. You, me, Drake, your Mom, and two cats and our dog."

She turns her head to me, surprised and amused. "The *animals* came with us in the car?"

"Yes they did," I respond. I smirk as I recall the unpleasantness. "Rico, our dog, bit your brother in the face and there was blood everywhere. That's why he has that scar on his nose."

"I didn't know that happened on the trip!" she says, shocked.

"Yep," I respond. Simone lets me rub her back.

"What if it happens again? What if there is a dictator or a war in New California?"

I pause to contemplate what she said. "It probably won't. Most things like that never even happen during someone's lifetime. If something like that does happen, we will be okay, just like we were when it happened ten years ago." I rub her back and she relaxes. "Also, Simone, it doesn't do you any good to worry about things you can't change. It will only upset you."

She sighs. I give her one last hug and release her. She jumps up, opens the door to the den, and descends down the stairs.

I stay on the couch and recall those days and days of driving. I had no job lined up, just an expensive apartment I signed a lease on, sight unseen. Jane was excited to go back to California where she is from—but also disturbed it became a different country. Her family members in California were not given the choice.

The car ride was long and grim, with very little conversation beyond keeping the kids happy. On the third night, we stopped at a Hampton Inn in Nebraska because no nicer hotels were available for hundreds of miles. I woke up early, choked with anxiety. I laid in bed, thinking about how our house from years ago in Chicago wasn't ours anymore, our house in New York wasn't ours anymore either. I was unemployed. The cats tromped around the hotel room meowing angrily. They didn't understand either. I sat up and looked around—Drake peacefully asleep, Simone in her travel crib, Jane asleep. *I have to take care of all these people.*

I rushed into the bathroom. I put the fan on and closed the door and melted to the floor with deep, wracking sobs. I put a towel over my head and laid face down on the cold floor and cried until I got it all out. Afterward, I didn't feel better. I felt calm, but not better.

Two nights later, before we crossed over, we stayed in Reno. After everyone was asleep, I went out on my own. It started with an idea to grab myself a drink and toss a twenty in a slot machine. Within five minutes, I turned twenty dollars into eighty. Five minutes later, I was down to forty. I bet it all and was up two hundred, which I turned into drinks at a bar, then drinks for a girl there. She had sultry green eyes and wore a stained tank-top. I drank until she didn't depress me. She said if she was going to stay up she needed some cocaine, so I bought it for her. We got a hotel room and I matched her cocaine consumption with whiskey straight from the bottle. A man showed up. He had cold, beady eyes that stung like pin pricks and a smile like a shark. He was pure cartoon predator, with a wad of cash and a perpetual cigar in his mouth. I'm not sure what happened next, but the splotches of memory still make me burn with shame.

The following day, hungover and down $1000, I surrendered my United States passport and became a citizen of The Republic of New California.

I pace around the room and land at a picture atop the mantel from our New York days. I was so young and wholesome. I had a different smile, with dimples. Jane's smile was bigger than it is now and matched Drake's. Simone was such a new baby she hadn't learned to smile yet. I pick up the picture and study her tiny innocent face. I'm glad she doesn't remember.

I wasn't going to drink, but I find myself on the rooftop deck with a Manhattan to quiet the memories of our immigration to California. Flights between the two countries were cancelled. We considered flying somewhere nearby and driving from there, but rental cars couldn't be taken over the border. That's how the four of us, two cats, and a Chihuahua ended up driving all the way from New York City to San Francisco. Previous to that I enjoyed road trips, but that time was different. I felt nothing but uncertainty.

I sip my drink faster. Slowly, the memories become more palatable and less like a knife in my chest. I take a deep breath and admire my view of the city. The sky is cloudy but not foggy. I begin to relax and melt into the outdoor couch. I set my drink on the adjacent table, lay down, and stare at the sky. My relaxed mood is quickly nullified by an unsettling sight. I jump up. Directly above me, about a hundred meters in the sky, is a drone parked in place. At the exact moment I lurch up, it speeds away at a clip so fast that I am certain it was a high-performance government drone.

CHAPTER 8

Tuesday omes and I can't wait to see Ashley. Our incipient relationship seems fragile, like something that could shatter and be swept away at any moment. I am hooked, but I suspect Ashley Doral discards people at her slightest whim.

Over the past few days, I kept my screen by my side at all times. Between messages, I browsed Ashley's social media pages for any updates. Many hours of my weekend were lost scrolling through hundreds of pictures of her, twisted with desire. We messaged several times a day, but it wasn't enough, like she was outside of my grasp. Our chemistry in person is undeniable, but anyone can write a flirty text.

I take a Lone to pick up Ashley. I want her alone longer than an UberAir can accommodate. I consider bringing a few splits of champagne for the ride, but decide that would be too cheesy.

Ashley lives toward the end of the colony. It's a long drive through a slow street until I reach her. Colony residents sit outside to enjoy the warm air. Some play with their kids. Others, seemingly childless, sit in cheap government-issue plastic chairs in yards and front stoops. They drink beer out of cans and share snack food out of large shiny bags that look retro to me. Further in, a fashionably dressed couple sits with a cheese plate and glasses of wine. Upon looking closer, the cheese is orange and the wine is Charles Shaw. I look away. In a green space between buildings, two men with tense throbbing necks and clenched fists pivot and scowl at each other. Other guys surround them, pat their shoulders, and try to reason with them.

Almost to Ashley's place, I jump as a large man in a tank top stumbles toward the car. He gets so close I am able to discern tranquilizer scars and prison tattoos. Everyone stares at the Lone as I pass. Some people glare, perhaps thinking I'm an American tourist. I see the friendly man I saw the first day I came to pick up Ashley in the Air. Several kids surround him and regard him with great respect. He speaks using expansive gestures and they listen, rapt.

When I arrive, Ashley talks outside with a young man I recognize from her social media accounts as Johnald. He examines the Lone with curiosity, hugs his mother and slinks back inside. He is smooth and subtle, like a panther on the hunt. I conclude he is definitely Ashley's biological child.

She opens the door and slides in to the middle seat next to me.

"Hi baby," she says. She kisses me, her hand on my cheek, and settles in resting her other hand on my inner thigh. "Is this the newer kind? Of Lone?" she asks.

"Yeah, but they came out like a year ago. They're more common than the old ones," I say.

Bored with that line of conversation, she runs her hand further up my thigh and meets my eyes. "We have a while in here, don't we? Are we going across the bay?" she asks.

"Yes, it will be about fifteen minutes."

She forms a sly smile. "I see why you didn't get an Air."

She sits up straighter, puts her arm around my shoulders and rubs my legs, my hips, my arms. My breath increases. We're still in the colonies, going back on the same road I came in on. The faint rumble of men fighting penetrates the thick windows. We creep around the corner. The tension between the two guys from earlier is now a full-blown fight involving multiple people.

"I saw that fight about to start when I came in," I say.

"Yeah, baby? Did it scare you?" she says.

"No," I say, "I wasn't scared."

She kisses me again and holds me. I stay still and let her touch me as she sees fit. I like that she is being more aggressive than usual.

When the car picks up speed outside of the colony, she moves her hand to my cheek and kisses me deeply. I match her intensity. A euphoric calmness washes over me and I lose myself in her kiss. Her tongue caresses mine. She stops and kisses me gently on the lips. Her dark brown eyes meet mine and I melt into her, letting my arrogance drift away. She starts to laugh a little. The deeper I stare into her eyes, the more her laughter grows and I turn away.

She kisses my cheek. "You're adorable, baby. Adorable and sweet," she says.

I smile shyly. She holds me as we drive across the Bay Bridge. I slouch to accommodate her arms around my shoulders. I'm only a few centimeters taller than her, but as we sit next to each other, I note her height is in her legs and mine is in my torso.

I turn to meet her eyes. "I really like you, Ashley."

She smirks. "I know baby, you told me before." She studies my face. "I like you too."

I initiate the kiss this time. My hands, acting on their own accord, seize her waist and wander upward, before landing on her back. She wraps her arms around my neck. We pull each other close, hard, like magnets, and keep pushing closer, creating a force I can't resist. She climbs onto my lap and straddles me. I want to freeze time and allow our bodies to take control, to consummate this brewing lust. My tan hands contrast with her soft, pale skin. I somehow know exactly how to touch her. She writhes and moans, confirming my intuition, and cementing our growing bond to one another.

My screen dings, alerting us we're two minutes away.

"Another time, baby," she says.

She gets off my lap, sits next to me, and rests her head on my shoulder. I meet her eyes and we smile, letting our gazes linger. I sigh and hold her hand until we arrive.

In the restaurant, we sit at right angles to be near each other. Concerned that earlier I was too aggressive, I tone it down and avoid contact with her while I study the menu.

"Did you see my boy Johnald, when you picked me up?" she asks.

"Yes, I saw him. He's very good looking, and the way he carries himself reminds me so much of you."

She beams. "Yeah, Johnald's mine. I carried Johnald and Jimothy. Misty carried Misty Jr."

"I recognized Johnald right away from your posts, but there is something about him in person that the pictures didn't capture."

Ashley smiles and leans her chin on her hand. "I saw the pics you posted of your family. Your children are beautiful. Seriously, you have the most beautiful family I've ever seen."

I respond with a smile and search for something to say. The restaurant is loud and without the comfort of alcohol, I feel awkward.

"There was a guy I saw right by your house with a bunch of tranq marks. He looked like he was drunk, do you know who I'm talking about?" I ask.

She rolls her eyes. "Yes, I know him, unfortunately. He is

exactly what he looks like. A drunk criminal. Whenever he's not in jail, he's causing trouble and bothering people. We're petitioning for him to get reassigned."

"What sorts of things does he get arrested for?" I ask.

"Usually just petty stuff, like getting drunk and being obnoxious, but he's been arrested for burglary before. He would get tipped off by people selling black market USD and then steal it back. Stuff like that."

"Wow, with how drunk he was I'm surprised he was able to pull that off."

"Yeah, I think he's gotten worse over the years. With people like that, sometimes I wish the police had real guns."

I stare at her, incredulous, and wonder if she is joking. "Really? But, remember in the U.S. how often the police would shoot people, oftentimes innocent people?"

"Yes, baby, of course I remember. But there are pros and cons to both sides. I mean, I guess I don't really hope the police shoot that guy. It's bad enough watching them shoot him with a tranq gun. It's just that knowing the police have real guns can really deter crime," she says.

"I just don't think it's the government's right to take someone's life, that's a philosophy of New California I've always agreed with. It's so tragic what happened this weekend, with that girl they shot," I say.

"Yes, it's unfortunate that the girl died, but she was trying to storm into the building. Do you think she would have even thought about it if the officers had real guns? I don't think so. This country is weak on crime, but then the government just manipulates and control everyone's lives as they please."

"What do you mean?" I ask.

"All the ministries, there is so much secrecy. There's so much that citizens don't know."

"Has Josh told you—"

She folds her arms and rolls her eyes. "No. Josh does not tell me state secrets."

Our drinks come and she gets right to work on hers, downing about a third of it immediately. I take a long swig of mine and recalibrate my view of Ashley after these conservative sentiments are revealed.

She continues. "I just get the impression that there are things going on that we don't know about—like, really disturbing things."

She stares into the distance and avoids my gaze. I contemplate what she might be hiding. Her odd mannerisms bring to mind her behavior at the park when we discussed the outage in the U.S. A chill rolls through my body. I wonder what sorts of dirty government secrets Josh has shared with her.

Later, on our way to her place in an UberLone, her face is twisted into a heavy contemplative stare. I take a deep breath, suddenly unsure whether or not our date went well. She sits next to me and holds my hand, but looks out the front windshield.

"Do they have cameras in here?" she asks.

"No," I say. "I'm certain they don't."

"They don't record audio or anything?" she asks. "Even for crime prevention?"

I study her face and freeze, confused about where these questions came from. "No. They don't."

"I need to know I can trust you," she says.

"Of course, absolutely. No matter what. I'm like the least vindictive person ever."

Ashley simpers and chuckles with her mouth closed. "You're so cute, baby." She kisses my cheek.

The car speeds up as we merge onto the Bay Bridge. I try to read her expression but can't tell if she's done with the topic or consumed by her thoughts. She turns her head toward me and stares directly into my eyes. Her intense stare cuts through my alcohol buzz and I lurch backwards.

"Do you love this country?" she asks.

"Yes." I answer immediately. "Of course I do. Don't you? Why do you ask?"

"Shut up." She lunges at me and kisses me hard. Her fingers entwine with my long wavy hair which she uses as leverage to pull herself onto my lap. Her tongue fills my mouth and I give into her, reveling in the thrill of letting her have me. I moan into her mouth and tune in to her, letting her place my hands where she wants them. She gropes me everywhere with her strong feminine hands. There is nothing gentle or subtle about her touch. We press into each other hard, like we can't get close enough until our skin is fused together. She grabs my hand, pulls her underwear to the side and lets me touch her wetness. She positions my hand so that my fingers slide into her. Her muscles spasm and I push harder. I open my eyes and drink in her face, eyes clenched shut, mouth open as she moans. She pulls my hair to bring my face back to hers and bites my lip.

"Does that hurt?" I ask.

Writhing with pleasure, she chokes out: "It's so good."

Her muscles squeeze my hand in rhythm with her breathing. She screams in pleasure and in pain. Not five minutes after she told me to shut up, she culminates in a deep, guttural, moan. I slowly, carefully, pull out my hand. She retrieves some wet wipes from her giant purse and cleans up her thighs and my hand, then we kiss for several minutes. She stops, stares into my eyes, and caresses my face.

"Cora, baby," she says, "I trust you, but you'll have to trust me too."

"What does that mean?" I ask.

"You'll see, sweetheart, you'll find out later."

We kiss again, until our mouths are sore, and explore each other's bodies with our hands. Between the alcohol, the sound of the wheels on the road, and the kiss, I am infinite. Like something is thawing deep within me and I am floating. But, like a dull ache that's forgotten until it creeps back up, Ashley's words unsettle me. Is she just concerned about trust? Has she been hurt before? *No*, I think, *it's something else.* I hold Ashley, both my arms around her, and study her dark eyes and crocodile smirk. I picture Josh's face, his impenetrable American flag-blue eyes. I never understood the Justin Trudeau comparison, there is something much darker behind Josh's eyes.

CHAPTER 9

Ashley and I continue to see each other a few times a week. Often on my lunch break only for a few minutes. The days pass by uneventfully, as days do in adulthood. I've yet to spend an entire night with her, but my desire to is strong. I want to see her without makeup, her perfect face gnarled with sleep. I want to wake up in the night and pull her to me, to wake up in the morning with her hands on me. I finalize the dates for my New York trip and one day, while we drink cappuccinos at a park in Oakland Shipyards, I ask her to join me.

"You want me to come with you to New York?" she asks.

"Yes, I'll pay for your ticket and for everything once we're there. I'll be in meetings during the day, but other than that we can spend time together, and sleep and wake up together."

She smiles, grabs my chin, and kisses me on my lips. "Baby, that sounds really exciting. It's like you're my real girlfriend."

I squeeze her hand. "So do you think you can go? Do you have to talk to Misty?"

"I'll have to decide what I'm going to tell her. I'll check in with Josh as well. He's going to New York soon too, maybe it's at the same time." She pauses, sips her coffee, and glances toward the bay, where a ferry boat full of tourists floats by. "That way I could see Josh while you're in meetings."

We hold hands, coffees in our other hands, content.

"It's been a long time since I last went to New York," she says. "It was just before New California partition."

"Really? That's when I lived there. Did you go there a lot when you lived in Pittsburgh?"

She turns to me, her head slanted. "*Please* don't tell me you confuse Pittsburgh and Philadelphia?"

"No! I'm familiar with the geography of the state. I was just asking since it's drivable from Pittsburgh."

She smiles and takes my hand. "No, I didn't go there often. Not at all. The last time I went was with a guy I was dating."

"What did you guys do in New York when you were there?"

She glances at me, perhaps to gauge how much I want to know. "I don't know, stupid stuff. He just wanted to hang out at the hotel mostly, but I forced him to do other things, like take me shopping, and fun little touristy things. I—" She interrupts herself with laughter and lets her hair fall over her face.

"You what?"

"If I tell you, you'll think I'm a horrible person."

"No, I promise I won't, whatever it is. I'm not judgmental at all."

She laughs once again and studies my face. "Baby, never mind I said anything. This was like my bitchiest, trashiest moment. And I have lots of those."

I meet her eyes and try to think of what it could possibly be. "Okay, Ashley, now you have to tell me. You can't say that much and then not tell me what it was. I'm pretty imaginative, I will probably assume it's something worse if you don't tell me."

She takes a deep breath. "So, keep in mind this was like ten years ago." Her sly smile returns and she rests her chin on her hand. "I've always been just a little bit of a party girl. Not, like, big obnoxious house parties, but more like go to bars by myself and get guys to buy me drinks and then stay out all night drinking those drinks, you know?"

I smile, squeeze her hand, and nod.

"So, I was in New York with this guy, and I decided on the drive over that I was getting tired of him, but like, we were already on our way to New York. Then, when we got there, one night, after he went to sleep, I decided to go out on my own."

I nod, urging her to continue. "So what happened?"

She takes a deep breath. "Alcohol. Lots of alcohol. I met a couple, they bought me drinks. They gave me a pill, I took it. I still don't know what it was. Probably ecstasy or something like that. We went to a jazz club and the music was so good, and I was sitting between them and we were kissing. Their hands were on me, but I almost wasn't sure whose hand was whose. Then we met another couple, and started talking and flirting with them. They took the pills too."

"Was it fun? Or was it, like, a bad drug experience?"

She smiles through her closed lips, and gauges my reaction thus far. "It was fun, baby, like, one of those nights where everything feels just right, you know?"

"Yeah, for sure, I know. That's how I felt the first night we were together at that party." I place my hand over hers. "So tell me what happened next, when is the part where you were a horrible person?"

She smiles and squeezes my hand. "So me, the couple, and the other couple, went back to one of their hotel rooms, and we're drinking and fucking, like, all of us all together, and separate little groups."

"Did you gravitate toward the men or the women?"

"The women, for sure, baby. I don't let just any guy fuck me. Though, I did let both of those guys fuck me. But anyhow, probably at like four a.m., right when I was ready to take a little break, I heard my screen ring, well, my phone I guess it was at the time, and it was the guy."

"The guy you came to New York with?"

"Yeah. So I pick up the phone, and people are fucking loudly in the background. There were five of us in a regular sized New York hotel room. He knew what was going on. What makes me a horrible person, is that I broke up with him right then and there—in the hotel room with people fucking in the background, I'm all like 'I don't think it's working out.'"

I cover my mouth and laugh. "Wow."

Ashley smiles coyly. "So do you think I'm a horrible person?"

"No, not at all. I mean, sure, definitely not the best way to break up with someone, but it was a long time ago, and actually I think it's a hilarious story."

"And baby, don't worry. I'm normally more sensitive when I break up with someone. I have a lot of practice. And anyway, why would I ever break up with you?" She leans against me.

I hold her gaze and smile. "I have very little experience breaking up with people."

"Really?"

"Yeah I'm usually broken up with."

"Huh. Weird, I've never heard anyone admit that. Why would someone break up with you?"

"I mean, never for like a legit reason. I think I just wait things out and stick around longer than I should, even when I know a relationship is doomed."

Ashley nods slowly. "That makes sense."

"So why did you break up with that guy who took you to New York?"

96

"He was an asshole. I mean, not to me directly. To me he was very sweet. And, actually, I should add that I got back together with him the next day."

I laugh. "Why did you get back together with him?"

"I don't know, I mean, he really was sweet. He was almost nurturing; the way he was with me, and the words he chose. Almost like a woman."

"Interesting."

"We didn't last long after that. I get tired of guys quickly."

"Do you think you'll get tired of Josh?"

"No, he's the exception to the rule, I guess."

"I thought you and Josh had only been together about a year?"

"I told you it has been over a year."

Oh. "How long has it been?" I ask.

She smiles coyly with her mouth closed, revealing a dimple. "It's been on and off and evolved over time. But really, it's barely begun."

"What do you mean by that?" I ask. An unexpected stab of jealousy strikes me.

"Just that I feel like he and I are at the beginning, like we have lots of adventures in our future." She turns away from me, toward the bay, with a sly, distant expression.

I ponder this and try to sort through the unease. "What about his wife? Does she know about you?"

She swats away the question. "I don't know if she knows. I don't worry about it."

I think about my image of Josh's wife from the media—a blank slate who avoids the spotlight. An odd match for a politician. But, when they got married he was just another tech entrepreneur.

"It's been my experience that there is a big difference between having a relationship with a married person whose spouse knows and one whose spouse doesn't. And the ones where the spouse doesn't know always end abruptly, and usually don't last long."

"I don't know about that," she says. "Some people can carry a secret and some can't. You just have to find the right person." Her mouth forms a devious half smile, and she takes my hand.

I smile back and a jolt of excitement hits me. She makes me want to do things I wouldn't normally do—bend the rules, carry secrets, go on adventures.

A government car catches my eye. Ashley turns to see what I am looking at.

"I feel like I've seen more government cars lately," I say.

Ashley examines my face and shrugs. "They're always everywhere."

"Yeah, maybe I just didn't notice them before. Ever since that girl was killed by those government protection officers I just notice them more."

She looks over my shoulder at the car. "He probably just came to see the view."

I shrug and return my gaze to the bay and the San Francisco skyline beyond. "Maybe."

We fall into a comfortable silence. She places her arm around me and kisses my cheek. I lean my head on her shoulder and she runs her hand through my hair. I lift my head, meet her brown eyes, and we kiss. Just when we reach the point where time seems to stop, I recall I need to return to work at a specific time for a meeting. I pull away and we regard each other for a moment, each with closed-mouth smiles, before we resume drinking our coffees.

CHAPTER 10

Flights between New California and the U.S. are about half first class, half coach. First class is almost entirely New Californians, and coach is almost all U.S. citizens. Ashley and I wait in the first class line and watch the Americans. They shuffle through the long line to the economy cabin, clutching their little blue passports with their bags ready for inspection.

Everyone in New California is issued a passport at no cost, and only professional class people pay passport tax. The plan was to give jobbers free housing and no taxes, so they could afford other things like travel, but it didn't work out that way. If a jobber is on this plane besides Ashley, they definitely didn't pay their own way.

We board, settle into our seats with a glass of sparkling wine, and take off. As soon as they announce we are free to walk about the cabin, we dash up to the small walk-up bar at the front of the plane and claim two spots.

I order my drink. The flight attendant smiles soullessly and gets to work, dutifully making a show of mixing it in the silver container. She retrieves tiny ice cubes, asks which bourbon I would like it made with, and pours it into a classic octagonal whiskey glass.

"Thank you," I say.

She nods and shifts her attention to Ashley. "…And you?"

"Gin mule," Ashley says.

She makes the drink exactly how it should be, with fresh lime and ginger beer. I'm sure in Coach they would use ginger ale. I slip my arm around Ashley's waist. She leans toward me and pulls my arm tighter around her. Everything is just right. I have so much anxiety about flying, but I'm okay once I'm in the air with a drink.

I claw my drink from the top of the glass and sip through the straw. Ashley gracefully cups her hand around the base of her glass. The music piped into the front of the plane turns from generic indistinguishable elevator music to a passable cover of 'Puttin' on the Ritz,' lyrics and all. I can't help but bob my head and sing along. Ashley doesn't know I discretely took a Xanax earlier in the stall of the bustling airport bathroom. Ashley watches with a charmed smile. When I become more enthusiastic, she throws back her head and laughs. Across the small circular airplane bar, two suit-clad men stare at me with unintentional smiles and raised eyebrows. I glare at them and they slowly reengage in their own conversation. Ashley grins at me, grabs my face and kisses my mouth. The guys across the bar peer back over casually, as if the sight of us is just one more stop on their generic scan of the entire airplane. I sneer at them, amused, as one of their gazes continues to the overhead compartments and onto the various other passengers who are all either asleep or engrossed in their screens.

We drain our first drinks fast. By the time we start on the second, the lights are dimmed and most people on the flight attempt to sleep because it's after midnight in New California. We are in no hurry because we're excited to be together and my meeting isn't until the day after tomorrow. I am jubilant and happy to be by Ashley's side with several days ahead of us.

We drain a few more drinks, and then I fade away. With the combination of the alcohol and Xanax, my mouth struggles to form words. Like my tongue fell asleep earlier or got drunk faster than the rest of me. I tell Ashley I need to sleep right now. She helps me walk to my seat, leading me from behind to ensure I don't bump into the limbs of sleeping passengers. She sits me down, presses the button to recline my seat, and tucks me in. I can't tell if she is embarrassed or amused, but a flash of shame penetrates my inebriation. I fall asleep immediately, without dreams, unable to appreciate Ashley's hand caressing my cheek.

*****

We arrive at the hotel at eight a.m. definitely not ready to start our day. I pay for an extra night to check in early. We look awful and exhausted, with our makeup smeared and clothing wrinkled. Upon arriving, I immediately take a shower and change into pajamas. Ashley takes a shower after me and emerges in a hotel-issued robe.

I'm unclear about what happened on the plane right before I fell asleep. I still don't think I am entirely sober. Ashley acts sweet and doting but distant, which I interpret as tired.

She is writing messages to someone, her screen angled, while stealing glances at me to make sure I don't spy on her. She doesn't hide the texts from Misty and I begin to enjoy reading them over her shoulder. Misty is apparently someone who overuses punctuation and thumbs up emojis. Example:

MISTY: Their safely?!?!?!

ASHLEY: Yes, we arrived safely and just checked into the hotel. About to take a nap. Tell our babies I love them!

MISTY: [Thumbs up emoji]

At one point, Ashley scrolls up to find a previous message and a series of pasty thumbs are displayed in nearly every other text. Ashley's texts are much more descriptive and warm.

Ashley sits down in the bed next to me while I go through work emails.

"I'm exhausted, baby," she says.

"Yeah, we should definitely take a nap, but I also want to make sure we don't sleep through the whole day since I have meetings tomorrow."

She wraps her hands around my waist and lies down. "Meetings all day tomorrow?" she asks.

"No, just in the morning for a few hours. Then, I think I can sneak away, but I'll need to carry a screen around in case something comes up."

I set down my screen and lay down next to her. I put my arms around her under her robe, pull her toward me and gaze into her eyes. Her eyelids look naked without makeup.

"You have freckles on your nose," I say.

She smiles and looks away. "So do you."

"I know, and I don't look like someone that should have freckles."

She caresses my cheek and her manicured thumb grazes my nose. "I noticed the first time I saw you."

I kiss her cheek. She closes her eyes and tilts her head toward me. I kiss her lips and move my hand to her hair and kiss her top lip, then her bottom lip. Leaning on my elbow, I examine her perfect face. She opens her eyes and meets mine. Her eyes are a dark, vulnerable void. I search them as if there is some sort of information or meaning I could grasp if I only stared long enough.

"I envy Jane," she says.

I pull back, confused and surprised, but excited and filled with affection for her. "Really?" I ask. "In what way?"

"What do you mean in what way? Isn't it obvious? Do you think I'm happy with Misty? I still wouldn't be happy with Misty, even if she had your life."

I sit up and ponder this. Is it a casual remark or is there more to it? "I don't know. It just seems like if things could be different, it would be Josh's wife you would envy, not mine." My eyes dart over to her, hoping she doesn't confirm my fear: that Josh is much more important to her than I am.

She puts her arm around my neck and pulls me back down onto the bed by my hair. I expect her to kiss me, but she just stares into my eyes. I stare back, and try to read her intense expression. Instinctively I understand it's not about her feelings, or her relationship with Misty, but something else entirely. Something I'm not aware of. A jolt of adrenaline shoots through me and I clutch her shoulders and study her.

"Ashley, what is it?"

"Not everyone gets what they want, Cora."

She kisses me hard. I kiss her cheeks and the salty flavor of tears coats my lips. I kiss her mouth tenderly and caress her cheek, but she swats my hand away. I give in and let her lead. She kisses me roughly, through tears, and pulls my hair. Her tongue penetrates my lips and caresses mine. She tastes like cheap toothpaste, gin, and something delicious and distinctly her. I kiss her back, matching her intensity. I want to help her, to find out what's wrong and solve her problems. She gets on top of me and pulls my hand to her. Her wetness practically forces three fingers inside. Her cries turn to moans. I stare into her dark eyes and try to figure out what she needs from me.

Afterward, she closes her eyes and rests her head on my

chest. I caress her hair. Such a light blonde, the contrast makes my tan skin olive. She holds me tight, her muscles still clenched.

"Ashley…" I say.

"Hmm?"

"Is everything okay?"

She laughs bitterly. "Yes, baby, I'm okay. Sorry about that."

"It's fine," I say. I adjust to get more comfortable, knowing I will fall asleep quickly.

"Do you sleep on your side, baby?" she asks.

"Yes, how do you like to sleep?"

"Here," she says.

She turns me to my side, facing away from her. Just as I am about to fall into a deep, dark, dreamless sleep, Ashley's voice pulls me back.

"Cora?" she says. She holds me tight, her arms tense.

"Yeah?"

Her muscles twitch. I open my eyes.

"You'll stay with me?" she says, her voice altered with sleep.

"Stay with you? When?"

"Just, if I have to go. When I go."

"Go where?" I ask.

"Never mind." Her arms relax until she's limp with sleep.

"Ashley?" I shake her arms. "Ashley, what are you talking about? Where are you talking about going?" I sit up and turn to look at her. Her eyes open, so much smaller without makeup, and impenetrable in the dark room.

"I don't know, Cora, I must have been dreaming." She pulls me back down. "Lay down, baby. Sleep in my arms."

She holds me and we fall asleep together. We sleep past noon, but it's only nine a.m. in New California.

CHAPTER 11

The following morning, I walk to my meeting. The air is humid but cold in a way it never is in New California, in a way unrelated to temperature. I breathe in the familiar New York smell, a medley of trash, food, metal, and people. A city so alive with all the glory and horror of life that it smells like blood.

I compare New York now with how it was pre-partition when I lived here. Back then, the parks weren't filled with squatters in tents and makeshift houses. I suppose this is what New California would be like if it weren't for the colonies.

I compare the low-income people in New York to those in San Francisco. In both places, they dress stylishly and shop at discount stores. But New York City is crowded with people outside with seemingly nowhere to go. I flipped through a photo deck recently about living conditions for recent college graduates in NYC. They live packed in tiny apartments, often four to a bedroom. They are barely better off than the families in the parks. So, rather than sit at home in squalor, they wander about the city. They haunt benches, trains and coffee shops, or trudge through the streets without a purpose.

Despite the bleakness of the lower class on display, it is great to be back in New York. When I'm away, the indescribable New York-ness fades from memory and turns my opinion neutral, but when I come back, I love it. A walk through New York is so different than San Francisco. The sidewalks are crowded but I float down them as if carried by the collective energy of the crowd. I pass by thousands of people, but remain unobserved.

In the stark light of a new place, something about Ashley seems off. Her slyness normally enchants me, but now I find it disturbing. It was odd to see her cry. I always thought of her as able to control her emotions, so perhaps I need to recalibrate my view of her.

I shouldn't be confused at her display of emotions, because I can tell she feels them. Perhaps her strength has metamorphosed into hardness. I've been called unemotional many times, but I'm very emotional. I'm just never emotional at people.

I find it odd that Josh is in town now too. Was that really just a coincidence? And what is he doing? We have little diplomatic relationship with the U.S.

I examine the situation objectively and feel worse. Despite the pleasure of sleeping in her arms, the sex, I can't summon pleasurable thoughts of her. All I have is this thud of awfulness pulsating through me. I realize I'm cringing and quickly change my face back to its resting stoicism.

What am I doing, anyway? A sultry married woman of a much lower class seduces me. Then, it turns out she is also having an affair with one of our countries most powerful politicians? It is the kind of drama I should avoid at all costs. Conversely, the opaqueness of it draws me in like a black pool, full of endless unknown pleasure.

*****

The meeting goes well, I successfully argue for a value proposition I don't believe in and they seem intrigued. The thought of leaving behind the deadweight of my company fills me with almost as much euphoria as spending the rest of my trip with Ashley.

Upon leaving, I receive a message from her:

Hi Baby, I'm with Josh right now and was thinking it would be nice if we all went out to dinner together. Meet me at his hotel tonight at 6. Waldorf, room 2231.

A stab of jealousy strikes me picturing her with him now. I trudge aimlessly down Church Street, unsure what to do until six. I check my screen again—only one p.m. Maybe Ashley thinks I will be working all day? I respond:

I'm actually done working for the day now if you want to get together earlier. I'm super hungry and could meet up for lunch.

She's typing. I am hopeful, envisioning staring into her dark sultry eyes over glasses of champagne and bacon-enhanced salads.

Busy!

Ugh. I don't like the thought of her with Josh right now. Normally it doesn't bother me, but I want her to myself for this trip. I pick up the pace. I don't want to amble along like a jobber, or whatever the U.S. equivalent of a jobber is. Gray, roiling clouds make the city dark and gloomy to match my mood.

New York City is the best city to walk in. It's full of endless

107

neighborhoods and a change of scenery every few blocks.

The longer I walk, the more nostalgic I get. I walked these same streets at Jane's side, a baby carrier on my back with Drake, and one on my front, with Simone. Simone was born here, in New York City. I'm flooded with a painful wave of nostalgia. My daughter was born within one mile of where I am right now. It was back when I was excited to make double the money of my previous job. Armed with a recent MBA, I realized I could make something of myself. I would go into Manhattan, walk, and revel in the warmth of the air on my face and the ache in my legs.

New California partition was just a rumor at that point. A rumor that spread dread and hope throughout the nation. After the Presidential Term Act was rushed through congress, the dictator announced the elections were cancelled. Later the same year, the truth laws were passed which suppressed the press and filtered the internet. Once 'Fake News' was outlawed, it was up to the government to define the truth.

Then, the Hardworking Americans Act was passed, which severely penalized companies that relied on foreign manufacturing and companies that created non-tangible technology products. At that point, what was a fringe secession movement in California became mainstream. Many feared violence, but Canada and Mexico allied with New California and the Dictator fought back with his usual weapons of threats, false claims, and irrational sweeping political policies.

Like any hard time, people coped. Many people ignored the news entirely. Others read the official news and read between the lines. I got my news on the deep web and followed the California secession movement.

My family still lives here, under the Dictator. My mother, my father, and two sisters. I was born here. Both of my children were born here: Drake in Chicago and Simone in New York, in the United States of America. Most of Jane's family always lived in California.

I smell the air. This is so much more me than San Francisco. This is so much more real. But, I cannot live here. I wander aimlessly, and turn down a residential street—fire escapes, pre-war windows, bricks. I love it and I hate it.

I hate it because I can't come back here. I can never live here again. I gave up my passport. I gave up my country, and now my destiny is at the whim of a very young democracy. All that money I have? Mostly just numbers on the NCD ledger. Supposedly hacker-proof, but Jesus knows that's never true.

I walk fast without poise. I turn down a street with classic New York stoops, like a fucking movie. People brush past me on the sidewalk. I feel small and entirely insignificant. My heart beats faster, racing to fuel my thoughts. Tears leak from my eyes. I search my mind for something—anything—to bring me pleasure. Money? Ambition? Ashley?

No. No. No. Who cares about another millionaire? I'm not anything special. I don't even *have* any ambition anymore. And Ashley? What the fuck is she up to? What does she want from me?

Ashley doesn't want to see me. Josh is fucking her right now. She is at the Waldorf. Being fucked by Josh. Right now.

I have everything I ever wanted, why am I jealous?

The more money I earn, the more horrifying basic emotions and common un-pleasantries are. Lines? Doctor's appointments? In a capitalist society, everything should be productized. With the wealth disparity, a first class service should be available for everything. It would create more service jobs, bring some jobbers up.

Annoyed and absorbed with my feelings, I walk faster. It's still business hours, so I dig through my purse for my screen. Nothing urgent, just a 'great job!' email from the board chairman. I roll my eyes.

I need a drink. I need to calm down my emotions. Down a side street, a bistro with outdoor seating draws me toward it. I approach a stand holding the menu. Vegan and no alcohol! I stalk off, deeply annoyed. It would have been a pleasant place to sit. Good thing I'm not with Jane. She would convince me to eat there and I would do it because she lets me do a lot of things other women wouldn't.

I find another place with outdoor seating. As I approach, I notice everyone wears business attire and the servers dash around as they balance beautiful salads, teas, and coffees atop ornate circular trays. Despite my own business attire, my gloomy mood has poisoned my sterile appearance and I storm away, stressed by the sight of the place.

I continue down the street. Two doors down, a dark bar that smells like beer and wood oil reminds me of my early twenties minus the cigarettes. A couple of sad men on stools stare at nothing and drink themselves to death. I dismiss it and continue down the street.

Finally, I find the perfect place. A small storefront restaurant so narrow only three tables fit outside and all are empty. I step in. A young girl in discount store clothes approaches me with a big friendly grin.

"Hi there, just one today?" she asks.

I am probably fifteen centimeters taller than her, which is awkward and I reflexively slouch.

"Yes, is it okay if I sit outside?" I ask.

"Of course! Sit wherever you'd like, I'll get you some menus."

She says 'you' like 'ya' and 'menu' like 'men-ya.' Strangely, I find her Midwestern accent comforting.

I sit down, take my leather wrap coat off, and let it fall back over the chair. She comes back and hands me both the drink card and food menu. I dig right into the drink menu, and order a glass of pinot grigio before she turns away.

The air is cool. I tighten my scarf and fold my arms. I cross my legs and lean back in the chair. In the storefront next door, a man opens the cellar door and disappears, as if the sidewalk consumed him. He reemerges with a box much bigger than his frame should carry, but he gallantly ascends the steps as if carrying nothing.

Across the street are classic New York apartments, with six floors of evenly sized windows and fire escapes. Storefronts grace the ground floor behind a narrow sidewalk and caged trees.

I think about Ashley, about my meeting today, and about Jane. I think about New York, New California, and the United States. Everything is out of sorts, not quite in its right place. I want Ashley. I miss Jane. I want to go home, but being here in New York makes my house in San Francisco seem so far away, like I can't believe it exists. It also never quite felt like home. I think of when I lived here, in a huge beautiful house on Staten Island, with the view of Manhattan and original dark wood. That house felt like home. I took a boat to work and would stand on the hull, headphones on, as lower Manhattan came into view. Back in the days when I was still climbing. I was so close to having everything I ever wanted, but I kept climbing higher.

The server returns with my glass of wine, a generous pour. I sip it fast, keeping it in my hand. I lean back in my chair and watch New York pass by. A man in business attire darts around slow walkers and tourists. A pair of NYU students amble along, coffees in hand, as if they just woke up.

Almost immediately, the wine begins to put the pieces of the world back together into something more palatable. I message Jane and tell her I love her and I couldn't be happier with her as my wife.

I eat a salad—exactly the one I envisioned, and finish a second glass of wine. I am fortified, armed, and ready to continue my day. I head out and spend the afternoon retracing the walks of my past.

*****

I arrive at the Waldorf hotel early. I do a lap around the block to entertain myself, but my legs are tired and the increasingly crowded sidewalks further my exhaustion. I find a seat in the lobby and sit. A chandelier the size of a car looms several meters above me. The hundreds of lightbulbs ablaze let everyone know: *this place is fancy*. Heavy burgundy curtains frame the windows, by which be-suited employees stand ready to be of service.

I don't want to seem over-eager. I decide to take the stairs to the twentieth floor. I stop on nineteen to pace and catch my breath. I knock at 6:02.

Josh answers the door, dressed, mostly. The panels of his shirt hang on either side of his unclasped belt. Ashley lies in bed under the sheets. Josh prances around, satisfied with himself, like a dog who was given a steak. I trudge over to the bed while he finishes getting dressed. Ashley, apparently undressed under the sheet, eyes me seductively.

"Hi baby, come lay down with me for a minute."

"No!" I say.

She rolls her eyes. "We didn't fuck in the bed."

I scan the room warily. She laughs, un-swaddles herself from the covers, emerges from the bed naked, and tries to kiss me. I turn my head. She puts on a hotel robe and saunters into the bathroom. I sit down in a chair, not sure what to do with myself.

Josh, now fully dressed, approaches me with a charming grin. "Hi Cora, it's great to see you again." He shakes my hand. "Can I get you a drink? They have those cool new minibars where you can actually make real drinks. Manhattan, right?"

I smile faintly without opening my mouth. "I'd love a Manhattan." The temporary relief from my lunchtime drinks has faded and stabs of anxiety and self-doubt have begun to bubble back up.

He trots into the other room to make my drink.

I check my screen. Jane never responded to the message I sent her during lunch. Her social media accounts won't load. A renewed anxiety courses through me. To distract myself, I turn to the window. The view is decent, not iconic, but decent. I approach the glass and peer down at the avenue. Several black U.S. government cars lurk by the entrance and I wonder if they're for Josh.

Josh stirs my cocktail in the adjacent room. A metal spoon clinks against a metal shaker. A cap unseals, and ice is scooped. Ashley is in the bathroom. The sink goes off and on as she washes up. The soundproof windows silence the city outside. Josh exhales and hums a tune while he replaces the caps on the bottles and pours my cocktail from the shaker into a glass. Ashley turns the water off and on again. The silence surrounding these noises hangs in the air, as unbearable as a shrieking alarm that cannot be disabled. Alone in the room, I pace in circles. I unlock the window and pull it up about five centimeters until it hits a barrier. The vacuum seal releases and the cacophony of New York City fills the room in one graceful *swoosh*.

Josh prances back in with a grin and hands me my cocktail.

"Wanted to hear the sounds of the city, huh?" he says.

"Yeah, it's such a distinctive noise, New York. So different than San Francisco."

He nods in agreement and stands beside me. I look over at him. His blue eyes focus on something in the distance, his delicate but masculine fingers wrap like an octopus around his glass of scotch. We stand, still, mesmerized by the sights and sounds of the city outside.

"So what are you doing in New York?" I ask.

He studies me. "Meetings. With some U.S. government officials, as well as foreign governments."

"I thought we didn't have much of a diplomatic relationship with the U.S."

"Well, we definitely have a major diplomatic relationship with them, it's just not necessarily a good one," he answers. "But we need each other. They'd be nothing without us, which is why things went so badly here after partition."

"What do we need them for? We have everything we need in New California, agriculture, industry, tech."

"We need our populace to be able to travel here. The majority of New Californians have relatives in the U.S." Agitated by this conversation, he pauses and takes a hard sip of his drink. "Also protection from foreign invaders."

"Really? Does that really matter to us? We have a military."

At that, he laughs. "Yeah, we have a military. A military of hackers and tranq guns. That's great if we can fend off an enemy that way, but we need something else as backup, and that is where the treaty with the U.S. comes in. Overwhelming force."

"Overwhelming force," I repeat.

This exchange unsettles me. Though, politics always seemed to me like a bunch of sociopaths and do-gooders teaming up to solve unsolvable problems.

Ashley emerges from the bathroom, dressed and put together. She shuts the window and the sounds of New York are sucked out as quickly as they came in. Ashley puts an arm around my waist, unexpectedly soothing something in me.

"Would you like a drink?" Josh asks her.

She does and he leaves to make it.

Ashley turns to face me and wraps her other arm around my waist. She touches my face, concerned.

"Everything okay?" she asks.

I hug her tightly.

"I'm fine now," I say.

She leans back and studies my face. "You're only fine now? Was something not okay before, baby?"

"No, everything's okay." I smile to convince her. "I just felt unsettled today, like something wasn't right, just for no reason, I guess."

"Baby! Why didn't you say something earlier? I would have come to you," she says. She kisses my cheeks, my nose, my lips. I am touched and surprised by her concern. She holds my head in her hands. "You're adorable, baby."

I kiss her, put my arms around her, and rest my head on her shoulder.

Josh prances in with his perpetual grin and I realize that's how he always walks. Like a trained horse at some sort of show. I don't think I ever met someone so pleased with himself. He takes note of our exchange and hands Ashley her drink, excusing himself. If etiquette school exists, Josh definitely went. I am both captivated and scornful of his every move.

He reappears at exactly the right moment, grabs his scotch and proceeds to initiate light conversation. He leads but does not dominate. It's surprisingly not awkward, being with both Ashley and Josh. The chemistry between Ashley and I extinguishes the chemistry between Josh and Ashley, and so we all mellow out into a comfortable level of social docility.

As my drink sinks in, I look forward to the night ahead of me. I want to relax, be at Ashley's side, and see what Josh Winston has planned for us.

*****

Josh, Ashley and I take a black car with a driver, apparently chartered by Josh, to a large South American steakhouse. We're taken to a table in the back, out of view of most people at the restaurant. Ashley sits between us and I note she is closer to me than Josh.

The service is distant yet attentive. As soon as any of us let our focus drift away from the table, one of the fleet of servers standing nearby with their hands folded jumps to attention to attend to our needs. New California is the same way, as is India, or any other place with a huge wealth disparity. The server to diner relationship is practically one to one.

We start with cocktails and switch to wine once the steaks come. We order giant cuts of tender, fatty steak, which we carve with sharp, skinny knives. I cut into the meat. My knife crosses Josh's. He chivalrously removes his knife and lets me sink mine in. The steak is delicious and the wine is smooth and dry. It feels primal, like we are on top of the food chain.

I cuddle closer to Ashley. Her hands explore my legs and my back. Josh's face relaxes after a couple drinks. His laugh is infectious and innocent like a child's.

After our steaks are ravaged, we order another round of cocktails. Josh is talking about campaigning when he was young, before he was elected to office. His distant, nostalgic eyes and large grin endear me to him. I'm not sure if it's the drinks, or more time spent with him, but my scorn and jealousy for him are gone in place of warm affection and a desire to truly know him, and for him to know me.

"In neighborhoods with older people, I went door-to-door to talk to people. I enjoyed it because I love meeting new people, but it was inefficient. Most people didn't want to talk and for those that did, there was often something off about them."

"Like what?" I ask, "I want to hear some crazy stories."

Ashley laughs, familiar with these stories. "Tell her about the woman who thought you were her internet hook-up."

Josh throws his head back and laughs. "Oh my God, I

almost forgot about that!" He laughs so hard he is nearly in tears.

I can't help but smile and laugh too. "Yeah, I definitely have to hear this story!" I say.

Josh laughs so hard he can barely speak. "So," he says, "I knocked on this woman's door, she opens the door, I was surprised that she was relatively young and nice looking. I quickly go over my 'hi I'm Josh Winston… etc.' and she interrupts me and says 'wow, you're much better looking in person' and pulls me in."

Ashley and I laugh as we anticipate the rest of the story.

He continues, "I'm trying to think of how she heard of me already, but then she pulls me in the house and starts kissing me, and not knowing what to do I just kiss her back."

"What?" I say, laughing.

"Wait until you hear what happened next!" Ashley says.

I turn to Josh, eagerly.

"So I'm kissing her, and just as I wonder if there's been a misunderstanding, the doorbell rings." He pauses, trying to calm down, and sips his drink. "She ignores it at first, then a message comes up on her screen. I can read it over her shoulder. She has him saved as 'John - Adult Friend Finder' and the message says 'I'm at your door.' She and I look at each other at the same time, she says 'so who are you?'"

"What did you say?" I ask.

He laughs so hard it racks his body. "I say, 'Hi I'm Josh Winston and I'm running for New California senate.' And then she says 'well, you have my vote' and sends me out the back door."

I laugh so hard that I rock back and forth, unable to speak. I shake my head. I glance down and note that Josh is holding Ashley's hand which doesn't bother me at all, I feel connected to both of them.

"I miss campaigning," he continues. "I really do. That was

when I was in my late thirties. My first few years in the New California senate, were some of the best times of my life."

"My late thirties were great too. And my early thirties."

"You guys aren't happy now?" Ashley asks. "Look where each of you are."

I contemplate this. "I miss striving for something. But yes, I'm happy. A lot of things make me happy, I just feel like I have no focus for my drive, right now, at this point in my life."

Ashley nods and tries to process this.

Josh catches my gaze, suddenly serious. "I understand what you're saying, Cora, and I've certainly felt like that before, but the climb is never over. There is always something greater." He makes unwavering, direct eye contact. His eyes are blue. A dark, pure, American flag-blue. "You and I have that drive in common, Cora."

I nod slowly, seduced by his words, and unsure of what to say. My drive is reawakened like a fire. Energizing, but dangerous without a focus.

"You've had an impressive career." He continues. His unblinking eyes rest on mine. "Do you know what your next move will be?"

"No," I respond. "It's really—I mean, it's—something I've been struggling with lately, actually."

A slight smile forms on Josh's face. He reaches across Ashley's lap and grabs my hand. He holds it, caressing it with his thumb. Ashley remains entirely still and uncharacteristically demure.

"Let me lead you Cora," he says. "Trust me, and trust fate, and opportunity will come your way."

I look down at his smooth, strong hand caressing mine. My breathing quickens and I'm on full alert, aware that this person is more strong and powerful than me in every conceivable way.

"People like you and me are different than others. It's not

that we're smarter—though we are—it's that we have a higher calling. We want to lead people, and not just companies. We're not money chasers, we're more. Do you want something more, Cora?"

I inhale sharply at my deepest desires, my most arrogant thoughts, reflected back to me from one of my nation's most powerful people.

"Yes," I say breathily.

He squeezes my hand before disentangling his.

Ashley looks down at her drink, then turns toward Josh. I can't see her face, but something passes between them. He smiles at me and heavy silence settles over the table.

Josh pulls up DinR on his screen, pays the check, and we're off. Ashley lightens the mood and takes each of our arms as we exit.

As soon as we enter the car Ashley kisses me hard. Her mouth tastes like gin with steak undertones. The kiss ends as abruptly as it began. She turns to Josh and rubs his chest through his shirt.

"Thanks for dinner, honey," she says.

"Yeah, thanks for dinner," I chime in.

"Of course," he says.

She called him 'honey,' and she always calls me 'baby.' I ponder this and decide I like the consistency. I've never been able to pull off calling people pet names. I'm just not feminine in that way.

The car lurches off. The driver is aggressive and the movement of a person-driven car energizes me. We lurk at red lights, ready to pounce at the whim of the man in the driver's seat. I never noticed how different the smooth ride of an UberLone is. We arrive at a dark building with a neon sign. Without reading a word of text, I can tell it's a jazz club. The driver puts the car in park and the engine relaxes.

"Just a minute, don't get out yet," Josh says. He fires off a message on his screen.

A man in a dark suit emerges and motions to us. We follow him into a side entrance and he escorts us to a dark corner—a place to see and not be seen.

We order drinks, and more drinks. Edges grated, cleansed, and polished by alcohol, we get into a sort of flow. Like we are bound to one another and in auto-drive. Once we are in the right place, effort is no longer needed. We have *arrived*. Ashley cements herself as the sultry, sexy glue that binds us together, and Josh and I bond in our shared secret, and shared weaknesses. The drinks blur one into another. We drink, we talk. Ashley's hands roam and Josh and I take turns kissing her like her mouth is the antidote for the sickness of bottomless ambition, and her ambition is realized on either side of her.

As the night goes on, I can't reconcile the Josh Winston in front of me with the Josh Winston on the stream. In front of me I see a man who laughs and drinks scotch until his throat is raw and his voice sounds huskier. On the stream, I only ever saw Josh the politician, not someone alive in the moment with a woman he loves and another woman—me—who he apparently trusts enough to be vulnerable around. I feel completely, and entirely, content.

Eventually, conversation slows, but Ashley hands, touching both of us, continue moving. We sit back with space in the conversation. We listen to the band, watch people go by, and take it all in. We talk about the little things that are different in New California, like a haircut, a makeup style, or a purse.

"You know what it's like here?" I ask.

Ashley giggles. "What, Cora, what is it like here?"

"I feel like it's 2020 in here." I say. I turn to them and laugh, but when I look at them I see a man in a white button-down shirt and pleated khakis, and a woman in classic makeup and a navy dress. Josh holds Ashley's hand and they regard me with the same blank expression. I glance down at my breeches and wrap coat and realize I'm the only one in my field of vision who looks like they're from New California. I feel a stab of self-consciousness. Ashley takes my hand and kisses me on the cheek, dismissing the issue, but something about it sticks with me.

The band exits and a more mellow, complex jazz band takes the stage. We become transfixed. My hand bumps Josh's over Ashley's thighs and he playfully pushes it away then takes it in, smiles at me good-naturedly, and lets it go. I smile back.

Josh digs in his pocket for his screen and Ashley and I turn to him.

"It's one twenty," he says. "We should probably get going, I have a call tomorrow at ten thirty." On his screen, he pulls up DinR, selects a tip amount, and pushes the button to pay out.

He motions to the man who brought us in, who signals for us to wait. Moments later, he reappears with two bouncers. They patrol either side of us while we make our way out the side entrance, unseen.

Back at the hotel, Ashley and I are tired and collapse into bed immediately without fanfare. She instructs me to take off my clothes. She takes off hers, holds me, and we are asleep almost immediately.

CHAPTER 12

Thirsty and weak, I wake up at about eight. Ashley is asleep on the other side of the bed after apparently detaching herself from me at some point in the night.

I drag myself out of bed and into pajamas. I mentally review my schedule for the day, relieved to recall my meeting is at two p.m.

I fill a glass of water for Ashley and place it on her bedside table. I crawl back into bed and swim through piles of poofy, cloudlike linens and find her, clammy from sleep. I wrap my arm around her and bury my face in her blonde hair. She stirs and pulls my hand to her breast. We lay in a comfortable state of half sleep.

Ashley succumbs to wakefulness and gulps down her glass of water in a single impressive sip. Water leaks from both sides of her mouth onto the bed. Despite messy hair, traces of last night's makeup, and water streaming down her cheeks, she looks as attractive as ever. She dives for her screen, reads something on it, and dismisses it.

"Josh is going to be on the stream later, he's calling in. We should listen," she says.

"Yeah, for sure," I say.

She stares at me, as if deciding whether to say something. "Did you have fun last night, baby?"

I reflect on the night. The delicious dinner, the drinks, the music at the jazz club. The way any jealousy, doubt, or reservations I had entirely disappeared.

"Yeah, I had a great time. I like Josh."

She grins. "I'm glad that you two get along so well," she says. She climbs out of bed and into a crisp hotel robe as she walks to the bathroom.

When she returns, I sit up in bed. She lays over my lap and wraps her arms around me. A touch of skyline fills the window across the room, reminding me where I am. My walk yesterday, fueled by those anxious panicky thoughts, seems like it happened to a different person, in a different place. I dismiss it entirely, purging it from my mind, and focus on the New York from last evening, the me of last evening. Josh Winston's friend, Ashley Doral's girlfriend. Josh Winston caressing my hand.

I call room service and order coffee, eggs, and bacon. While we wait, I drink free hotel room coffee while Ashley uses the landline to call her wife and children. I check my screen—it connects to the internet but messages are not delivered.

I sit on the couch and listen to Ashley talk to her wife and kids. I'm surprised at her sweet tone toward Misty. She calls her 'baby' like she calls me.

I find I am relieved Jane doesn't answer when I call. I leave her a voice message, brusque and self-conscious with Ashley studying me.

The doorbell rings, Ashley saunters to the door in her hotel robe. A lanky young man pushes a cart into the room with two metal-covered plates, glasses of water sweating with condensation, and a pair of cappuccinos. He removes the plate covers with a flourish and announces the food. Jolted by his standard American accent, I realize I expected him to be foreign. Of course he's an American, immigration ended over a decade ago.

Ashley brings both plates to the table and I follow behind her with the cappuccinos. The diffused sunlight highlights her high cheekbones and beautiful skin. Free of makeup, she is almost more attractive than usual. Her manicured hand selects a piece of bacon and brings it to her full lips while she gazes out the window. I follow the glow of light to the point in which her long neck meets her shoulders, where the hotel robe opens up and exposes the side of her breast.

She laughs and swats me with a napkin. "What are you looking at baby?"

"Nothing," I respond shyly, "you just looked really beautiful."

She swallows her bacon, wipes her hands off, and stands up. She comes to me and places both hands on my shoulders. My arms reflexively encircle her waist.

"You always look really beautiful, Cora."

At the sound of my name from her lips, a wave of pleasure shoots through me so sudden I nearly moan. I breathe harder and so does she. She hugs me, my face pressed against her breasts, and kisses the top of my head.

"I adore you," she says. "Cora, I absolutely adore you."

I hug her tighter and breathe harder, inhaling the scent of her morning skin. I kiss her chest. "I…" I start, "…adore you too."

We hold each other for a long time. She lets go and kisses me gently on my lips. We smile, ending the episode. She sits down and resumes her meal, and I begin mine. Her leg touches mine under the table as we eat.

My whole body glows from her touch in a way I've never experienced before. The connection I feel to her is so strong, that it surprises me every time. Yet, I can't fathom how I managed to subsist before I met her. It's like she was always there, that what we have is predetermined.

Ashley grabs her screen. "Cora, baby, Josh is on the stream," she says. I stop eating and Josh's voice fills the room:

"...New California is committed to preserving and strengthening diplomatic and military ties to the United States of America. We are respecting the Naval Treaty of 2028 and have, as agreed to in that treaty, seized all surveillance—including electronic surveillance—of the 32nd Street Naval Station in San Diego, New California. Additionally, all United States Naval Officers captured in the military conflict of 2024 are no longer in New California custody and have not been since 2025. The Republic of New California..."

His voice sounds deeper than usual and scratchy from all the laughing, talking, and drinking he did last night. While still star-struck that I hung out with him, his message disturbs me. The words themselves are not what bothers me. Everyone in New California knows we respect the naval treaty and that those naval officers were freed long ago. In fact, while in captivity, they probably lived in nicer conditions than when in the Navy. But what is the point of Josh announcing this on the stream? And why would the U.S. government allow someone to go on the national stream—or, I guess in the U.S., 'cable' for a lot of people—and debunk their conspiracy theories? Ashley turns it off as soon as Josh is done.

"I love when Josh is on the str—"

"Can you turn it back on?" I interrupt. "I want to see what they say afterwards."

She stares at me through her thick eyelashes. "No," she says. In one leap, she is on my lap kissing me sensually. My chair nearly falls over. I kiss her and enjoy the taste of her mouth and her weight on me. I melt into her, but the thought of Josh spreading propaganda on the stream distracts me. My uneasiness from yesterday comes back and I cannot shake the feeling that something isn't right.

CHAPTER 13

I returned to New California without Ashley. She and Josh wanted me to stay and travel to D.C. with them, but I declined the invitation. After several days of excessive alcohol, sex, and mourning my former country, I was ready to return to the stability of my wife, kids, and daily routine.

After dinner, I trot up the steps to my rooftop deck. My body feels taut, healthy, and aglow with the effects of a few days of healthy habits. I sit on the wooden bench, my arms outstretched on either side, and take a deep breath, trying to relax. The sparkle of city lights, drawing painterly lines down the hill, soothes and excites something in me.

In the months since I met Ashley, I always wanted more time with her—a common phenomenon in extramarital relationships. Now that I spent several days with her, I am oddly sated. Extramarital relationships are like alcohol. In order to appreciate them, you need some time away.

Upon returning, I gleefully launched back into my routine and found myself excited again about work. Simone dropped her glum mood and turned back into her cheerful, giggly self. Drake's basketball team is on a winning streak and he's one of the best players on the team. I haven't had a drink in four days.

I walk to the ledge and soak in my surroundings—the clean air, the recycling cans at the end of the block, the silent cars and whir of drones in the air. The grit of New York feels like a skin I shed.

Then, it comes creeping back.

Like a voice in my head. It begins as a whisper and escalates to a feverish, moaning demand. It returns: the great, needy wanting. The restlessness. It weaves its way through every cell of my body. No thought can quiet it. Not my money, not my past accomplishments, not my wife or my children. I need something else. I need passion with a woman I feel great affection for. I need to kiss her, hard. I need Ashley, and I need a drink. Now.

Every day I wonder if I will drink.

If I do, and it's a weekday, I can almost always drink just one or two—maybe three. But, on the weekend—defined as Friday through Sunday—I always drink, but only three or four. Maybe five or six if I start early, and occasionally maybe seven or eight on a special occasion, or if I'm on vacation.

I message Ashley a picture of myself as well as:

Are you around? I miss you so much! I'm really craving you.

I stare at the screen. I think of New York, of the streak of morning sunlight that framed her face while she ate thick bacon slices. I think of her tongue darting out to wash the bacon grease from the corner between her plump lips. It was the morning Josh was on the stream. A rush of emotions courses through me when I recall how her voice broke when she said she adored me.

I sit down and pull my jacket tight around me. Clouds cover the sky and a cold wind rampages through the city. I curl up, my knees to my chest and take in the gloom. I check my screen again and double check that the sound is on. The stench of marijuana wafts into my space. Normally omnipresent but unperceived, it brings to mind its absence in New York.

I picture pouring whiskey into a glass, making the ice crackle. A little vermouth and then some Angostura. I think of the hard, sweet, smoky yet floral taste. The glass in my hand, smooth and hard, while the cool condensation drips down my fingers.

I jump up and lope down the stairs to make myself a drink. Jane is at some sort of yoga thing, Drake is at basketball practice, and Simone—shockingly—is at a friend's house.

I deposit four large ice cubes in a square glass and fill two-thirds of it with bourbon. I top it off with sweet vermouth and a dash of bitters and stir. The clink of the ice cubes hitting the side of the glass brings me comfort.

I return to the deck and sip my drink. Warmth and comfort flood my senses. The flight of delivery drones overhead mesmerizes me. They land, drop packages, rise, and then proceed to land and drop other packages. I try to predict where they will land next, what their next move will be, but the programmatic flight pattern deceives me every time.

Ashley hasn't responded. The rational part of my brain understands that perhaps Ashley is busy, but the emotional, animal part of my brain wants Ashley. Right. Now.

I stand and pace around the rooftop, like a caged animal in heat. Camouflaged by darkness, I study the glow of streetlights snaking down the hill.

I can't decide what I want to do. I am both proud and disturbed by the thought that, with age, I am less lazy and more motivated by things like sex and power. But when will it stop? I feel guilty and ungrateful whenever people mention simple dreams, like obtaining a decent salary or conceiving a child. I have everything anyone could ever want and more, what am I still climbing for?

I check my screen again—still no message from Ashley.

I go downstairs and refill my drink. I return and find myself mesmerized by the tiny lights of the drones and their robotic movements without the context of their outlines.

Someone walks up the stairs, quiet like on cat feet. *Jane*.

Drake's walk is heavy and masculine. He stomps and walks louder than he's naturally inclined to. Simone walks like me—fast with long heavy steps, but jumpy around the house. Jane walks like a ninja and slinks in out of nowhere.

She emerges, dressed in workout clothes and an elegant long brown leather coat.

She smiles at me and tilts her head. "*There* you are," she says. She sits down next to me.

I claw the top of my drink, bring it to my mouth, and sip. "Yes, here I am," I say. The wind howls and I lean away from her to aerodynamically let it through.

The wind passes and she scoots toward me. "It's cold out here," she says.

"It is."

She holds me, I lean into her, and we watch the drones hover like sparkles over the lights of the city. The familiar sound of her breath, and her slim arms around my shoulders soothes me. I close my eyes and wish this was all I needed.

My screen dings and displays Ashley's name. Of course I can't check the message now that I am in my wife's arms. It always works that way. When I writhe in restlessness and desire, nothing, but when I'm busy I get messages.

"How was your yoga thing?" I ask Jane.

"You mean my yoga class?"

I shrug and display my hand, as if to say, *whatever*.

"It was good, I had a nice time." She pulls her screen out of her pocket to check it. No new messages are displayed, just reminders she sets for regular household chores, which deeply annoys me at this moment. "I messaged your sister this morning and she hasn't responded," she says.

"Yeah, messaging is spotty in the U.S." I say, "De-digitization."

Her mouth drops open and she pivots her head toward me. "What? Again? Is the internet down there again?" she says.

I'm annoyed at her alarm. This is not news. I don't react right away and allow for a dramatic pause.

"No, the internet is not down entirely, it's just spotty. No one knows why," I say.

She calms down. She rests her chin on my shoulder. I follow the street lights down to the black pool of emptiness where the city meets the bay, then onto tankers slithering past one another.

"Oh! I totally thought that drone was going to the blue house!" Jane says.

"What?" I say, distracted from my reverie.

"Sorry, I thought you were looking at that drone too," she says.

I was looking further ahead than she was, and missed what she saw right in front of us.

*****

Ashley's text said:

I miss you too, baby, but I won't be able to see you for a few days.

I respond:

How long is a few days? I'd really love to see you, even if it's just for a few minutes. Maybe we can voice call?

I try to take solace that she called me 'baby,' but I remember she calls everyone that and I am even more anxious than before.

I put on my headphones, play music and pace. A song I never heard comes on, full of energy, defiance, and dissonance. I add it to my library. As soon as it's over, I play it again. I retrieve a new drink. I pace around the deck with long heavy steps, palm my drink, and sip it.

Jane went to bed a while ago. Drake and Simone are home and asleep and I'm the only one up. I stalk around our roof like a cheetah in a cage. The air is thick and cold. I breathe it in. It tastes fresh, invigorating.

I check my screen. No response from Ashley. No messages from anyone at all.

Sometimes I notice people who seem to constantly receive messages on their screen. Whether they respond or not, their screen glows, alive. I often find I am self-conscious around those people, and I compulsively check my screen, like maybe I missed something. I wonder why I care when I decided decades ago that a social life would not be something I would devote resources to.

I decide to go for a walk. I don't bring a purse, what would I need it for?

I put my boots on in the dark room, lit by city lights diffused with curtains. I slip out and trot down the steps, still listening to the same song on repeat. Energy, defiance, and dissonance.

It's late and quiet out. I hike down my street, the rim of a steep hill which allows us views of the bay. At each block, narrow residential streets shoot downward, framed by electrical wires and the gray roiling bay beyond. My boots clop with each step. My walk is angry and assertive. It always was, even when I was young, quiet, and meek. My senses overwhelm me, the song I listen to, the cool air, the smell of San Francisco—marijuana, salt water, and Asian food. Why don't I do this more often? Why do I pace around my house every night?

I pass Victorian mansions, Victorian mansions split up into apartments, and then bars, restaurants, and people walking by. I pass a bar aglow with neon lights, packed full of young people. A few shiver outside and lean moodily, smoking e-cigarettes, which glow and highlight their perfect skin. I hold my breath to avoid the vanilla mist of their exhale clouds.

A handsome young boy says hi to me.

"Hi." I say. I don't bother to look at him with anything but my peripheral vision. A power move, I know.

I don't worry about safety and never have. I don't allow myself to be tied down by the tales of danger lurking at night, ready to prey on women.

I find myself in the Tenderloin. Everyone is younger and hipper than I am, and stares at me like you would at a high school party if someone's mom walked in. I guess I am a high schooler's mom now. Whoa.

I increase my pace. After several minutes the perfect bar presents itself. Several open seats, mellow music, and the people inside are closer to my age than my children's.

I sit down and order a bourbon Manhattan. While the bartender makes it, I check my screen. Still nothing from Ashley, or anyone else for that matter.

The drink is served and I pay for it immediately with DinR. The cool, foggy air outside calls for me. The bar, lit exclusively by a few large screens and backlit liquor bottles, shields me from the sobering stare of strangers. A few other people sit alone and I get the impression they are regulars. It reminds me of a dive bar I frequented in Chicago when I was in college. The same people came every day. Some were drinking themselves to death, and some were single lonely men who used it as their living room. They sipped cheap beers, watched television and chatted with the people on the stools near them. The reality of it was quite mundane, but once in a while something would happen. There would be a fight, or someone would become unruly, or someone would finally drink themselves to death and the bar and the world would move on without them.

My Manhattan is almost gone. I contemplate having another and try to assess my state of intoxication. I'm at the point of thoroughly enjoying doing absolutely nothing but staring into space and listening to music. I zone out and savor my last few sips.

Suddenly, a collective gasp rockets me out of my trance. I sit taller on my barstool and my head pivots left, then right. Everyone in the bar gapes at the screen mounted on the wall. I turn toward it and see why:

"... All internet services in U.S., including mobile, completely down."

I immediately think of my sisters. My older sister just got a landline and cable TV installed, but my younger sister is still on a waiting list. I feel an overwhelming empathetic ache for her. She lost her job at a software company, one of the few remaining ones. She's been trying to find a new job, but how will people even do that without the internet? How did people apply for jobs before the internet? Did they use fax machines? I try to let go of my feelings. She has two young kids. Her husband still has a job. She's totally fine. So many people are much worse off.

Everyone thought the intermittent outages would be all, and that the Dictator would just hold up de-digitization as a threat.

The fact that he followed through is almost more disturbing because that's how dictators wear people down. Repeated threats became mundane, and by the time they are enacted, everyone is already numb.

I consult my screen for more information. I scroll through the headlines; *"Internet Down in U.S.," "De-Digitization Starts Now," "U.S. Outage: This is Not a Test."*

I check the time—midnight here, so 3 a.m. in New York. They rolled it out in the middle of the night.

My questions and shock take on a new shape, solidifying into a hardened anger. The Dictator destroyed democracy, destroyed a country—one of the best countries—in the history of the world. Because of him, my sisters and their children are being deprived of opportunities. Because of him, I gave up my passport and moved to a different country.

I take a deep breath and reign in my anger. As an adolescent, anger fueled me, controlled my every mood and action. Letting it go, gradually over time, was like cutting out a piece of my heart—but one that allowed the real me to bloom. Once in a while it flairs up again. I need to center myself, and remember that I am in a great place—in a country that I love, even more than I ever cared for the U.S. I have two amazing children and a wife I love.

I gulp the last of my drink and drag myself home, disturbed and deflated. Everyone I pass is glued to their screens. The vanilla e-cig kids in the Tenderloin talk rapidly and trade theories. I no longer listen to the same song on repeat. I try a different station but decide to take my headphones out and walk home plain. I overhear bits of conversation. Everyone talks about the same thing. Once I am back in mostly residential Pacific Heights, the only sound is the distant din of the city and the loud footsteps from my boots.

CHAPTER 14

After my night out drinking by myself, I sleep until the first hints of sunlight peek through the curtains. Jane holds me and gives me kisses on my back and neck. I drift back to sleep, melting into her skin. I dream I'm on a ship off the east coast of the U.S. and an old woman hoists her leg over the railing and heaves herself off. I gasp and jump forward to stop her, but it's too late. She sails through the air gracefully until she hits the water. The dream is so vivid I lurch back to wakefulness with a gasp. Jane is gone. The sunlight draws large abstract shapes on the walls.

The events of the previous evening come back, loading slowly, like web pages from my childhood. I am anxious and unsettled, so first I go over the logistics—did I black out? How did I get home? I recall the sound of my boots on the sidewalk and the glow, like sparklers, of vapers outside of bars and the buzz of their chatter. All at once, it comes back to me: the internet outage in the U.S. I sit up on my elbow and grab my screen from the edge of my nightstand. I unlock it and scroll through the headlines. The Dictator has held a press conference. I press play. Like a child, he is unable to stamp out his arrogant, jubilant smile. He sits in the oval office in a perpetual shrug, his billowy suit hanging off of him, somehow simultaneously bloated, overfed, and frail, while spewing out his exhausting lies.

"Ladies and gentlemen," he says. *"It shouldn't come as a surprise, that we've shut down the internet. What once was a platform of freedom, where Americans could voice their opinions, buy things, and learn new information, has become overrun with foreign propagandists from New California, Mexico, and Russia, masquerading as Americans. These propagandists, funded by malevolent governments and tech billionaires, clock in, and spend each day spreading hateful lies, half-truths, and harmful anecdotes and rumors, which threaten our freedom, our democracy, and our very existence as humans. But!"* His right-hand index finger shoots into the air. He continues. *"We're going to bring you something better. Rather than allowing our foreign adversaries to dictate what we see on the internet, your United States government is building a new platform, an unbiased platform, for legitimate business interests, freedom of speech, and a single source of truth and fact, which cannot be accessed or manipulated by foreign interests."*

I close the video. It's amazing how convincing he is. If I were younger and less educated, I would entirely believe him. Like when I was fourteen and was shocked to find out that in fact, President Clinton *did* have sexual relations with that woman, and there wasn't a vast right-wing conspiracy.

I hold my face in my hands, recalling my nieces and nephews, back there still. Maybe in hushed tones, their parents confide that the 'president' is full of shit, but probably they think it's not that bad. Their parents are just total nerds, unable to let go of the past. My oldest nephew was only five when the election was cancelled. This is his normal.

My head throbs. I drag myself into the bathroom and find some ibuprofen. With four capsules in hand, I stumble back to the bed. I swallow all of them at once and proceed to gulp the rest of my water. I lay face down on my pillow and wait for relief.

The door opens and Jane walks to the bed and lies next to me. I turn my face toward her and she runs her hand through my hair.

"Did you hear?" says Jane.

"The internet outage? Yes, I was still awake last night when it happened."

Jane kisses my back. "It's so fucked up," she says. "I'm so glad we don't live there anymore."

"Yes," I say. I turn around, sit up, and pull the covers up to my neck. "Let's call my parents tonight when I get home."

"Yeah that sounds like a good idea. I think it will make the kids feel better to talk to them, to know we still have a connection."

"Have you been up? Have you talked to the kids?" I ask.

"Yeah, I talked to both of them. They're okay, but I think you should talk to them too. You're so good at that sort of thing."

I check the time. In about ten minutes, they will walk to school. I jump out of bed and put on clothes.

"I'll go do it now," I say.

I climb down the stairs and emerge on the main floor where Drake and Simone eat breakfast. They chew their food and observe me with serious expressions on their faces.

I greet them with a bright smile. "Good morning," I say.

Their eyes follow me as I saunter over to the espresso machine and push the button.

I whip around. "So!" I say cheerfully. "We'll never see or talk to your grandparents, aunts or uncles, or cousins on my side of the family ever again!"

Drake laughs and spits out cereal. Simone cocks her head

and drops her fork. I rush toward her and hug her shoulders. I hold her head in my hands and kiss her thick curls.

"I'm just kidding! I promise!" I say.

I put my hand on the back of her head and a small smile breaks out on her face.

I retrieve my espresso from the machine, take a sip, and lean on the counter. "We're going to voice call your grandparents tonight."

"How will that work when the internet is down?" Simone asks.

Drake answers without looking up from his cereal. "Landlines. It's a non-digital phone line where everything is connected through wires."

"How would that work, Mom?" Simone asks me.

I wave my hand dismissively. "No idea, Simone. I don't understand how anything works that isn't digital. I'm sure Drake or your other mother can explain it to you."

Simone takes another bite of her bacon and stares into the distance in wonder. Drake pours another quarter of the cereal box into his gigantic bowl. I put my hand on Simone's shoulder.

"It's important to understand that everyone in the U.S. is going to be okay. Don't forget, anyone my age remembers when all phones were landlines. We might have to communicate with people in the U.S. in different ways, but we can still talk to them and visit them."

Drake looks up from his cereal with hopeful eyes. "Are we really going to voice call our grandparents tonight?"

"Yes," I respond.

"Cool," Drake says. He loves all his grandparents. Simone is more awkward around them.

I sit at the table with them and sip my espresso. Drake devours his cereal with a faint smile on his face. Simone scrolls through her screen with one hand while her other hand feeds bacon into her mouth. They never lived in a world not connected to the internet, and I barely have either.

*****

When I arrive home from work in the evening, Jane informs me we will call my parents shortly. Drake stages himself in the sitting area where the call will take place and scrolls through his screen. Simone asks questions about why landlines don't support video chat and paces aimlessly. Drake creates an agenda of news and accomplishments to share with his grandparents.

"Do Grandma and Grandpa know how well my basketball team is doing?" Drake asks.

"I put some pictures on the PhotoShare of you playing a few weeks ago, but they haven't seen anything new since then. Let's make sure to tell them about how many more games you've won."

He nods, smiles, and reengages with his screen.

Simone wanders toward me, her face twisted in genuine confusion. "What will Grandma and Grandpa do all day when the internet is down?"

"Well, I really wouldn't worry about that, because Grandma and Grandpa were almost as old as I am now when they first got the internet."

She cocks her head. "Really?" she asks.

"Yes, and when I was a kid, we didn't have the internet either. I first had the internet when I was a little younger than you. At that time, they didn't even have mobile, just wired—not even Wi-Fi—wired."

Her mouth drops open. "It had to be plugged in?" she asks.

"Yes, it had to be plugged in. It connected through a phone line and was slow. I didn't even use text messages until I was in college."

"What did people do all day, then?" she asks.

I wave my hand, dismissing the question. "People always find things to do."

Jane walks in, gestures with her screen, and announces my parents are on the line.

"Hi, everybody!" my dad says.

"Hi!" says my mom. They sound even more cheerful, wholesome, and Midwestern than they do in person. I smile and picture them at their lake house in Michigan crowded around the cordless phone.

"How's the outage?" I ask.

"Oh, well, it's not that bad," my dad says.

"We don't like it, but we're coping just fine," my mom says. "Don't worry about us—we're fine."

"I know that you kids—Cora and Jane included to some extent—don't remember a time without the internet, but we do. We're fine. We can easily go without it. I just don't like that the decision was made for us," my dad says.

"Why do you think they turned it off?" Drake asks.

Everyone is silent.

My dad clears his throat. "Well, Drake, that's a good question. There are rumors—"

I lean forward. "What are the rumors you're hearing?" I ask.

"Well, you can read the official reasons in the news. However, some of the rumors indicate it's a cover up for some type of secret transition."

We are quiet. The information bounces through me, inflicting a vague nervousness.

Simone's shoulders tense up. "What type of transition?" she asks.

"It might not be a bad transition—" I try to explain.

Simone glares at me. "I asked Grandpa."

"Your mother's right," my dad says. "The Dictator is in his eighties now—the transition could be a change of power, and chances are it will be someone better than him. His last few speeches were about unity and freedom." He clears his throat and pauses. "He always meant well, the Dictator. He genuinely thought he could make positive changes. It just didn't happen that way."

My kids stare at the floor, stunned into silence by their grandfather's defense of the Dictator who made us flee the country of their birth.

"But we don't believe him," my Mom interjects. "He's always said he wants freedom, that everyone has freedom, but they don't. We're hoping, that if he steps down, maybe someone better will come in."

"But we're not getting our hopes up," my Dad says.

"It could be someone worse," I say.

My Dad exhales loudly, in annoyance or perhaps fear. "Cora," he says. "I highly doubt that will be the case. He's old, he's concerned about his legacy, he'll probably install someone who has the potential to unite the people. That way, if the United States of America comes back from this, and we regain what we had before the Dictator, he may wind up with a positive legacy. If he installs someone more divisive and ruthless than he, the opposite will happen."

"Well," I say, "I hope you're right."

After a few moments my mom chimes in cheerily. "We really are fine! It's not a big deal to us. The worst part is that it is more difficult to communicate with our grandkids."

"I agree," my dad says. "That's the worst part, we already miss seeing your pictures on the stream."

"So how are you guys doing other than being disconnected from the internet?" I ask.

"Good," my Mom says.

A note of uncertainty in her voice makes me nervous. Jane and I glance at each other.

"You don't sound too confident about that, Mom."

"I've not been feeling well," my Dad says. "It's probably nothing. I'm probably just getting old. I've just had a general sort of exhaustion. It's mild, but it's new, so I'm a little bit concerned. I'm seeing my doctor next week. But Cora, don't worry about it, it really is probably nothing, just my age catching up with me."

Jane chimes in with a description of a similar thing that her Dad had, but I don't pay attention. Simone, adorably, offers to research his symptoms on the internet and call him back.

My parents have always been healthy and full of energy. I used to joke that they're in better shape than I am. At the news of my Dad's health concerns, I feel a deep sadness, and a reawakened lifelong fear of losing my parents.

I tune back into the conversation.

Drake's face lights up. "My basketball team is doing really well!" he says. "And now you won't be able to see any pictures."

"Well, you can call us as often as you'd like to tell us about it," my dad replies.

Drake smiles.

Jane adds, "I'm sure there's a service that will mail paper photos to you. I'll look into it."

We end the call. Jane and I study the expressions of our children. They sullenly lounge on the couch, regarding us with sad beautiful eyes. Drake's earliest memory is of tattooed movers with thick New York accents roughly hauling his whole world into a moving truck.

When partition happened and the Hardworking Americans Act in the U.S. caused me to lose my job, Jane was more disturbed than I was. I felt so hopeful, so resolute. I always felt drawn to California. Not for the glamor of Hollywood, but for the beauty and history of San Francisco and the chance to fully erase my Midwestern upbringing.

I peer down the street to our view of the bay, partitioned by utility poles. I turn around and study my children, now lost in their screens.

"You guys okay?" I ask them.

They meet my eyes with identical polite smiles. "Yes," they say in unison.

"Let's get delivery tonight!" Jane says.

Drake excitedly initiates the order on his screen. We pass it around and enter our selections.

Once the drone drops off the food, Drake sets out plates and uncaps the takeout containers. We parade through the line of food and chat inanely, inexplicably in good spirits. I pour glasses of wine for Jane and me and the four of us ceremoniously sit at the table. Simone gushes about some new band or something she's a fan of now. I smile and listen to her, but an uneasy feeling creeps through me. Something tells me to hold on to this moment, because soon things will change. I can't ignore it. A secret transition? What could that mean?

CHAPTER 15

De-digitization in the U.S. becomes the new normal. My parents and sisters quickly adapt to communicating on cordless phones, meeting people at specific places at specific times, and having limited entertainment options.

With a flourish, the U.S. launches the first two websites of its new intranet. One is the official news website. Another is a technology company enrollment site. Companies fill out a form, sign a contract, and—upon approval—can obtain a website or mobile app on the intranet and do business in the U.S. My company applies. We are not concerned about being denied. Our innocuous business-to-business application shouldn't raise any alarms, but I am worried the uncertain political climate will further delay an acquisition.

I distract myself from stress over de-digitization and limited contact with Ashley with work. I focus on morale and anxiety reduction among employees. Only fifteen percent of our customers were in the U.S. anyway, I point out, despite the U.S. economy only being marginally smaller than New California's.

Plus, untapped markets are plentiful right here in stable New California—where tech is safe.

Six days into de-digitization I'm at work, focused on my screens, when my personal screen buzzes. Across my desk, I recognize the length and shape of Ashley's name. My stomach drops. I freeze, and momentarily fear I won't be able to handle the disappointment if it's not her. I lurch for the screen and my wish comes true—Ashley Doral.

Hi baby! I'm so sorry that I haven't been in touch. I miss you so much that it hurts, I need my baby Cora! I know it's last minute, but can you get together tonight? Maybe you can pick me up in a Lone instead of an Air?

My mood soars up like a drone. *Tonight.* I could be alone with her in the back of an UberLone. It's not 'could,' I *must* see her. My hand twitches with urgency, despite the fact she hasn't contacted me for days. I am irrationally afraid if I wait too long, she will drift off again and exist somewhere without me, like she's done in the past week. I reply and stare at my screen impatiently.

*****

My UberLone merges onto the self-drive only lane and shoots me through the streets of San Francisco. Over the Bay Bridge, I open the window and study the skyline. Tufts of fog drift by obscuring the hills. I pull my jacket tight around me and wrap a silk scarf around my neck. A government car drives alongside us, nearly at the exact same speed. I'm not alarmed when I see it, in fact—it's like I expected it to be there. It fits into the landscape so naturally that it becomes invisible, barely registering within my conscious thoughts. I close the window and the car speeds away.

My UberLone slows once it turns down the road toward the colonies. Some people in the colonies drive manual cars, which doesn't make any sense to me. They get free public transportation and they waste their money on obsolete gas-burning cars. The faint smell of gas permeates the area, which triggers nostalgic memories of the U.S. where most cars still run on gas.

The car turns into Ashley's colony. No one is outside. The heavy clouds necessitate lights on in the apartments which highlight their inhabitants. Despite the lack of pedestrians, the car creeps through at a pace so slow I consider getting out and walking alongside it. Several meters away, by the playground, two men discretely exchange something as their eyes dart around, surveilling the area.

The car halts at Ashley's building and she emerges moments later. Her door is about ten meters from the road and I watch her walk toward the car—slow and sultry with her chin high. She's not small, but she carries weight in all the right places. I feel a stab of jealousy. Whenever I gain weight, it goes right to my stomach.

She looks up into the sky, slowing down as she examines something. I follow her gaze to a drone parked overhead, so high in the air it's barely visible. When I look back at Ashley, she's looked away and once she's closer, she beams at me. I open the door for her and scoot to the middle seat. Once inside, she grabs my cheeks and kisses me on the lips. She pulls away and holds my face. Staring into her brown eyes, I am overcome with a sense of absolute calm and relief. I hug her and inhale her intoxicating scent. The car glides back onto the road. I hold her, tight, and wish we were back in New York again. Just the two of us, in a hotel room, our bodies pressed together between crisp white sheets. There is something different about how she makes me feel that I've never quite experienced before. Something final. Like there is another power entirely brewing just below the surface that

I have no control over.

She grabs my face again. "Cora," she says, "if you knew."

Before I can ask what, she kisses me deeply. Her tongue down my throat nearly gags me. She pulls my hair and moans. Large tufts of hair come loose from my ponytail. We kiss for a long time and stop only to gaze into each other's black-lined brown eyes. We only stop once we're on the Bay Bridge, speeding into San Francisco. I turn to look out the window and she wraps both of her arms around me and rests her chin on my shoulder.

"Are you taking me to a restaurant, baby?" she asks.

"Yes."

"Good, I'm hungry," she says. "Baby, we need to fix your hair, move forward a bit."

I move forward as she re-sculpts my hair into a high pony tail, wavy pieces come out on top in every direction. I fold down the mirror and inspect it.

"I didn't know there were mirrors in here," she says.

"Really?" I ask.

She laughs. "Yeah, baby, really. I never ride in these things when it's just me."

We settle in, and hold hands.

"Yeah," I say. "I guess I only ever really poke around in them when I'm alone."

"Right?" she says. "Like when you first get to a hotel room and shut the door and inspect the entire thing."

I laugh and she squeezes my hand. She smiles wide, more relaxed, and less sultry than usual, revealing her faint, pretty dimples.

The big question of what she has been up to these past days re-enters my consciousness. Was it family issues? Was she in the U.S.? Was she with Josh? Problems with her kids? Some sort of illness?

As my thoughts race, Ashley caresses my upper arm and I turn to her.

"Cora," she says, "Cora…" Her voice shakes.

I search her eyes. "Yes?"

She closes her eyes, puts her arms around my shoulders, and whispers in my ear: "I love you, Cora."

I hold her but my eyes open wide. I stare at the dark metal geometry of the Bay Bridge. My heart thuds and I feel an overwhelming surge of love for her. I bury my head in her hair, rendered speechless by my emotions. Finally, I say, "I love you too, Ashley."

I relax, close my eyes, and savor the familiar shape of her body against mine. We remain like that and listen to each other's breath, until we arrive at the restaurant.

Ashley looks at me meaningfully as we climb out of the car. I return her gaze. I close the door and place my hand on the small of her back. I let her set the pace with her slow, sexy gait. I am euphoric, and overcome by unexpected emotions so intense they border on unpleasantness.

Once we're seated, Ashley squeezes my hand and regards me with her more wholesome, less seductive smile.

"How are your kids?" I ask. A sly tactic to possibly explain her recent mysterious absence.

"Good," she says, "really good."

Our drinks come. I nod and encourage her to continue. Her drink is garnished with a sprig of rosemary, which she contemplates and pushes to the side while she takes a large sip.

She continues. "Johnald's basketball team is doing really well, they're going to the playoffs."

"I didn't know Johnald played basketball," I say. "Drake's team is going to the playoffs too."

"Is Drake on the varsity team?"

"Yes. And he is very proud of it," I respond.

"Impressive. He's only fifteen, right?"

"Yep, just a sophomore."

Ashley nods. "I bet they'll play each other," she says. "My boy versus your boy." She eyes me slyly.

"They probably will. Do you go to all of his games?" I ask.

"Yes, I rarely ever miss one," she says.

I take her hand. "Well if they play each other, we will be at the same game." I say. "Maybe you can meet my daughter Simone."

"I would love to meet Simone, she's yours, right?"

"Yes."

"Same donor?"

"Yes."

"Did you guys do IVF?"

"Yeah. My wife carried her. Jesus knows I can't quit drinking for nine months." I respond.

Ashley laughs. "Will I meet your wife too?" she asks.

"Do you want to? I don't know if she wants to meet you. I bet she will though, she's intensely curious about you."

Ashley pauses. "Hmm, yeah, it sounds awkward, but I think I do want to meet her." She sips her drink, then removes the sprig of rosemary and places it on her plate. "Unless, of course, you think it would be difficult for her in some way." She searches my face.

"No, well, I don't think so. It used to be a requirement for her to meet whoever I was involved with."

"Really. Hmm. How odd."

"Will I meet Misty?" I ask.

"I don't know, hopefully not," she says.

"Why hopefully not?"

"Misty is not a nice person," she says.

"Well, it's an inherently delicate situation, but I would like to meet her," I say. I leave out the fact I have already met her.

"You met Jimothy already, the day I met you," she says.

"That's right, I did," I say, "but I was too busy noticing you."

She laughs. "As soon as you walked in I knew I wanted you, and I knew that I could have you."

I contemplate this. What strange confidence. Ashley and I are perhaps equally good-looking, but I don't have that appeal. Not a lot of people are attracted to me.

"I knew I wanted you right away too, but it didn't occur to me that I could have you," I say.

She grabs my face and kisses me on the lips. "I knew you'd have me, and so I took you," she states.

Later, we enjoy expensive steaks with béarnaise and wine. As our blood alcohol levels rise, so do our proclamations of love. We say it again and again.

On the way home, in the UberLone, we keep the lights off. Almost as soon as we're off, she kisses me slowly and sensually. She places my hand up her dress on her inner thigh and unbuckles my belt. We kiss the whole time and hardly say a word.

When I drop her off, detaching ourselves seems impossible, but when we do it's like she's still there. Afloat with love for her, I drift home, mesmerized by the sparkle of city lights.

CHAPTER 16

Drake's at basketball practice when Jane, Simone, and I receive a group message from Drake:

Our next playoff game is Friday at 6, against Vallarta!!

The three of us briefly confirm schedules and I respond:

Awesome! I'm so proud of you! We'll all be there.

Simone, who normally finds the pageantry of sporting events deeply annoying, paces excitedly.

"Do you think Drake is the best player on the team?" she asks.

I shrug. "He's one of the best players, for sure."

She smiles. "Where's Vallarta? Is it nearby?" Simone asks.

"Yes, it's a jobber school over in Oakland," I respond.

Jane regards me quizzically.

Simone is confused and curious. "Don't we usually just

play other professional class schools?"

"Yes, during the regular season, we do. But during the playoffs, we just play whichever schools made it to the playoffs and then we come up with a regional champion who plays another regional champion."

She considers this and nods slowly, impressed with the logic of it. "Do they figure out who the best team in the whole world is?"

"No, just in the country, which is still a lot of teams. When I was in high school in the U.S., they only ever figured out the best team in the state."

"I hope Drake's team is the best in the country!" she says.

"Me too!"

Simone darts out of the room and disappears through the door to the den.

I turn to Jane. "So," I say, "Vallarta is where Ashley's oldest son goes."

"Is she going to be there?"

"Yes, he's on the basketball team."

"Oh my God, that's so weird," she says. "So our son will be playing against her son?"

"Yep. Do you want to meet her?"

Jane shakes her head, her hand on her forehead. "Yes, I think so. Will we meet her wife as well?"

"Possibly."

Jane nods slowly and sits down. "Yeah, I definitely want to meet both of them."

*****

Like Simone, I also do not like the pageantry of a high school basketball game. The cheerleaders, the chants, the fervor of teenage hormones—it all makes me cringe. On top of that, every time I turn my head there is someone I must greet. It seems like everyone who works in tech and venture capital has a kid at Drake's school.

Worst of all, they don't serve alcohol and I don't want to be the only person who brings their own. The wine I drank before I came has begun to wear off. The jobbers across the gym, however, apparently think drinking alcohol is appropriate. A large man hands out cans of beer to the people around him who open them up, throw their heads back, and chug. We had a donation drive to give free snacks to the jobber visitors and they were not shy about accepting them. A few women have purses bursting with free snacks which they ration to the outstretched hands of their whining children.

The jobbers appear markedly different than our side of the gym. They dress differently, many in shorts and flip-flops. On the professional class side, a few people wear suits and many wear nice jeans with expensive leather shoes. Both sides of the gym are ethnically diverse, though the jobber side is much whiter. The pro class from Drake's school is less than half white, mostly due to educated immigrants who are—according to the U.S.—from 'enemy states.'

I scan the jobber crowd for Ashley. I spot her platinum blonde hair near the front row in the middle. She sits next to Misty and her younger kids. She wears a large Vallarta High School sweatshirt that I suspect she shares with Johnald. I thought I might be less attracted to her when she isn't dressed sultry for me, but she's adorable. She and Misty sit close together and hold hands, which confuses me, though I am not jealous.

I reach over to take Jane's hand. She is surprised, but she looks at me adoringly. I return her gaze.

At each entrance, government protection officers armed with tranq guns stand and surveil the crowd. Others patrol the perimeter of the gym. Most pool on the professional class side with their eyes fixed across the court, as if protecting us from the rabid jobbers. An officer stops right in front of me, perhaps a meter away, and I stare at his tranquilizer gun with dart rounds ready to fire. He is so close I can see the metal transponder on the end which sends GPS coordinates to capsule ambulances. I can see the fluid in the dart. The fluid that has taken lives, despite preventative measures. I squeeze Jane's hand and glance at her. Her eyes are on the tranq gun too. The officers speak into their headsets and then drift toward the back of the bleachers.

Jane exhales. "There aren't usually this many government protection officers, are there?" she asks.

"No, definitely not. Normally there are just maybe two or three."

"Maybe because it's the playoffs? Or because of the jobbers?"

"Maybe they're recruiting the jobber kids," I say.

Jane glares in response to my joke.

The lights dim and cheesy electronic dance music engulfs the gym while the teams jog out. Everyone stands up, claps, and cheers. Drake smiles wide toward the stands and waves at everyone. I'm perpetually puzzled and in awe of my handsome son's extroversion. A group of annoying-looking girls yell his name and giggle.

Across the gym, Ashley cheers and jumps up and down. I cringe at her enthusiasm. Jane and I remain reserved and clap politely.

"Which one is Ashley's son?" Jane asks.

"Number seventeen," I whisper.

Curious and callous, she eyes him.

The game starts and both teams play hard and steady, pacing themselves for what could be a close match. Drake scores the first basket of the game and Jane, Simone, and I cheer with enthusiasm. Johnald gives him a pat on the back before he jogs down the court. Impressed with Johnald's sportsmanship, tears form in my eyes.

Johnald is taller than Drake by a few centimeters and slimmer. He is good looking, but not as handsome as my boy Drake. Johnald is cool and calm, but ignores the crowd and remains focused on the court and his teammates. Drake on the other hand, feeds off the crowd.

During a time out, I check my screen and find a message from Ashley:

Hi Baby, you're looking sexy over there. Want to meet up during half-time?

I respond that I do. I tell Jane, who gives me a wary look.

"We'll have to bring Simone as well," Jane says to me.

I place my hand on Simone's back. "Simone."

Her lip quivers in disgust. "What?"

"During halftime we're going to go meet a friend of mine."

Her eyes widen. Halftime is the least fun time to walk around. She and I share a dislike of crowds.

"Why can't your friend just come over here?" she asks.

"She's from the other side."

Her eyes light up. "From the jobber school?" She's always been curious about jobbers and disadvantaged people. She's even proclaimed she wishes she were a jobber.

I respond. "Yes. She's a good friend of mine, we're just going to meet up with her and talk to her for a few minutes. We'll all go, you can walk between us."

"How do you know her?" she asks.

We are distracted by the roar of the jobber crowd after Johnald scores a three-point shot. He smoothly turns around and trots toward the other end of the court like nothing happened.

"You know how I go to jobber schools and do talks

sometimes?" I say.

Simone nods.

"I met her at one of those talks."

"Does she work at the school? What was she doing there?" Simone asks.

"No, she doesn't work there, her son was in the class so she came to hear the talk. At jobber schools, a lot of parents come into the classrooms and help out."

Simone absorbs this information, focused and distant as it sinks in.

The game continues. The score vacillates between each team's favor. Toward the end of the second quarter, Drake's team is ahead. Johnald and Drake are each stars of their respective teams.

I am curious and nervous about how this meeting will go. My blood alcohol level is not high enough to deal with this awkward situation. My stomach turns as the time in the second quarter counts down.

The buzzer rings. We spring up to beat the indecisive crowd. I glance across and spot Ashley make her way out with Misty and their two youngest children. Most of the jobbers stay in their seats because the free snacks are gone.

We exit the gym and trudge through the crowd toward our designated meeting spot. I spot Ashley. Misty stands next to her, arms crossed, glaring. Jimothy and Misty Jr. glance around warily. I hug Ashley in a way I hope appears platonic and friendly. Misty rolls her eyes as Jane approaches her and introduces herself. Misty half-heartedly attempts a smile at her, but it comes out as a grimace. Ashley shakes Jane's hand, smiles, and introduces herself. Jane grins and introduces herself as Jane Broussard, giving our last name extra emphasis. I whip my head toward her, but am relieved when they continue to chat in a genuine warm tone. I attempt to shake Misty's hand.

"So the home wrecker wants to shake my hand." She growls in my ear. "Yeah, hi, I'm Misty."

I cock my head and smile. "Cora," I say.

"Mm-hmm," Misty responds. She looks me up and down with contempt. "You're not even wearing your team colors?" she says. "Why even bother rooting for your team?"

I shrug. "My son doesn't mind."

I glance at Ashley and Jane. They introduce the kids to one another. Nervous and fascinated, Simone greets them with an intense smile. Jimothy stares at her with his mouth open. Misty Jr. starts a conversation about the game, and she and Simone speak with pride about their older brothers.

Misty rolls her eyes, retrieves her screen from her jeans pocket, and dismisses me.

Behind Misty, a government protection officer observes us. He holds a screen in his hand pointed in our general direction. His eyes meet mine and he shifts his body the opposite way, but his screen remains pointed toward me. I look away. My breath quickens. I tell myself that when I look back, if the officer and his screen are not focused on me, that it was nothing. I give it a few seconds and look back. He stares directly into my eyes and I gasp. He stuffs his screen in his pocket and scurries away. His tranq gun bounces with each swift step.

I attempt to calm myself. My eyes dart between Ashley, Jane, and Misty, but no one looks at me and I was apparently the only one who spotted the officer. Maybe he was curious why a jobber family and professional class family were talking? I try to relax and forget about him, but I can't stop picturing the unnatural way he held his screen. It wasn't the typical way someone holds a screen, like an extension of their hand.

I tune to Jane and Ashley's conversation to distract myself. Ashley compliments Jane on her cardigan.

"Thank you!" Jane says. "I got it in Italy when Cora went

there for work."

"Oh, do you come with her sometimes on business trips?" Ashley asks.

"When I can. It's harder now with the kids in school but not old enough to stay on their own." Jane responds.

Ashley nods and shoots me a quick look of jealousy. She glances at Misty, who stands with her arms crossed and her head turned away. Ashley pulls her gently by the arm and welcomes her back into the conversation. I'm surprised Misty acquiesces. Ashley meets Misty's eye and pleads with her. Misty visibly relaxes and replaces her scowl with a look of sad resignation. Her eyes toggle between Jane and Ashley attempting to pick up the conversation. Ashley takes her hand and squeezes it.

In a flash I understand Ashley's relationship with Misty and what she needs from me, and from Josh. She takes care of Misty, almost like a wayward child who she loves but doesn't like.

Ashley's disadvantaged position is only partially financial. She takes care of all of these people, and only Josh and I take care of her. She can't leave because she loves Misty and her children, but if her life consisted of only them, she would implode.

As I overhear Jane and Ashley talk, I am grateful to be married to a happy, emotionally stable woman, but I also have deep respect and affection for Ashley. I do love her. Here, at this moment, I intensely hope everything will stay exactly as it is right now.

CHAPTER 17

Saturday morning, the day after the team's big loss, I wake up early to make omelets for the family. I was not disappointed at the outcome of the game. Drake and his teammates are privileged and will be successful in life no matter what happens. For some of those jobber kids, if they go on to win a championship it could be the most exciting thing that ever happens to them.

Drake was disappointed and quiet while we walked home, but he seemed to take it well. He let me place my hand on his shoulder while Simone talked in detail about how awesome various points of the game were.

Drake clops down the stairs and emerges at the end of the staircase.

"I'm making omelets," I announce.

He mumbles pleased acknowledgement and wanders over to the couch with his screen.

"What do you want on yours?" I ask.

He shrugs. "Whatever."

"Great!" I say.

Simone walks in and gasps with excitement when she spots the omelets.

The front door opens, stirring the air and casting dramatic chards of light throughout the room. Jane enters with a yoga mat and a wide dimpled smile. I scrape the last omelet out of the pan and onto the chopping block. I chop each omelet into squares and create an omelet bar. We grab plates and hobble through. Drake, predictably, takes two entire omelets.

"Drake, I know you're disappointed, but it really was a good game. You played great," I say.

Jane and Simone nod in agreement.

"Thanks," Drake says. His eyes remain cast downward toward his omelet.

Simone leans forward and places both her hands on the table. "At halftime we met some people from the other school that Mama Cora knows," she tells Drake.

Drake eyes me, curious. "You know people from Vallarta colonies?" he asks.

"Yes," Simone answers for me. "Their son Johnald is on the team. He has a brother, Jimothy, and a sister, Misty Jr. They have two moms too. One of their moms is named Ashley, and she's really nice, and the other one is named Misty, and she's really mean." Simone speaks quickly, apparently excited about Ashley's family.

Drake turns to me. "You know Johnald's mom?"

"Yes," I say. It feels odd to hear Johnald's name from Drake's mouth. "Do you know Johnald?"

"No," he says. "I just met him for the first time last night." He takes a bite of his omelet and cocks his head. "I'm surprised to hear you're friends with someone who named their kid Johnald."

Jane and I laugh, surprised at his snarkiness.

"That was over sixteen years ago," I say. "Actually, I believe he is seventeen years old."

Drake shrugs. "Well, how old is Jimothy?"

I laugh, conceding, "Jimothy is seven."

"How old is Misty Jr.?" Simone asks.

"Thirteen," I say.

Simone visibly deflates at the news that Misty Jr. is two years older than her.

Jane sips tea and listens with her brow furrowed at our children's knowledge of Ashley's family.

With finality, Jane hits her hand on the table. "I thought they were very nice people," she says. "What do you want to do today, Drake?"

He shrugs and mumbles incoherently.

"We can still have a celebratory day for you," Jane continues.

After the game, Jane and I didn't get a chance to discuss how she felt about meeting Ashley. I'm very curious what her impression was. It amazes me how many days pass between meaningful conversations.

Simone and I finish our omelets first and return to the kitchen to clean up while Jane stays at the table and quizzes Drake on things to do to cheer him up. Ice cream? A day trip somewhere? His favorite restaurant?

"Do you think maybe Misty Jr. would want to be my friend, even though I'm two years younger than her?" Simone asks me.

I consider this possibility. I don't think Jane would like that, and I am absolutely certain Misty Sr. wouldn't like it.

"I don't know, Simone. I think most thirteen year olds wouldn't want to be friends with an eleven year-old. Misty's mom told me she's really busy with activities and stuff, and going out and seeing her friends, so probably not." That last part I made up.

Simone regards me with sad puppy eyes. "I want to be friends with a jobber," she says.

"Well, we should look up some sort of program where they

have jobbers and pro-class kids together," I say.

She waves away the idea. "I hate programs."

I laugh. "They're not all the same, maybe we'll find a program that you'll like."

"I don't think so." She bolts out of the room to go down to the den.

I motion to Jane to meet me in our room. I walk up the stairs, lay down on the bed, and wait for her.

She walks in, closes the door, and lays down on the other side of the bed. "Hi wife," she says.

I reach over and rub her back. "Hi," I say. "We haven't really had a chance to talk, but I'm so curious what you think of Ashley."

"Well," she says, "I definitely liked her, and she was very attractive..." She trails off. "She was just not what I expected. Does that make sense?"

"No, not really, what do you mean? In what way was she not what you expected?"

She opens her mouth and pauses. "You just described her as this sultry hot woman, and then we walk up and she's wearing a giant sweatshirt and little makeup and just seemed wholesome and nice. I mean, we were at her son's basketball game—it's not an occasion to be sexy—but, I mean, you had on your leather coat and boots and everything, and looked exactly like you always do."

"Yeah, I understand. That makes sense. I can see how that would throw you off. She was definitely more casually dressed than I've ever seen her."

"I just think she seems different than other women you've been with in the past, and I guess I just don't understand what you get from her that you can't get from me."

My breath quickens. I consider Jane's words. "It's hard to explain, but there is something I get from her that is similar to the other women I've been with. She's assertive and knows how to get what she wants. But at the same time she lets me take care of her, which I like. There is something mysterious and strong about her, something I've enjoyed watching slowly unfold." I pause and consider what else I mean to say. "We have a lot of chemistry together and it just feels good being with her."

"Okay… I guess I see that. I'm not upset, I'm just trying to understand."

"So, we're okay? You're all right with it still? With Ashley?" I ask.

"Yes, I'm okay with it," Jane says. She kisses me. I lay my head on her lap and hug her. She runs her hands through my hair and kisses my forehead.

I sit up. "Hey, while we were talking to Ashley, did you see the government protection officer nearby?"

Jane cocks her head. "No, why? What was he doing?"

"He was standing nearby and it seemed like he was listening to us."

"What do you mean? Why is it weird that he was eavesdropping?"

"I mean, he had his screen pointing to me, like he was using something on it to listen to us."

A tense silence seizes us.

I continue. "Like, he was definitely not holding it in a natural way and he made eye contact with me. It was weird."

"He was probably just curious what professional class people and jobbers were doing together. I mean, we did look kind of strange," Jane says.

I nod slowly. "Okay, that makes sense, so maybe he was listening to us with his screen, but just because of that."

Jane pivots her head toward me. "Why else would it be?"

I shrug.

Her eyes bore into mine. "Cora?" she asks. "You thought it

was something other than that? What else could it possibly be?"

"I didn't have anything in mind. I just notice government protection officers more often, ever since I met—well, I guess it's been ever since that girl Emma was killed. I just notice them all the time and it seems like they're paying attention to me. It used to be I saw them all the time, they were everywhere, but they didn't even notice me. Now, it seems like I see them more often. And that they're older-looking more experienced ones, and that they're looking at me."

Jane stares at me. I meet her eyes. Blue around her pupil, then hazel, then green. Murky like the sea, but her meaning is clear. After a long pause, she says, "Do you think it has to do with Ashley?"

I skip a breath at my paranoia echoed back to me.

CHAPTER 18

A t work on Monday, my screen buzzes, and I'm surprised to find a message from Josh Winston.

Hi Cora! Great to see you in NYC! Would love to catch up over lunch soon. Sound good?

I picture myself at lunch with him. Just me and Josh Winston, and I find myself dazzled by the idea. I knew Josh tolerated my company, but this is different. He sought me out. I allow myself to indulge in my fantasy, and picture us—Cora and Josh—having frequent lunches and drinks together, accompanied by long, meaningful conversations.

Hi Josh, sure! Just let me know when.

He answers:

Great! How about tomorrow at noon? I'll send a car for

you.

*****

The following day, I leave work at noon and wait outside. He didn't message again to mention any specifics about the car. Outside my office building, I stand awkwardly and check my screen for messages. I contemplate messaging him, but it seems weird to reach out to a high-ranking politician to ask questions about the logistics of transporting myself to lunch. As I ponder this, a government car pulls up and a man in a suit steps out and approaches me.

"Cora Broussard?" he says.

"Yes, that's me."

He opens the door and I expect to find Josh inside, but the car is empty when I get in. Unsettled, I check my messages again but find nothing new. The driver takes the car out of park and manually drives forward. He doesn't use auto drive or any sort of navigation device. I try to breathe evenly and relax.

We pull up to a restaurant behind an identical black government car. Two government protection officers, dressed in their trademark uniforms and armed with tranquilizer guns, motion to the drivers. One of them leans over to open the door to the car in front. I jump at the sound of the other officer simultaneously opening my door.

"Ms. Broussard. Come along please."

I gather my things and climb out of the car. As soon as I'm on the street, I'm standing next to Josh. I am flustered by the weirdness of it all, but I can tell Josh is used to it. He is taller than I recall, maybe twelve centimeters taller than me.

He shakes my hand and grins, making his eyes crinkle at the corners. "Cora," he says.

People in business attire bustle in and out of the restaurant

167

eyeing us discreetly. The place is upscale enough that people pretend not to be impressed by Josh's presence.

I force a smile. "Hi."

Josh places his hand on my shoulder and turns toward the restaurant. We walk in alongside one another. He wears a suit and a red tie. In my wrap coat, jeans, and boots, I appear small and underdressed next to him and I rarely feel either of those things.

We're escorted to a table in the corner. I am incredibly uncomfortable, but Josh is all charm. I realize I've seen him as his true self, and when he's vulnerable, but I've never interacted with him when he's in his element. Perhaps this is a power play. Something to do with Ashley. Though I can't think of why a man with prime minister prospects would bother trying to intimidate me when I'm just another eccentric tech CEO.

Once we're settled in and the star-struck jobber waiting on us finishes introducing herself and the specials, Josh flashes me a grin. He seems like the Josh Winston from the stream, not the Josh Winston who mixed drinks for me and our girlfriend in a New York hotel room.

"Cora," he says, "it's great to see you. I had such a lovely time in New York getting to know you. I just had to reach out and see if you could meet for lunch."

His intentions seem earnest and I try my hardest to relax and act like a normal human being.

To occupy my hands, I open the menu. "Yeah, New York was fun," I say. I meet his eyes. "I was glad to hear from you."

He smiles with his mouth closed and cocks his head. I return my gaze to the menu and he does the same. I glance at him and notice he appears nervous and begins to sweat. I feel the power dynamic shift and feel more comfortable.

He closes the menu, places it in front of him, and folds his hands over it. "So what's been happening with you?" he asks. "I hear you have a basketball star for a son!"

"Oh yeah, did Ashley tell you? My son Drake's team played Johnald's team in a playoff game, but Johnald's team won."

"So I hear! Isn't that something? A jobber team beating a professional class team." He shakes his head.

I shrug. "Yeah, I would never mention this to my son, but I was actually happy with the outcome."

"Really?" He purses his lips on his straw and sips his water. "How come?"

"I guess because I'm always rooting for the underdog."

"Hmm. I can empathize with that. I've certainly been the underdog before."

I clarify: "My son's only fifteen, he's a sophomore, he will have other opportunities."

Josh nods sympathetically, understanding.

"Plus," I continue, "the fact that it was against Ashley's son certainly helped."

He smiles and nods. "Mm-hmm, *Johnald*." He meets my eye like we share an understanding, but fidgets when I give away nothing. "I'll never get over that name."

It's not what I expected and I laugh. "Yeah, me either."

"He's a wonderful young man, but for Christ's sake, call the guy John!"

We laugh, and the tension eases all at once.

"You don't have kids, do you Josh?"

"No," he says. He meets my eyes and reminds me more of the lovely man I hung out with in New York than Josh the politician. "My wife and I never made that leap."

Our drinks come. Tea for him, a cappuccino for me. He gives his tea bag a few vigorous dunks before topping it off with the contents of a sugar packet. He opens his mouth to speak and then hesitates. I remain quiet and wait.

"When we were in our early thirties, we discussed it. I think I wanted kids more than she did, and she just ended up never being ready."

I nod. "I never wanted kids until my early thirties, and even then it was a gradual process. If my wife didn't push so hard, I'm not sure I would have ended up with kids. Of course, now I'm glad I have them, and really can't imagine my life without them."

His brow furrowed, he stares into his tea and nods. "I'm fine with how things turned out now. Sometimes, I wish circumstances were different, that everything was different, but I can't change decisions from my past, I can only move forward," he says.

"My perspective is the same. I don't let things get in my way, I always look to the future. Is your wife still happy with the decision?" I ask.

"Yes. As far as I'm aware. I don't think she feels any absence for not having children. If anything, I think she is relieved that the topic is closed."

I nod and sip my cappuccino. "Does your wife know about Ashley?"

"No. I don't think so. Not really. Not specifically. She doesn't ask where I am, where I go or what I'm up to. I don't believe we have an expectation of monogamy anymore."

"You don't think? But you haven't discussed it?"

"Correct, but—"

I cut him off. "Well, in my experience, when someone says that, they are mistaken."

He chuckles and points at me with his tea. "You are right, most of the time that is true."

"So what makes you think you don't have the expectation of monogamy? What makes you different than everyone else?" I ask.

He gathers his thoughts and prepares to present his case. "A few times, she found evidence of me being with other women, little things—a gift I bought for Ashley, lipstick on my collar—"

"No! Seriously? That's such a cliché—lipstick on your collar?"

"Yes, I know, that's exactly what I thought," he says.

"Man, I'm glad I only wear black shirts. You know, thinking it through, I did come home to Jane once with lipstick all over my face, so I shouldn't judge, but anyway, go on."

He laughs and shakes his head. "Seriously? Wow." He sips his tea again, punctuating our conversation. "When my wife found those things, she wasn't upset, she acted like a teasing best friend and said she was glad I was out having fun."

I nod. "Interesting. I guess that works for some people. I don't know though, for me personally, I just couldn't go behind my wife's back."

"That's great that you have that level of trust and open communication," he says.

"So what is your relationship with your wife like? What do you get out of it?" I ask.

He stares upward as he prepares an answer. "I genuinely like her and enjoy her company. I have a lot of stress in my life and I like coming home to her, being able to wind down by chatting inanely. She's totally fine when I'm away and enjoys her alone time"

The conversation pauses as the server takes our order. After placing mine, I contemplate what Josh said. I picture her greeting him each evening with a smile and a glass of scotch. I'm interested in her side of the story. Is she happy?

The server dramatically places her pen back in her apron and departs.

"I'm really enjoying this conversation, Cora. I like that you aren't shy about asking the personal questions," Josh says.

"Yeah, I'm not big on small talk."

He daintily sips his tea. "I'm big on any kind of talk, I just love communicating with people. I think you need to sometimes have the real conversations, but I love filling the time with small talk, just, having all these quick connections, quick exchanges with different people. It makes you feel good. You know?"

"No," I say.

He smiles. "Introversion is something I don't understand. Whenever I think I do, it turns out I don't. My wife is introverted, yet she can't wait for me to come home so we can talk. Then, all day while I'm gone, she chats to her friends on social media. Yet, she's way too nervous to do an interview with me on the stream." He shakes his head.

"It doesn't sound like your wife is introverted, it sounds like she's shy."

He cocks his head and considers this. "Hmm…"

"Or maybe she has a hard time trusting people."

"Yes, yes, she does." He grabs for his tea like it's a glass of scotch.

I apparently opened some wound. A silence befalls us and I fear I went too far. I sip my cappuccino and scan the room, then glance at my screen for the time.

Josh smoothly breaks the silence. "Cora, have you ever considered going into politics?"

I am surprised by the question. "No, why?"

"Oh, it just came to mind, I think you would be great at it. You have a good mind, Cora. Even more importantly, you're composed, and you have an authoritative presence about you."

"Thanks. Honestly, yes, I have thought about going into politics before, but never seriously. I think what is holding me back the most is that I am really not a people person. I'm truly introverted, meeting new people is exhausting to me."

"Really? Exhausting? Hmm… interesting. That's the exact opposite of how I feel about meeting new people."

"That doesn't surprise me," I say.

He leans forward and meets my eyes. "Seriously though,

you should consider a political run. I can help you. Sure, there is a lot of interacting with people, but it's easy to avoid interacting with people directly. Are you okay with public speaking?"

"Yes, I actually really enjoy public speaking."

He points at me. "Thought so. With technology, and how the world is now, you don't need to knock on doors, or shake hands at train stations. There are much more efficient uses of your time."

I nod slowly. "Yeah, going door-to-door doesn't sound like any fun. Unless of course someone thinks I'm her sleazy website hook-up."

Josh slaps the table and laughs to the point of choking on his tea. "Yes, that definitely makes it more interesting!" He shakes his head. "You know—Kev King is a total introvert. He avoids talking directly to constituents. Always has. He schedules alone time every day."

"Intersting." I say. I smile at the thought of our handsome prime minister re-charging in a room all by himself.

Josh nods. "Yep. Just last week I had a late afternoon meeting with him and when I asked what's next on his schedule, he said 'a glass of scotch alone in my man cave.'"

I laugh. "Interesting. I can see the introvert in him now that I think about it. He seems like a plotting and scheming alone in a dark room kind of guy."

He points to me. "I see that in you too."

"Yeah, totally," I respond.

"The Presi—I mean the Dictator, he's actually more introverted than you would think. Spends hours every day just watching T.V. by himself. Won't let anyone interrupt him."

I nod, uninterested, having heard that before about the Dictator.

Josh continues. "My take on the guy, is that it's all a game to him. His whole interest in people. It's about power. It's about projecting an image."

"Yeah, he's a true sociopath," I say.

"I don't think it's that simple," Josh says. "He's very loving and loyal to those who obey him. Really, Cora, you'd be surprised." Josh fidgets with his tea, his silverware, and avoids my gaze.

"Have you met him?" I ask abruptly.

Josh inhales sharply, removing his shaky hands from the table. He sits up straight in his chair, smiling. "Yes, of course. I mean, in the course of official business we've had a few meetings. You'll recall his meetings with Kev years back. I was there as well. And, well, Cora I can't tell you everything of course, but the public efforts to restore our relationship with the U.S. aren't the only ones. Not everything makes it into the news." He smiles pleasantly.

I lean back, finish off my cappuccino, and push the saucer to the side of the table. I flag down the waitress and motion that I want another cappuccino. She nods, conveying duty and efficiency. I turn back to Josh. Sweat forms on his forehead.

"Well," I say, "everyone's nice *sometimes*."

"Very true, very true." Josh sips his tea before topping it off with more from the kettle, busying himself. I lean back in my chair and watch him, waiting for him to break the silence, which he does.

"You're from the Midwest, correct?" he asks.

"Yes, Michigan."

"I would never guess that if Ashley hadn't told me."

"Thank you," I say.

He laughs. "I'm a proud Minnesota boy myself."

"You don't have the accent."

"Yes I got rid of it," he says. "I'm guessing you did the same?"

"Yeah, starting when I moved to Chicago. Most of my

friends weren't from the Midwest, and I realized how nerdy my accent sounded, so I just worked on not talking in it. It comes back a bit when I see my family."

"Do you go back to the U.S. a lot?" he asks.

"Yes, I go to see my family a few times a year. Do you go back to Minnesota?"

He shakes his head. "No. My mom died when I was in high school and I never knew my father. I'm not close to any of the people I knew back there. Too many bad memories."

"Yeah that sounds terrible, I wouldn't go back either."

He smiles. "Do you ever miss it? The U.S.?"

"Miss it? No, not at all. I was never patriotic—at least not toward the U.S."

"Why's that?" he asks.

I contemplate this. "I don't know, a lot of things. The guns, the lack of education, the ignorance. The complacency. The greed—and not just greed itself—but the way wanting things slowly became disconnected from working for the things you wanted. It's a lot of things. Basically, I just think Americans are a bunch of fucking idiots."

He leans forward. His eyes widen, simultaneously shocked, offended and amused, and I think: *Oh no, I've just let it slip that I'm awful!*

He laughs and shakes his head. "You've got a sharp tongue, Cora."

He reaches across the table and places his hand over mine. I'm surprised to find that his warm soft skin feels nice.

I retract my hand and change the subject. "Do you miss the U.S.?" I ask.

He lowers his eyes and regards me with a tight smile. "Sometimes I do."

"But didn't you go to college in California? Weren't you here from the beginning? Working in tech?"

"Yes, but that was when it was part of the U.S." He sips his tea. "It was different as soon as we left the U.S. Almost immediately. I didn't want to secede from the U.S., despite all that was going on. Everything in Washington seemed so far away. I was successful by then, thinking about getting into politics. I thought I could be the president of the United States. It was in the U.S. that I turned myself into a young man with no family and no money into what I am today. I just don't think there is that same spirit here."

He swallows and closes his eyes. Josh's stately charm makes it easy to forget he didn't come from money, that he was raised by a single mother with addiction issues. Perhaps I brought back some bad memories, something he doesn't share. His clenched fist rests on the middle of the table. I squeeze his hand and smile at him. Surprised by my nurturing gesture, he meets my eyes and smiles back.

"I get what you're saying about New California not having that same spirit, the—I don't know, whatever the hell it is that they say—the boot strap thing. But yeah, I agree, you don't see that as much here. Though, I definitely don't see that in the U.S. anymore, and I really hadn't in a long time."

"Things just kind of fell apart over there," he says.

"Americans choked on their own greed and privilege," I say.

"Perhaps."

Our salads come and they require further assembly, they're basically salad kits. Intensely focused, we dive into them with our steak knives.

While I eat, I reflect on this experience of being here with Josh. It seems odd being with him without Ashley, yet very comfortable. I become more curious about Ashley and Josh's relationship. She's secretive about it and he hasn't said much to me about it either.

When we're done, Josh pays with DinR and we stroll out.

The twin black cars lurk outside the restaurant with doors open and government protection officers beside them. Josh gives me a light hug and we each climb into our respective cars.

Once I'm settled, the driver whisks me away toward work. A sense of excitement about my potential friendship with Josh livens my senses. I'm at a point in my life where I don't pursue friendships because relationships that are not intensely emotional bore and disappoint me. It always surprises me which friends stick and which ones disappear. It's never who I would pick, but maybe it will be different this time.

CHAPTER 19

De-digitization continues to push the U.S. backwards down the path of progress. I talk to my parents every few days for updates. Just like everything related to the loss of democracy has been, it starts out slow and subtle. Then there is a distraction and that's when they strike. I've seen this before. I've been watching this for fifteen years, and something is definitely going on.

"The 'news stories' or 'propaganda'—whatever you want to call it—have changed since de-digitization begun," my dad said on the phone the previous night. "The focus is now on New California."

"In what way? What are they focusing on?" I asked with alarm.

"It's not that the tone changed necessarily, but just that the stories are more frequent. Nearly every night, there is some story or another about how life in New California is not what it seems, that the quality of life is terrible for most. They profile crime in jobber colonies, corruption, classism, and lack of freedom."

No nation has ever successfully fully suppressed the ability to disseminate information. Bits and pieces of information are smuggled back and forth on screens of New California residents.

I think back to what my dad said weeks ago when this first started, the rumors about a secret transition. It would make sense. The Dictator is now in his eighties. The assumption was the vice president would take over, but somehow that always seemed unlikely to me.

As I walk home from work, I think of the situation in the U.S. and worry about my money. While I still have some money in U.S. mutual funds my dad holds for me, and some in various international bank accounts, most of my money is a number on the NCD ledger. Back when partition happened, a lot of people's money was confiscated or held by the U.S. government. Some people were able to petition the New California government to credit their ledger for that money and then create an IOU for the U.S. government. Luckily, I was one of the first to come and didn't go through any of that. However, the fact they credited people for money that isn't backed in any way unsettled me. Hence the reason I diversified. I do some quick calculations and figure about eighty percent of my net worth is in NCD. Mostly because I haven't moved any money around in over five years and somehow I keep piling up more money.

I'm so engrossed in my thoughts, I jump and gasp when a New California government protection officer blocks my path on the sidewalk.

"Cora Broussard?"

"Yes?" I say.

He flashes credentials. "Officer Felix Wentworth. I need to see a form of government-issued identification please. For verification."

I fumble through my purse for my New California passport. His hand rests on the barrel of his tranq gun. My hands shake. Terror pulses through me. The omnipresent tranq gun-armed government protection officers normally blend in like sidewalks, but being approached by one and addressed by name? Something must be terribly wrong. I soothe myself, for a moment, by recalling that I've never committed a serious crime, but that makes this even more confusing. What could it be?

He inspects my passport, examines me, and nods.

"The Ministry of Catastrophe Anticipation needs to speak to you. You must come with me now. This is mandatory."

"Do you know what they want to talk to me about? Is it mandatory that I go right now?" I ask.

"Yes, Ma'am, you must go immediately. You must give me your screen and any other communication devices you have on you."

My hand trembles as I hand him my screen.

"Do you have any other digital devices on you at this time?"

"No."

My mind races through a spider web of scenarios. Did I black out and do something? Fuck. On the rare occasions in which I black out, I usually later learn that I was either very quiet, or ranting inanely about inconsequential annoyances.

Did my kids do something? Secretive Simone. Could she be involved in something? Maybe hacking? Jesus fucking Christ, that can't be, she's only eleven.

The officer retrieves a small black device from his pocket, presses a button on it, and scans me with it from head to toe. A green light turns on and he returns it to his pocket. The rear door of the government vehicle opens and he nods at it. I walk toward it, my ankle boots clanking loudly. I try to walk gently, avoiding any provocation. I settle into the seat and Officer Wentworth closes the door behind me, not bothering to check that I'm ready.

The car comes to life with a hybrid vehicle growl and he immediately puts it in auto drive. The car turns right on Market

Street and I absorb the familiar sights, the beginning of streets shooting up into hills, swarms of pigeons, the square that used to be full of homeless people. Yet, through the terrifying haze of forced government custody, the familiar sights look like ominous facades created by a malevolent force in service of some sort of fucked-up joke.

The car speeds up in the direction of the Office of the Ministry of Catastrophe Anticipation, which is separate from the other government buildings. Most of their work involves researching the potential of problems which do not yet exist. Very little information is available about them, but everyone agrees they are the most secretive of government agencies.

I twitch as fear slices through me once again. What would they possibly want from me? What sort of trouble am I in that's so bad that they sent someone to hunt me down and find me?

Josh, I think. They must have been sent by Josh. I don't commit crimes, so what else could it be? But no, that can't be it. Part of how the Ministry of Catastrophe Anticipation prevents catastrophes is by having no contact with other branches of government. They have access to all government documents, networks, and communications, but it's a one-way system. They take information in, but nothing ever comes out. So this could be *about* Josh. Maybe they think I have some sort of plot against Josh? Maybe they just screen his friends? Hopefully that's all this is.

Then I recall a venture capitalist I worked with a few years ago who knew Kev King. He explained a whole process where he had to be screened by the Ministry of Security and go in for an interview, but that it was an official, open process. This is different. This is not *routine*.

Officer Wentworth is the only protection officer in the car and I wonder what would happen had I run away. While the car shoots through traffic on its own accord, he enters something into the functional yet distasteful user interface of an official government app.

He turns to me. His face is smooth, with intermittent poofs of soft facial hair. He couldn't grow a beard if he wanted to. His eyes are pure green, like a light that says go. "I just got confirmation they'll be able to see you right away."

I nod and open my mouth to respond, but resort to an incoherent mumble.

Officer Wentworth flashes a tight smile and turns back toward the road. He retrieves his personal screen from his loose dark gray government pants. He has a message that I can't read, but is at least seventy-five percent emojis.

My thoughts swirl and I try to calm myself with the hypnosis of passively observing the city go by from the back seat of a car.

Upon arrival, Officer Wentworth unlocks my door with a fob, and motions for me to walk beside him into the building. The brutalist architecture alone must play a part in preventing catastrophes. No one wants to enter. Some enter and are kept for days, others seem to disappear entirely.

We approach a desk where a blond-haired woman with empty blue eyes sits behind a screen. Officer Wentworth gives her my name with a proud smile, like a hunter dragging in his kill. We stand and wait in complete silence, other than the woman typing. I take a deep breath. Inhale. Exhale. I jump at the sound of oxford shoes on marble floors echoing off concrete walls. Officer Wentworth and the blond woman turn their heads, bored and sedated. I snap my head in the direction of the footsteps. A man my approximate age and height walks toward me and stops about a meter away.

"Cora Broussard?" he asks.

"Yes."

He nods. "This way."

He escorts me to a room on the first floor, perhaps twenty meters from the entrance. His large build conceals excess fat. Where I am tall, curvy, and reasonably slim, he is compact and sturdy. His perfectly ovular head features small crystal clear blue eyes and short balding hair. His expression reveals nothing. We are in a cinderblock room designed to convey the message: *you are being interrogated.*

We sit down. Officer Felix Wentworth enters. He hands me a tall glass of water with crescent moon ice cubes, meets my eyes with his pretty green ones, and scurries out of the room. The water is lukewarm but quickly gives way to the coldness of the ice cubes. I take a long sip and realize I was thirsty. The man sitting across from me stares into my eyes intrusively. His emotionless face suggests a life void of laughter or smiling.

"Please state your full name," he says.

"Cora Renée Broussard."

"Date of birth."

"May 14, 1984."

"City, state or province, and country of birth."

"Grand Rapids, Michigan. United States of America."

He pauses to check his tablet. He does everything slowly, barely blinking, gravely serious. An odd taste forms in my mouth. Something chemical. A taste designed to leave nothing behind. I examine my mental state, my alertness, the speed at which I recall information and calculate. The sharp edge of anxiety that lurks over most of the long hours of the day. Everything is intact.

"Ms. Broussard. This is what we call a data mining session. We believe there is a possibility you have some information which may be of use to our agency, but you are not suspected or accused of any crime. Your participation is mandatory, if you do not participate, you will be arrested. Do you understand, Ms. Broussard?" he says.

"Yes, Sir."

"Your citizenship in the country of New California is contingent upon cooperation with any and all government agencies, so failure to cooperate can result in citizenship revocation, deportation, or imprisonment. Do you understand, Ms. Broussard?"

"Yes, Sir," I say.

He pauses and glances at my water glass. I follow his eyes to the glass half full.

He continues. "This meeting must remain entirely confidential. You must not mention the fact that this meeting occurred with any individuals. When we are finished, we will inform you what you may tell people about your whereabouts this afternoon. If you tell anyone that this meeting occurred, or any information *at all* about this meeting, you will be arrested and charged with treason. Do you understand, Ms. Broussard?"

I pause, disturbed by the fact that I can't even tell Jane, and wonder how many people have been through this. Has this happened to Jane? Drake? Simone?

"Yes, Sir," I say.

"Please summarize what you are confirming."

"I can't tell anyone this meeting occurred or any information I may glean from it." Just as I speak, my anxiety slips away and a warm tingle crawls up my neck like a spider and out my mouth like a yawn. My eyelids drop slightly while my brain snaps into crystal clear focus. An alliance forms between my mouth and my brain and I lean forward, perfectly poised and ready. The effect is subtle, like something that could happen naturally with a lover, a fast European car, or a beautiful day. But in a cinderblock room with a cold man, is conspicuously manufactured.

He stares at me with his tiny blue eyes, bored and ruthless. Cruel and courteous. "Do you know Josh Winston?" he asks.

"Yes," I say.

"Who introduced you to Josh Winston?"

"A friend. A woman I met—"

"What's her name?" he asks.

"Ashley Doral." I answer immediately. My voice quivers with excitement and I try to calm down.

"What is Ashley's relationship with Josh?"

"I'm not entirely certain."

"Is it a sexual relationship?" he asks.

"I believe it is, from what Ashley told me and from the impression that I have."

He nods. "Do you have a sexual relationship with Josh Winston?"

"No."

"Did you enter the United States of America with Josh Winston and Ashley Doral?" he asks.

"No—yes—well, it was a coincidence, really. Josh was going there at the same time that I had a business trip to New York and then Ashley came too. So, we just all ended up getting together."

He stares at me for a long time. "Did you fly together? With either of them?"

"Yes, I flew there with Ashley. I bought her ticket, but then she stayed longer and flew back with Josh."

His eyes penetrate mine in a way that feels obscene. "Did you visit Washington, D.C. with Josh Winston?" he asks.

"No, I was only in New York, I did not go to Washington, D.C."

"Did either Josh Winston or Ashley Doral invite you to visit Washington, D.C. with either of them?"

I pause, thinking. "Yes, they both did. I didn't want to go, so I didn't."

"Why didn't you want to go?" he asks.

I search my brain, but it's fuzzy. Why didn't I want to go to

D.C. with them? I pause for a long time, as my interrogator's ice cold eyes stab into me. I glance up at him and he raises his eyebrows.

"I had to get back," I say. "To my family and to work."

He stares at me as if I said nothing at all and my hand jerks, as if searching for a mute button to un-press, to make him hear me. He leans forward.

"Why else?"

I stare at him and take a deep breath. I follow the pattern of the cinderblocks on the wall, as if they will lead me to a truth I can't quite express.

"I don't know," I answer. "I just didn't want to go. I don't like Washington D.C. It makes me think of what the Dictator's done to the country. It makes me sick."

"It makes you sick? Does it make you want to do something about it, to change things?" he asks. His tone is angry and mocking.

I meet his eyes. "No," is all I say.

He consults a paper in the file and the questions continue. I realize the information they are after: what was Josh doing in D.C.?

Then, he leans forward and asks a question that throws me off: "What do you know about the paternity of Jimothy Doral?"

"Jimothy? Nothing. We've never talked about it."

"You never talked about your children with Ashley Doral?" he asks.

"Well, yeah. Ashley and I talk about our children all the time. I know I mentioned to her that we used the same donor for my kids, so they are half siblings, but I don't think she ever mentioned anything about sperm donors or anything for her kids. I never asked."

"Wouldn't it be a natural question?" he asks. "Especially when you shared information about how your children were conceived?"

I shrug. "Oftentimes, it doesn't occur to me to ask natural questions."

"What do you mean?"

"I mean—I see what you're saying about it being a natural question. But when I'm talking to people, I don't tend to ask obvious questions like that. I tend to ask unusual questions, or to not ask any questions at all."

"Have you ever been diagnosed with Autism Spectrum Disorder?"

"No," I say. "I definitely don't have that. I took an online test."

He nods. "How long has Ashley Doral known Josh Winston?"

"I don't know. In fact, she has always been vague about that exact question. She said over a year, that it's been a long time. I don't actually have any idea when they met."

He regards me with a cold blank stare, then resumes asking questions about Josh's trips to Washington D.C. Then, his tone changes, matching the opening tone in what must be a scripted outro.

"Ms. Cora Renée Broussard, I want to remind you—the fact that we spoke at all today must remain confidential, or you will be arrested. Any information gathered from our conversation today, no matter how seemingly insignificant, must remain confidential, or you will be arrested. The government of New California has many ways to gather information, more than any one citizen knows about. More than Josh Winston knows about. Certainly more than I know about. No one knows the whole story, Ms. Broussard, but I do know that if you tell anyone about this interrogation, you will gravely regret it. Do you understand, Ms. Broussard?"

"Yes, sir," I respond. The mild euphoria begins to slip away.

Just enough that his words deflate something deep within my chest, something that used to be important.

"You must not tell Jane Broussard, or you will be arrested. You must not tell Josh Winston, or you will be arrested."

He says the phrase 'or you will be arrested' with such ease and with little enunciation that I wonder how many times a day he says it. It strikes me that the phrase is rather beautiful when extracted from its meaning.

"…you must not tell Ashley Doral, oryouwillbearrested. You must not tell Drake Broussard, oryouwillbearrested. You must not tell Simone Broussard, oryouwillbearrested…"

My stomach turns as he lists the names of those closest to me. He knows my children's names. He knows my sister's names, and my parents.

"… You will be released now. We will return your screen, but it will not work for half an hour. When your screen is automatically reactivated, it will send your GPS coordinates to us. At that time, you must not be at your home, your place of employment, or the home or place of employment of anyone you are acquainted with. We understand it is difficult for many people not to share information about this meeting with their loved ones. The purpose of the half hour after this session is for you to come to terms with that. Do you understand, Ms. Broussard?"

"Yes, sir."

"We sent a message from your screen to Jane Broussard informing her you are working late. That will be your story if anyone asks where you were at this time. During this short time that we've been speaking, you've received one message from Jane indicating her acceptance of you working late."

I am disturbed someone from the Ministry of Catastrophe Anticipation was so easily able to hack into my screen and contact my wife, and that she would receive it and think the message is from me. I imagine them reading all my texts, from

Ashley, Josh, my children, my parents.

They courteously offer to drive me anywhere, other than the places they told me I couldn't go. I decline and decide to walk to fill the half hour. A government protection officer escorts me down a long, narrow corridor adjacent to the parking garage. At the end, I see a full height turnstile, through which the sun shines, drawing long bars of warm light on the concrete walls. I reach for the gold light, so close I can taste it like a warm soup. But then that thought disturbs me. The silky glow I felt minutes after drinking the water has warped into something more dissonant. My teeth grate against one another to suppress a wave of unpleasantness, which immediately crashes into a burst of excitement. Back and forth, the feelings dance. Synapses firing and crashing and burning.

My shoes echo with each step. I walk faster and the officer matches my pace, too timid to tell me to slow down. At the turnstile, he nods and I walk through. I glance back to make sure it's okay, and he has already turned around. On the other side, the block is lined with government protection officers and no pedestrians at all. I slink by them and they eye me suspiciously, armed with tranq guns and male bravado. Past them, I turn a corner to a normal block and increase my pace.

My thoughts swirl and I can't piece anything together. The trip to New York, Josh and Ashley, Washington D.C., Jimothy? What is going on? They weren't concerned with Josh and Ashley's relationship, just about what they did in the U.S. Maybe Josh ordered this to confirm he can trust me? Should I have lied to them? I decided long ago I don't want to be involved in anything illegal, and would never risk being arrested. I am traumatized by the thought of riding in an elevator for a few seconds, what would I do in a jail cell?

I dig into my purse for my screen to check how far I am from home. Ugh, of course, it won't work yet. I check the message history to and from Jane and that's blocked as well.

I pass by a non-descript dive bar, hesitate, then turn around and walk in. I sit in the darkest corner and order the usual. The bartender adds the bourbon, the vermouth, the bitters, and the dark red cherry.

I turn toward the door. With my eyes adjusted to the shadowy bar, the sunlit evening casts a blinding glow. A distorted impressionist shadow forms in the doorway. My eyes adjust to the outside light. Across the street, a New California flag hangs limply on a building. I avert my eyes and readjust to the bar's darkness. The bartender strains the drink into a glass. A giant tattered New California flag hangs on the wall behind him. It is the old version, the first one, with a slightly different shade of yellow. When the new one came out, everyone criticized it, as people do with any sort of new logo, but then the old one started to look retro.

The bartender delivers my drink. I retrieve my screen to scan my DinR code, but recall I'm offline. Instead, I scan an offline NCD token and the bartender gives me a strange look.

I study the New California flag. It lurks ominously, like an actual being, or the taxidermy animals haunting walls of homes and dive bars in the U.S.

I turn my experience at the Ministry of Catastrophe Anticipation over in my mind. I am not accused or suspected of any crime. I might know something that will be of use to them. All the questions were about Josh and Ashley. I can't tell anyone. I consider whether I should comply. If I tell Jane, then she certainly cannot tell anyone. It would upset her and not fix anything, so why should I tell her? That's decided. I won't tell her.

I sip the last of my drink and eat the cherry. Whatever was in the water they served me either wore off or lost the battle with my stiff hastily drank Manhattan. I catch the bartender's eye and lift the empty glass to signal I want another. He gets right to work and scoops ice into a shaker. He is tall and thin, dark hair, tight t-shirt with some sort of indiscernible logo. Probably in his thirties. I ponder what his life must be like. What colony he lives in, if he likes it there, if he's happy with his jobber status or if he wishes he'd made different decisions and gotten a professional class job. It occurs to me I can stay here and keep drinking and start that conversation, but I need to go home to my family. I check my screen and find a message from Jane. Apparently the thirty minutes are up.

What time do you think you'll be home? Are you cooking dinner or should we order delivery?

I check the timestamp and she only sent it four minutes ago. I respond:

Let's get delivery, I'm fine with whatever. I'm just finishing up having a drink with a co-worker and then I'll head home.

She responds:

See you soon! No need to hurry if we're getting delivery.

The whiskey soothes me and dissolves my anxiety. I can pull this off, I can forget this happened.

A message from Ashley comes in and I dismiss it immediately. I'm not in the mood.

I study the flag hanging on the wall, its shapes and colors, the fabric itself. The fact that it's sewn together, not painted or dyed. I stare so long that it loses its meaning, and a part of me does as well.

CHAPTER 20

As distance grows between the present and my interrogation at the Ministry of Catastrophe Anticipation, it continues to loom over me, but slowly starts to haunt me less. I try to ignore the vague anxiety and dread it produces, and get nowhere trying to decipher what it meant. I go over it again and again. Each moment, each question, a distinct memory—a bullet point in my brain with smaller bullet points below it with more questions, possible interpretations, and motives. No matter how hard I try to sort it out, or organize it, I can't. Eventually, I stop trying to find answers and let it blur into one distinct but unpleasant memory.

De-digitization in the U.S. continues. The U.S. government announces that once they are confident the entire country is fully functioning without the internet, they will slowly roll it back out with reliable government-approved websites. I wonder how they managed to build an 'off' switch for the labyrinth of the internet, and which tech traitors helped them.

I am glum, walking to work and thinking of this, like I've been deflated. I feel my weight, where normally I am propelled.

It's cloudy and cooler than usual. A cold wind comes out of nowhere and makes my long walk to work arduous and unpleasant. I ignore the ornate, Victorian apartments and modern micro-apartment buildings, fully suffused with hip, attractive young people, and stare at the pavement while I tread. I listen to music, but continuously skip tracks. Nothing sounds right.

I jump at the unfamiliar sound of my ringtone, when my thoughts and music are interrupted by a voice call. I don't recognize the number, but it starts with 616—my parents' area code. Terror strikes me. Put on the spot, I can't decide if I should pick up the call. I stare at the screen, mentally calculating how long I have to make this decision. My shaky hand accepts the call.

"Hello?" I say. An analog white-noise fizz responds. My muscles tense as I anticipate what this call could be about. Finally, a familiar voice responds.

"Cora?" My Mom.

"Yes?" I say with urgency.

"Sorry, you didn't sound like yourself. It's your Mom, sorry to call so early." Her voice shakes. "I'm calling from the hospital."

"Why?"

"Your dad is here. He's in here, in a room—"

"Like as a patient?"

"Yes, he's checked in as a patient."

"What happened?" I ask.

"He had chest pains. It's probably nothing. They're running tests. They said the first test looked okay but something was a little off, so they need to run more tests."

"Did he have a heart attack?" I panic, remembering my dad's father died of a heart attack at sixty-five and my dad just turned eighty-one.

"No, well, they don't know, but if he did—it was a mild one. But they are concerned enough that they admitted him. As a patient."

I duck into an alley and lean against the brick wall. "Okay. Wow. Are you okay?"

"Yes, thank you Cora, I will be fine. I'm just worried about your dad. He wasn't himself last night, he was tired and went to bed early and now this."

"Should I come visit?" I ask.

"No, no—not yet anyway. Let's wait and see what the tests say."

"Okay, well, will you call me right away?"

"Yes. Absolutely."

I end the call and put my screen back in my pocket. I remain in the alley, unsure of what to do—should I still go to work? My parents were always so healthy. This was completely unexpected. Though—it occurs to me—it shouldn't be. My parents are not young anymore.

I message Jane to inform her what happened. I exit the alley and head toward work, still unsure what to do. An urge to go home—and perhaps to Michigan—causes me to pivot and lurch back in the opposite direction, but no, that doesn't make sense. Not yet. I turn back and trudge down the hill.

I stop again and message Ashley. I haven't seen much of her lately. She has been busy, or with Josh.

I resolutely decide to head to work. I walk briskly with purpose. I can be strong about this. This is something that starts to happen when parents age. I should be thankful this is the first major medical scare. But, I realize this could be it—my dad could die today. He could be dead, gone, and I would never see him again.

I think of what that would mean—one less person to be proud of me. My parents are the only people I try to make proud, but I think my dad in particular is who I most want to be proud of me. When I was growing up, I always said I would never be more successful than my dad and I thought that meant he would never be completely proud of me. Instead, I am more successful than him and with each success he only becomes more proud. With my mom, of course—she's proud of me as well, but in a less emotional way.

I think of my dad's relationship with my kids, and how close he is to Drake. He's such a sweet man to the children. Though, he was kind of an asshole to my sisters and I when we were teenagers.

My eyes burn and I try my hardest not to cry. I calm myself down and try to be level-headed. They're still unsure if it was a heart attack.

I begin to relax. I need to be an adult and deal with it. It might be nothing. I try to think of other things. Work things. Ashley. Jane and the kids.

My thoughts are interrupted by a message from Ashley so generic I roll my eyes. She's sorry about what's going on with my dad. She's thinking of me, etc. etc.

Something about it makes me feel worse, especially when I reflect on the last time I saw her. It was several days ago. I took a Lone to the colonies. Barely glancing at me, she entered the car with her brow furled. I tried to hold her hand, but her arm was tense. She messaged back and forth to someone on her screen while stealing glances at me and angling her screen so I couldn't see it. This went on for several minutes while she mumbled apologies and excuses. I patiently waited and reserved judgment. Eventually, she put the screen away and met my eyes. She ran her fingers through my hair. I returned her gaze and tried to figure out what was wrong, but got nothing.

"Everything okay?" I said.

She laughed bitterly, stared out the windshield, and focused on the oncoming road. "Yeah," she said, "everything is fine."

She cuddled close to me, but continued to stare forward at

the road ahead. We both became distracted by a manually-driven gas-powered car ahead of us. The driver gesturing angrily at the UberLones around him.

I turned back toward Ashley. "I love you and you can talk to me about anything," I reminded her.

She searched my face and the vulnerability I saw scared me. Her strong, solid demeanor was gone. I squeezed her hand and urged her to open up to me. Her breath quickened.

"I love you too." Her voice shook. She grabbed my head in her hands, kissed me deeply, turned around, and pulled my arms around her shoulders. "Hold me," she said, and I did. We stayed like that all the way to the restaurant. Once inside, she regained her composure and apologized. I spoke softly and treated her tenderly. Back in a Lone, she told me I am the sweetest woman she ever met, and that she loved me. I had the car idle somewhere while we had sex. She let me lead and I went slow and touched her gently. She moaned my name when she finished. I held her and caressed her face for several minutes afterward.

On my way home I tried to focus on the sweet things she said to me, the 'I love you's,' the sex, and a part of me felt calm and satisfied—but something was different. An air of finality. She acted like someone weighted down with a secret too arduous to carry.

I knew I loved her, that I needed her, but I felt disconnected. I ran through some scenarios in my head and tried to figure it out. Could it be problems with Misty? With the kids? No, it was something bigger, something I couldn't guess. I am perceptive enough to understand that much.

Lost in my thoughts, I almost pass my office building. I trudge up the stairs, thinking of Ashley, of my dad, of everything. I stop, sit down on the stairs, and hold my face in my hands. I take a deep breath, get up, and keep climbing. Once at my desk, I check my screen again, but still nothing. I torture myself mulling over how long it will be until I receive an update.

The time drags in a way that feels physical. Minutes upon minutes drag through mud. The blood runs through my veins, the air through my lungs. All the things my body does to show it's alive continue to happen, marking time in their wake. I browse my work messages, then check my schedule. The uncertainty of where I'll be and the lack of control torture me.

Jane finally texts me back and unlike Ashley, her text soothes me a bit.

I step into my first meeting. Everyone talks about what they did the previous weekend. I sit down and project my screen onto the wall to signal the meeting is starting. I briskly launch into my agenda, and notice most people are actively paying attention. I draw energy from them and let myself be in the moment. In a world where I am a respected executive who can motivate a team, and not someone who might be on the brink of a major family illness. I push forward and become my most charming self. I make an unexpected joke and everyone roars with laughter. I end the meeting revitalized and centered.

I throw myself into my work and accomplish much more than I normally do. I am so focused I barely perceive time passing. When I allow myself to think of the situation again, it is two p.m.

I decide to call for an update and think through the logistics of this. Should I just call back the number that called me? I wasn't told the name of the hospital.

My thoughts are interrupted by a message from Ashley:

Hi baby! I'm thinking of you. Have you gotten any news about your Dad? I love you very much!

I smile at the sweetness. I'm glad she is concerned enough to follow-up and didn't send an obligatory empathetic message and then forget about the situation. I respond:

No news yet, which is actually really surprising. I haven't heard from my mom at all. I'm going to attempt to voice call the hospital. I just wish I knew which hospital it was! I love you too, and getting your messages cheered me up and made me smile.

I decide to call the number that called me. It rings, and rings. As soon as my attempt fails, the need for an update becomes more urgent. I search my screen for hospitals in Grand Rapids. I map them to find which one is closest to where they live. I call the first one, and spend five minutes going through a retro phone directory. I get someone on the line who informs me Robert Broussard is not a patient.

Exasperated and annoyed, I set my screen down. I think back to my childhood, before the internet or cell phones. What did people do in this situation then? The pathways in my brain that knew how to survive without digital technology are apparently gone, and I can't come up with anything.

A voice call interrupts my thoughts. A voice call from Grand Rapids. My hand shakes as I answer the call. I expect my mother's voice, but it's a man. I listen to the tone and accent of his voice to discern who else it could be—an uncle? A brother in law?

But no, I do not recognize this voice.

"Ms. Broussard, I'm calling from Saint Mary's Hospital in Grand Rapids. Your mother asked that I call. You are aware that your father was admitted to the hospital this morning, correct?"

"Yes."

"I am calling to inform you he remains in the hospital due to a minor heart attack. He is awake and we do not anticipate any subsequent heart attacks, but at his advanced age there are no guarantees."

"So he's okay now? Can I talk to him or my mom?"

"No, I'm sorry, I'm afraid that won't be possible. We have limited phone connections and are not allowing patients to make calls at this time."

"Okay, how long will he be in the hospital?"

"I'm sorry, that is not known."

I end the call more anxious than I was before.

CHAPTER 21

I'm in the First Class cabin of an A320, too distracted to do anything but think and drink. I replay the call in my head over and over. I try to focus on the facts, but then I feel worse.

With the way the man spoke, he simultaneously seemed overqualified and under-informed. Who was he? He was not a doctor or a nurse, yet he was confident and smooth.

He also sounded distinctly un-Midwestern.

I sip my drink faster until it's finished. I catch the flight attendant's eye and hold my glass in the air. He approaches moments later with a new Manhattan.

Later, feeling tired and heavy, I lay my seat back and drift off to sleep quickly, without dreams. Like time travel all the way to Detroit.

The first glimpse of morning sunlight and collective click of window shades opening wakes me. The pilot announces the final descent. The flight attendants pry beverages out of the hands of nearby passengers. It's too late to ask for coffee. My drinks from hours ago cling to my bloodstream, but only the last bitter remnants remain. I dig a mint out of my purse and turn my screen camera toward myself. A halo of frizz frames my hair, which I quickly gather back into a bun. I remove my smeared makeup with a wipe in my purse. The flight attendant returns with a wastebasket and I discard it, now streaked with my heavy dark eyeliner and gold eyeshadow. I look at my reflection again—small, deep-set brown eyes now naked and vulnerable. I lock my screen and place it face-down on my lap. Downtown Detroit is framed through the airplane window, visible between intermittent clouds. Then the river, and Canada beyond.

I anticipate turning my screen on when we land and watching the messages come in. A jolt of excitement strikes me at the thought of Ashley's name on my screen. Then, I recall my screen will not work. Before I left, I found a pen and paper and wrote down my confirmation numbers and driving directions. Two hours, twenty minutes to the hospital. Being out of communication with my parents made me crazy in San Francisco, but the lack of communication with my family and Ashley in San Francisco will make me crazy here. The only way I can communicate is through voice calls, and I am particularly awkward on voice calls.

The plane pitches forward and the familiar Detroit airport grows larger in my window. The wheels hit the runway with a jolt. My seatmate clutches his armrests and gasps, but I smirk knowing it's just a rough landing. The brakes screech until the plane settles into its normal runway gait.

In my childhood, my family used to change planes here on our way to Florida to visit my grandmother. Now, in adulthood, I can't deal with the tiny planes that fly the forty-minute flight from Detroit to Grand Rapids, so I always drive. I like getting a chance to deal with being both home and in a foreign country.

*****

At the rental car garage, I pace up and down the aisles until I find the perfect car: a gas-powered Camaro Sport with all-wheel drive. I like electric cars, but the nostalgia of being in Michigan makes me want something gas-powered. Even in Detroit they're hard to find.

I settle into the plush upholstered seat and exit the garage. With my useless screen still in my purse, I consult my sheet of directions and manage to get on the correct highway. I revel in the fiery gasoline power of the car. With my hands tightly clutching the leather steering wheel, I hug curves and go double the speed limit. The weather is void of any life: gray, no wind, and about twelve degrees Celsius. The highway is nearly empty.

Once I bore of driving fast, I put the car in auto-drive. I examine the interior of the car and sip my cappuccino. Even the design of the interior lacks taste, like the car itself is plagued with the same Midwestern accent I imagine the team of engineers who designed it have.

I lean my seat back and become reacquainted with my home state. The corn fields and flat forests look so pathetically boring compared to the beauty of San Francisco. The billboards are the most interesting. Dictator propaganda is the most common, followed by sad little ads for truck stops, restaurants that sound awful, hunting-related merchandise stores, and strip clubs. This time, the usual ads appear as expected, but many billboards are empty, and I'm surprised at the lack of propaganda.

A secret transition. My dad's words come back to me. I put the car back in manual as my mind races. I imagine what might fill those billboards, in a few months, weeks, or even days? The transition could happen while I'm here. I pick up speed, try to push all thoughts out of my head, and drive forward toward my hometown.

*****

I arrive at the hospital two hours after I left Detroit—extraordinarily good timing. I wait to turn into the parking garage at a red light and scrutinize the hospital's cinderblock 1960's architecture and find that it depresses me. I wonder if this is what it was like forty-eight years ago when I was born here.

I walk through the revolving door into the main entrance. I wish the guy who called me provided more details. Perhaps the room number or a doctor's name would be useful. The lobby is tastefully decorated, despite the low ceilings and stark white floor. A woman with a friendly smile stands behind a large wooden desk.

"Hi, my dad is a patient and I'm here to visit him."

"His name, please?"

"Robert Broussard."

She nods and types his name into a computer. I confirm the spelling.

She cocks her head and smiles blankly. "Robert Broussard is not a patient," she says.

"Is he, was he released?" *If he wasn't released, then…?*

She types again into her computer. "No, we just don't have a patient by that name."

"Are you sure? Maybe your database isn't updated because of de-digitization?"

"It's an internal network," she says.

I meet her green eyes, which would be quite pretty if on a different person. Frustrated, I try to collect my thoughts. "I got a call yesterday at what would have been six p.m. here. The guy said my dad had a heart attack and would stay in the hospital."

"You got a call?" she asks. "Was it from his doctor? Maybe his doctor is affiliated with Saint Mary's?"

"No, the call wasn't from his doctor. It was someone who

worked at the hospital."

"We don't generally make calls like that, not unless it's the doctor or perhaps one of the nurses."

"It wasn't a nurse. Are you sure he's not here? Was he transferred elsewhere, like to another hospital? Can you check an alternate spelling of his name?"

She tries all possible spellings of his name. To appease me further, she tries searching by address, date of birth, and even checks the names of all patients named "Robert."

She looks again at the computer and shakes her head. "No Ma'am, I'm so sorry. There is no record of a patient named Robert Broussard."

"Thank you," I say. I turn away and walk toward a bench. I sit down, confused and not sure if I should be relieved. Maybe the guy used to work at Saint Mary's and said the wrong name? That seems unlikely.

Seized with certainty of my next move, I jump to my feet and race out.

*****

I drive fast to my parents' house. I know the way. I stop questioning the call, stop wondering why I never heard from my mom. I just drive. Fast.

Once I pull into my parents' driveway, the garage door is closed so I can't tell if they are home. I park and exit the car immediately, without my suitcase. I hike down the sidewalk to their house. At the top of the hill the lake is visible through the trees, on either side. The lights inside cast a warm glow against the bleak, gray day. My breath quickens. When I approach the door, I can hear a series of loud clanks and footsteps. My parents habit of putting away dishes as loudly as possible used to annoy me as a child, but comforts me at this moment. Everything seems so normal that for a moment I wonder if I imagined the whole thing. The phone call from my mom, the call from the hospital, and the terror about my dad. But of course I didn't. Only a day has passed since my mom and I spoke and already my father is apparently pivoting around the kitchen roughly tossing plates onto stacks of other plates.

I ring the doorbell. I recognize my mom's loud footsteps as she approaches the door. Her face appears in the long window. I wave. Her eyes widen and her mouth drops open. The door opens.

"Cora! What are you doing here? Where is Jane? Where are the kids?" She gives me a hug and grabs the sides of my wrap coat. "This is cute! Where did you get it?"

"They're at home. Where is dad? Is he okay?"

He approaches behind her. He appears healthy, but shocked. I worry for a second if my surprise presence will give him another heart attack.

"Yes, I'm fine," my dad says. "It wasn't a heart attack. We tried to call you, and Jane too, but I think there is something wrong with your phones. When I called it just kept ringing and no one answered."

My mom nods. "I called your office and talked to a woman named Kim. She said you got the message about your dad so I figured one of your sisters called."

"A man called and said dad had a heart attack. That was the only call I got," I say.

They are visibly shocked. We enter their living room and sit down. My mom offers me food, coffee, water, but I decline.

"I went to Saint Mary's and they said that Dad wasn't a patient."

"I wasn't at Saint Mary's," my dad says. "Are you sure that's what they said?"

"Yes, I'm sure, I remembered because it's where I was born."

My mom's face is mangled in confusion. "What a weird call!" she says.

My dad is more rattled. He begins to pace, brow furled.

"Did you give anyone at the hospital my phone number? Is there any way they would know to call me if something did happen?" I ask.

"No," they say simultaneously.

I pace until I reach their coffee maker and pour myself a cup.

I am confused and disturbed by the events of the past day. Something is definitely not right. There is no use in talking to my parents about it any further.

CHAPTER 22

I start drinking wine early, as soon as it begins to feel appropriate, at three or four or so. I try to call Jane again and again. It rings and never goes through. My mom and I chat, about everything and nothing. My dad stalks around the house, distracted, and tries to piece together what could be going on, what any of this could mean. I want to tell him to stop, to not worry. I will find out soon.

Most of all, more than anything, I am troubled I cannot get in touch with Jane and the kids to tell them my dad is okay.

I go to bed early. My fitful three hours of airplane sleep last night wasn't enough.

As I sink into the pillows, I fall into a light dream-filled sleep. I dream I'm walking down a city street, and up ahead I catch a glimpse of Ashley in San Francisco, but it looks like Grand Rapids. Delighted at the sight of her, I walk toward her familiar body, clad in a red dress and high heels. I increase my pace but she turns a corner. I almost reach her. I call her name, but I can only walk in slow motion. She stops, but before she spots me, a New California government car stops in front of her and the door opens. She climbs in and is whisked away. No matter what I do, she remains ahead of me.

A knock on my door wakes me. I gasp and sit up. The unfamiliar dark shadows in the room remind me where I am. I check my screen—three a.m.

"Yes?" I say.

The door opens and my dad enters holding an object with a red light like a pin prick of blood. "Cora, Jane is on the phone. She says it's not an emergency, but she needs to talk to you."

He hands me the phone, exits, and shuts the door.

"Hello?"

"I've been trying to call you since you left. Are you okay? Is your dad okay? I'm sorry to call so late, but I need to talk to you."

"Yes, my dad is fine. He never even had a heart attack. What's going on? Is everyone okay?"

"Everyone's okay. What do you mean your Dad never had a heart attack? What about the call you got?"

"Yeah, he never had a heart attack. Still trying to figure out what was up with that call. But what is going on with you?"

My stomach drops at the sound of an unfamiliar voice in the room with Jane.

Jane responds. "What? Someone called and lied to say your Dad—?"

"It could have been a misunderstanding. I just don't know yet, Jane. Who are you with? Please tell me what's going on."

"Okay, sorry, this is so confusing. Anyway, I think my screen was blocked somehow. It hasn't worked since you left. The reason I'm calling is because Ashley's wife, Misty, and Josh Winston's wife, Cheryl, are here. We've been talking for a few hours."

"What? Why are they with you? What's going on?"

"Ashley and Josh are gone. They left last night. Their wives thought maybe you were with them, or that you had talked to them."

"No, I haven't heard from either of them since I've been here. Did they say anything to anyone?" I ask. I wipe the sleep from my eyes and try to process this, but my brain comes up with nothing, like an error message.

"No, they just disappeared. Misty said there was also suddenly a deposit for 10,000 NCD in their account. We don't know what that means."

"Jesus." I say. "Trust me, I am just as shocked as you all."

Jane relays the information to Misty and Cheryl. A disappointed silence lingers.

They appear to struggle with the phone. Jane barely has time to announce Misty would like to speak with me before I am on the phone with her.

"Cora, I don't believe you," she says in her shrill, clear voice. "It just seems like this is all connected. Why are you in the U.S., anyway? It turns out your Dad is fine? Seems suspicious to me. Time to speak up, Cora."

Her aggression wounds me. I take a deep breath and summon the strength to respond. "Misty, I don't know anything, believe me. I am just as confused as you—"

"She targeted you, Cora. She targeted you from the beginning. Do you remember when you and I first met and we talked? It was because my wife was targeting you. For what, I don't know, but she was planning whatever scheme she has going on long before you two met, and she knew you would be a part of it from day one. She was using you, and she probably still is."

"She targeted me how? How would you know this?" I ask. The idea is too difficult to process. Ashley using me? I shake my head, trying not to let my vulnerability bleed into my voice and over the phone line.

"When I went to your first talk at the school, she was already running searches on you and learning everything she could. She was there that day too. I saw her come in even though she told me she wasn't coming. She sat in the back and disguised herself. She wore old clothes and a hat. She slipped out before it was over. Then, in the parking lot later, I saw New California government cars follow your car. They were probably sent by Josh. It's all part of a scheme, Cora. I knew she was up to something, she and Josh. They've been up to something."

A shred of calm slows my drumming heart. I think this through. I can't decide if Misty is paranoid, or if there is something to this. In my opinion, and my experience, anytime anything mysterious is going on, the truth turns out to be the most boring possible explanation. Also, what could Ashley have possibly been using me for? Not money or power, because Josh has me beat there, so what, then?

"Misty, I just don't know what to say," I respond. I roam over to the window and pull up the shade. The full moon carves a shimmery yellow path through the dark, silver lake. "I'm shocked by all of this," I continue. "I'm sorry this is happening to you. I absolutely promise that if I hear from Ashley I will do the right thing and let you know what's going on."

Misty breathes into the phone. "Okay," she says. "But don't think I trust you! I will do whatever it takes to get to the bottom of this!"

Misty and Jane struggle with the phone. Jane says something to her in a scolding tone.

"I'm sorry to wake you," Jane says.

I take a deep breath and collect myself. "No, don't worry about it, I'm glad you called. I've been so worried and anxious. It's terrible not being able to communicate. And I wanted to let you know that my dad is okay."

"I'm certainly relieved to hear that. I'll tell the kids about their grandpa in the morning. But Cora, I'm really freaked out about that call you got. Please keep me updated and come home as soon as possible. It just makes me so nervous that someone possibly tricked you into coming to the U.S. and you're still there, just at your parents' house. If someone is up to something, they know where to find you."

"I know, Jane, it freaks me out too. Though I'm sure whatever the explanation is, it's less dramatic than you're insinuating."

"You always think that," Jane says.

"And I'm always right. I miss you, Jane, and I love you."

"I love you too. Come home soon."

*****

I'm not sure if I slept again or not. Eventually, at seven, I hear my mom downstairs. Excited to drink coffee and spend a morning normally, I get up. I put my hair up into a high bun, and check the mirror to verify I look okay. I pause momentarily and wonder what my mom knows about the call. After I hung up, I told my dad the gist of it.

I descend the stairs with my screen in hand out of habit. My mom sits in a chair in the corner—the one with the best lake view. She looks up from her book and is surprised and delighted to see me. I realize that in my mind, I picture her as much younger than she is. I left home for Chicago when she was my age.

"Cora! I didn't expect you up so early."

"I went to bed at like eight."

"Yeah, but I know you got a late night call from Jane! Is everything okay?" She can't wait for the gossip.

I get coffee and sit down next to my mom. In distant, general terms I explain some friends of mine ran off together. I make sure not to let it slip that one of these people is my girlfriend.

Loud intentional footsteps interrupt us. We turn to the stairs and my dad rushes down. We regard him, tense and silent.

"The news is reporting that there is an internet outage in New California," he announces.

"What!" I say.

I'm shocked. New California literally can't function without the internet. How could it happen? We even have satellite redundancy! I immediately doubt the legitimacy of the story. So, maybe wired is down, for one ISP, but not mobile, and certainly not satellite redundancy. It can't be. My dad turns on the TV and tunes in the news. The headline proclaims: "INTERNET OUTAGE IN NEW CALIFORNIA WREAKS HAVOC," along with the sub-headline "Complete outage disrupts transportation, communication, and commerce."

We watch, spellbound and horrified. The newscaster asks where the Minister of Technology is.

Misty's words from last night come back to me and a deep sense of dread mushrooms through me. Maybe she was right. Maybe I am embroiled in a political scandal. The wife of the Minister of Technology was at my house last night. According to the U.S. news—which I of course do not entirely trust—the internet is completely down, wired and mobile, and satellite is only working intermittently.

Once the news starts repeating itself, I can't watch anymore. I turn away and put on my jacket and shoes. Heavy with a sense of impending doom, I open the sliding glass door and walk down the concrete steps to the dock. The familiar sound of my footsteps on the wooden dock contrasts with the international emergency at hand.

The rhythmic sound of metal on metal distracts me. A few houses down, an old man pulls a rope to raise the American flag. Full mast. I wince and look away.

The air is cold and crisp, but the sun, which has just started to come up, is warm. The sunlight only hits the very end of the dock. I turn toward it and it blinds me. I cover my eyes and admire the silhouette of my parents' house in the shadows. I remove my hand and let the sunlight blind me once again.

Emotions stream to the surface and I almost can't take it. The wood of the dock is stained and weathered, but each summer, year after year, my parents install it. It was over thirty years ago that we replaced the old dock. I was in high school and the wood was fresh and new, at a time when I felt like my heart was ugly and rotten. One night I brought a sleeping bag and a pillow to the end of this dock. I laid on my back, smoked cigarettes, looked at the stars, and wondered who I would grow up to be. I slept peacefully that night. Here I am, thirty years later. The same faded dock is here, but I'm a foreigner, an alien, a tourist.

Whatever I got myself into is deeper than I know. In some ways I enjoy remaining blissfully ignorant. Whatever is coming is something new, something I have never dealt. Something I greet with dread, but also intense curiosity. I turn back around toward the lake. The water is flat, like glass, without wind or any movement at all. One hour from now, it will not be like this. Tiny ripples will appear. Then later, tiny waves. It's rarely this flat, so easy to glide over. No boats on the lake other than a few idle fishermen. It will be a beautiful day, unseasonably warm. Yet, I already know this day and this weather is something I won't be able to appreciate or participate in.

"Cora," my mom yells for me. She holds up an object. "Phone."

"Okay," I respond. "I'm coming up."

She turns to go back in. I turn back to the lake for one more moment, to the beautiful day approaching, savoring it, and I think: *this is the beginning of the end.*

CHAPTER 23

It's Ashley.

The sound of her voice gives me no pleasure other than the thrill of knowing I will soon discover what is going on.

"Josh and I are in D.C. and we need to talk to you. You need to come here today."

I respond with silence and plot my response. "Why do I need to come there? Why can't you just tell me what's going on now?"

"Just come, Cora."

"Misty and Josh's wife called, they were with Jane," I say. "What the hell is going on, Ashley?"

"I talked to Misty. I called her this morning before the outage."

"So the outage is real? Did Josh know it was going to happen?"

"Cora, I'm not having this conversation now. Just come to D.C. We need to talk. Come here today. We booked a flight for you today out of Detroit, okay? Come."

"What for? Why should I come?"

"Don't argue with me, just do what I say. Okay, baby? Come here. I love you, baby. We need to talk and it has to be in person. You have to come to D.C. Let me know when you're ready for your flight information."

I pause while I hold the phone to my ear and pace around a spare room in my parents' house. What would happen if I don't go? Would I never discover the truth? Of course not. Whatever is going on is so big everyone will find out. But one thing I am sure of is not going means there will be no resolution, no ending. Or, at least I won't find out what my role would have been.

"Okay, give me a second." I exit the room and find a pen and paper in the kitchen. "I'm ready for the flight information."

As I write it down, my parents stare at me, making no attempt to hide their curiosity. I end the call without fanfare and reserve my judgment for tonight.

*****

I drink two glasses of wine at Detroit Metro Airport but do not take a Xanax. I need to stay focused and alert. Ashley said Josh will send a car to pick me up in D.C. I don't know where the car will take me, or for how long I will be gone. My only comfort is this: whatever Josh and Ashley are up to; they aren't evil people. Perhaps more importantly, it wouldn't benefit them to harm me in some way. Everything Misty told me floats in and out of my mind as I try to sort out what I learned. There is no use in mulling it over too much because I will find out soon enough.

I spent the day withdrawing $50,000 USD in cash. My dad and I made several phone calls and drove to three different banks to come up with the bills. It's surprisingly difficult to obtain so much money in cash in a single day. I separate $25,000 which I distribute through my clothing, purse, and suitcase. I overnightship the rest of the cash to Jane.

On the flight I try to distract myself with an inane movie, welcoming the simplistic plot line and one-dimensional characters. When the flight attendant announces our initial descent and the plane gradually pitches downward, my dread increases. I peer over the shoulder of the man next to me. In the distance, the mall, museums, and propaganda houses come into view through the overcast sky. I look straight ahead and ignore the landmark buildings of the country that used to be home.

When I disembark, it's late and I'm tired. I wait for my bags at the conveyer belt and scan the airport, unsure where I should go next. I was not given details about who will pick me up or where to meet them. I expect a piece of paper or screen with my name on it, but no one is around at all except for guards with assault rifles searching people.

After I retrieve my bags, I follow the flow of the crowd and find the location of the car service pickup. A dense crowd of drivers hold up cards with names scrawled on them while their cars idle at the curb. I trudge through the sea of confused people and scan for my name. Some of the drivers have cleverly attempted to alphabetize themselves by their placards, while others stand still, clueless, and wait to be approached. I find the B's, then the C's, and read all the names. Nothing.

A heavy hand grabs my shoulder. I tense up and jump.

"Ms. Broussard?"

"Yes?"

"Your car."

He motions for me to follow him. A guard with an assault rifle walks beside him.

I'm not sure if he's here to protect me, or to keep me from returning to the airport and buying a ticket to San Francisco. Perhaps it is too late. The guard tails me while resting his hand tenderly on the barrel of his gun. I follow the driver to a vehicle much larger than a sedan, but not quite a limousine.

He swings around. "Passport," he says in the firm manner of a border patrol officer, as if I should expect this request.

I fish through my purse and locate my passport. My hands shake when I hand it to him. He inspects it and I'm relieved when he returns it to me.

The guard opens the door and indicates I should slide across to the seat behind the driver. At the metallic click of my seatbelt, the car whisks us away. With both hands on his gun, the guard patrols in place from the passenger seat, detecting threats. I pay close attention to where the car drives, intensely curious where we are going. Perhaps they will take me to the New California embassy, or maybe a hotel. Maybe we will go to some sort of government guesthouse. I almost wish I came to D.C. with Ashley and Josh before, so I could guess what to expect.

I examine the billboards and posters of the Dictator along the banks of the Potomac. Many of the billboards are blank where pictures of the Dictator used to be. We cross the river and drive toward the mall. The armed guard speaks into a walkie-talkie. Two identical cars surround us. In the distance, the spotlighted White House glows ominously, flanked by darkness. We turn left and drive toward it. For a moment, I am interested to see it. A long time has passed since I last visited Washington, D.C. But then, a sudden surge of absolute dread hits me as it occurs to me that perhaps we are going to the White House.

I stare forward, out the front windshield, and the White House enlarges in front of us. The armed guard, the motorcade. *Oh God, no. I don't want to go in the White House.*

I went inside before. In the nineties with my parents, during the Clinton years. 1996. I was excited, and proud to be an American. We waited outside in the cold for over an hour. Once on the tour, we strolled from room to room and gawked at the high ceilings and intricate details. We saw the pressroom, which I recognized from TV. Most of all, we basked in the thrill of being in the same house as the president of the United States. Later that day, we walked through the mall. I was twelve, surly, and not in the mood to socialize with my parents. I had thought the mall was a shopping mall. After the novelty of the White House, wandering around in the cold to see statues I recognized from currency felt tedious. My bra came undone, or I thought it did. Something about it felt wrong and I felt mortified my fellow pedestrians would somehow know. The trip fell during my most painfully self-conscious years. If, then, I could catch a glimpse of myself now, in a motorcade cruising toward the White House, I would feel proud and vindicated.

But in that glimpse I wouldn't know I was no longer an American. That democracy was a thing of the past.

We slow down as we approach the White House. *Keep driving, keep driving,* I command the driver in my head, but we don't. We turn. I am being taken to the White House. We stop at the tall black gate and a pack of armed guards point assault rifles at us.

"Passport," one says.

His gun, now draped casually over his shoulder, points obscenely at my face. I hand him my passport and he hands it to another guard. Another guard hoists my suitcase out of the vehicle. He instinctively points his gun at it, as if the suitcase itself might be armed. They motion for us to come into a tiny structure while they hand-search my bag. They riffle through my clothing with some sort of stick, as if it is too filthy to touch with the same hands that caress their assault rifles. After a few minutes, they pack everything up. Miraculously, they either don't find the cash or it doesn't surprise them, and my passport is handed back to me.

We return to the car and it slowly slinks forward a few hundred feet. Another litter of guards, armed with assault rifles, awaits us in front of the bone-white spotlighted White House, no longer iconic in such close proximity. The driver unlocks the door and I disembark and follow the guard into the White House.

A man in a suit awaits us. His lively, amused gray eyes endear me immediately.

The guard from the car gestures toward me. "Cora Broussard, passport verified. Foreign national."

The guy in the suit dismisses him with a flick of the wrist and nods at me, motioning for me to follow him. I follow calmly, un-phased at this point. He takes my suitcase and walks beside me.

"It's a bit of a walk, Ms. Broussard, is that okay?" he asks.

"Yes, that's great actually."

He smiles warmly, revealing matching dimples. He is the first person I encountered in D.C. who seems like an actual person. Matching my pace, he daintily treads down the hall.

"What would be the other option if walking wasn't okay? Do you have like an indoor car or something, like at the airport?" I ask.

He throws his head back and laughs. "I wouldn't be surprised if we did! No, we don't have one of those. We are supposed to warn people if there is a walk. In case they want to take a break, or request a wheelchair."

I nod. I want to ask him about Ashley and Josh. I worry for a moment that I will be forced to fall asleep at the White House before I learn why the hell I'm here.

He seems to read my mind. "Ms.—Doral will meet you in your room shortly. She's been alerted of your arrival. You have a meeting scheduled with Mr. Winston tomorrow morning."

Despite my anger and skepticism toward Ashley, the thought that she will join me in my room excites me. More than potential answers, I crave Ashley herself, right here in front of me.

Feigning lack of excitement, I nod, like this was what I expected. Another thought strikes me, and I blurt out: "Is the president in?"

"No," he responds abruptly.

I exhale, relieved. I hope whatever is going on does not involve collusion with the Dictator.

He regards me and smiles. "Ashley's really looking forward to seeing you. She'll explain what's going on," he says with a wave of his hand.

I nod. We walk several paces in silence. A muffled, haunted thud rings out with each step. A sound unique to ornate buildings over 200 years old. We approach a carved wooden staircase.

"Ashley said you'd prefer the stairs?"

"Yes, thanks."

We climb up and walk a short distance to a door marked "Lincoln Bedroom." He retrieves a key from his pocket and lets us in. The carved mahogany bedframe commands my attention first. My eye traces the high ceilings, the understated but exquisite furniture, and finally the wall-to-wall carpeting—like a mix between a fine Persian rug and a Vegas casino. I feel like I'm in a museum and I can't fathom the idea of actually sleeping in this room. He walks me through and explains the historical significance of each piece of furniture. With each former president he name-drops, I am dazzled, but then I recall the turn in history that ruined the office of the U.S. president, and ruined my home country forever. The man departs and I trace the carved shell of a beautiful couch. Such subtle, smart, class. Relics from the past when quality mattered, when class mattered, before the word 'presidential' lost its meaning. I take a deep breath, pushing these thoughts from my mind.

I open every drawer and they're all empty. I'm not sure what I expected to find, as if the other people who stayed in this room didn't do this exact same thorough search. It's not like I'm going to come across a former president's kid's old pair of jeans or something.

A light knock on the door makes me jump. I check the peephole and see Ashley, blonde hair freshly dyed and draped over her shoulders. She looks beautiful in some sort of presidential pajamas. The sight of her makes me both exhausted and desirous. I want to pull her in and melt into her, taste and touch her, let her kiss away my anxiety. But—just as strongly—I want to keep the door closed, and turn around and go to sleep.

I open the door and let her in. *One last time.*

*****

Suspicious, I stand back. Ashley passes me and sets a bottle of wine and two glasses down on a table. She is then quickly, and completely in my arms. Her arms encircle me. Her wrists, turned, work on a second round. My anxiety deflates. She squeezes me, tentacles digging in. My face is pressed into her hair and neck. My arms rest on her shoulders. I kiss her neck, the side of her head, her forehead. She puts her arms around my neck and kisses me gently, then more intensely. She stands on her tiptoes, surpasses my height and moans. I feel her soft breasts against me as she squeezes tight. I put my hands on each of her hips, squeezing them, and pull her to me.

"Cora," she moans. "Cora, baby, I missed you. I love you, Cora."

I don't say it back. Her desperate stare meets my untrusting eyes.

I tear myself away from her, step back, and shake my head. "Ashley," I hiss. "Ashley. What the fuck is going on?"

Her brown eyes look up at me with desperation. "We'll talk tomorrow, baby, we'll tell you everything. You and me and Josh. We love you and we brought you here to tell you first, everything that's going on. We love you, Cora, we want you to stay in our lives, baby. You and Josh could be best friends. He doesn't open up to people, it's all surface, but with you he doesn't act like he does with most people, baby, he loves you and respects you so much, he—"

"Shut up." I say. I stalk across the room. I sit on a velvet chair and lean forward with my hands over my face. She remains where I left her and watches me. "Shut up, Ashley. Whatever is going on, it's fucked up, it's, it—"

"Cora, you can't judge," she says. She crosses the room toward me. "You don't even know. You don't know, Cora. Everything is so easy for you, you always had everything." She stands before me.

Incredulous, my mouth drops open. "That's not true, Ashley. I've suffered a lot in my life."

"Baby, please, you don't know everything, please don't judge until we all talk—"

"What the fuck do you know anyway? What do you know about my life? I've told you little about my past. Things weren't always easy."

"Baby, I'm not saying you didn't feel pain, but that's beside the point. Baby, please, just don't judge, keep an open mind until we talk tomorrow. That's one of the things that I love about you, that you're so open minded."

I lean back in my chair and regard her blankly. Her hands grasp my shoulders and I don't react. I try to make sense of everything. Misty's words come back to me. That Ashley was using me. It doesn't ring true, and now, seeing her here, it makes even less sense.

She drops to her knees. She's at my feet, on the floor of the Lincoln Bedroom in the White House in the United States of America. Her dark brown eyes plead with me. She wears silk pajamas with a presidential seal embroidered on the pocket.

All I know with certainty is that for the entire time I've known her, she has been dishonest with me. I cross my arms over my chest, feeling vulnerable and like I've lost something of great value. Ashley squeezes my leg and pleads with her eyes. The feeling I've always had when I'm with her is entirely extinguished and replaced with a desperate yearning for how things used to be.

"Cora, please, I love you. You can do whatever you want. You can go now, or tomorrow, or whenever, but I want you to stay right now. Spend tonight with me. Talk to Josh and I tomorrow. Then you can decide what to do. Please, baby."

I ignore her and wander to the window, stepping over to her like a discarded object. The White House lawn is splayed out before me, a deep green, beautifully lit, patrolled by guards armed with assault rifles. Beyond, the Washington Monument splits the sky, spotlighted and crisp on this clear night. A symbol of the west, of American power. This room—all the ornate details—the carved wood, the antiques, the high ceilings. This is it. The center of American power. The highest American class.

I turn to Ashley, still on the floor. Her sad, wet eyes plead with me.

I catch my reflection in a circular mirror lined with carved mahogany. Funny how we've changed roles. I thought I was part of the upper class, in an unlikely relationship with a smart, confident jobber. Yet through her, I befriended one of New California's highest ranking politicians and now, for reasons that remain unexplained, I'm in the castle of America's dictator.

Anger and jealousy surge through me and I stalk away. Ashley settles back, sitting on her feet, on the ground, observing me with interest. Waiting to see what I'm going to do. What the fuck does she want from me? And why the fuck won't she tell me what the fuck is going on?

I step over to her. Her hands reach to me, but I don't take

them. I loom over her with my arms crossed. She rises to her knees and places her hands on my hips, looking up at me expectantly, with uncharacteristically submissive eyes. I run my thumb over her cheekbone, down to her cheek. I trace her lips with my fingers. She savors my touch, closing her eyes and breathing slowly. I run my fingers through her hair, and then the anger comes back, and my fist grabs her hair, firm but gentle, holding her still. She opens her eyes.

"I really did love you, Ashley," I say.

"Baby, I love you too, I still love you, please tell me you still love me baby?"

I say nothing.

"Please take me now, don't be sweet and shy. I want you, Cora."

Using her hair to guide her, I slowly push her onto the floor, on her back. I glare into her eyes, searching for an explanation, but I don't see deceit. I see vulnerability, arousal, and love. I let go of her hair and pull off her smooth, dark blue silk pajama pants, and unbutton her shirt. When she's entirely undressed and I have her naked, underneath me. I intertwine my fingers in hers and kiss her roughly. She spreads her legs and I rest my weight on her, kissing her greedily, her hands above her head. She moans into my mouth, kissing me back. We're sloppy and rough, her teeth knocking mine. I squeeze her hands as hard as I can and she matches my strength. I flip her over and get on her back, I hold her head sideways, against the floor. My right hand squeezes, pinches, penetrates, grabs all the rest of her. We pant and moan. When she finishes she screams like an animal, and I worry the secret service will come to investigate. When she's done, I tell her what I want, and she obeys. We start to go again nearly right when I'm done. Wrestling and grabbing at one another with urgent needy hands, like those of someone falling from a great height.

I try to memorize every piece of her, every sound. I try to touch her everywhere, every strand of her hair, down to the tips of her fingers and her toes. I try to give myself to her and take everything she has. I gaze into her eyes and love her. One last time.

We sleep lightly, entangled in each other's limbs, waking only when we come apart. I wake up to her soft kisses on my back and fall back asleep. I awake again relieved the room is dark with no hint of sunrise. I dread the morning and want this night to continue. My desire to savor my final night with Ashley feuds with my perception that tomorrow, I need to be at my sharpest.

CHAPTER 24

Before I open my eyes, I sense the morning light seeping through the corners of the drawn curtains. Tense and still, Ashley lies next to me pretending to be asleep. She faces away and holds my hand to her breast. Already, the seduction of darkness has faded away for both of us. I open my eyes and stare at her messy blond hair. I squeeze her heavy breast. My body tenses as sleep wears off and I think of what is to come.

A peculiar slyness comes over me. I coolly disentangle myself from Ashley and hop up to get dressed. I return to the large bed, sit up, and lean against the pillows. Ashley remains on the other side of the bed. I eye her manicured fingernails clutching the overstuffed comforter and the smooth skin on her back. I want so badly not to desire her, to be able to navigate clearly through this day without the fog of lust and tenderness for her. She turns around and studies me, her brown eyes somber.

"Do you want coffee?" she asks.

"Yes, please," I say.

"Okay," she mumbles. She slithers to the nightstand where

a phone sits, picks up the receiver, and dials a few numbers.

I gaze at her curved back and familiar hand clutching the handset. Her trademark red nails brush hair away from her face. She lifts the handset to tuck hair behind her ear. I yearn to kiss her between her shoulder blades, but I don't. I stay where I am and observe her.

"Yeah, hi David, it's Ashley... Mm-hmm, everything's good... Yes, coffee, for both of us... Cora takes hers black, right Cora?"

She turns and I nod affirmatively.

"Yeah, black....Great, see you soon. Cora will come to the door."

She glances back at me and I meet her gaze with a glare. She returns the handset to its base.

"I'm not dressed," she says. She rolls over to expose her breasts. I look at them blankly.

"Okay," I say.

She searches my face and moves closer to me. I turn away and reveal nothing. Her hand touches my leg.

"Are you okay, baby?"

I shake my head and laugh cynically. I turn back toward her and stare. "Yeah, Ashley. I'm fine."

She removes her hand from my leg and takes a deep breath. "I know you want to know what's going on, baby, I know. I'm sorry to stress you out. We'll talk to Josh this morning." She resumes eye contact and touches my leg once again. "Baby, just know I love you, okay? That much is true."

I laugh once again. "That much is true, hmm?" I shake my head.

I'm jolted when she jumps on my lap and straddles me. She kisses me. Her mouth tastes like toothpaste and I wonder how long she's been up and when she brushed her teeth. She kisses me harder and pulls my hair. I am instantly, and completely, turned on. Just when I approach the point where I can't resist her, a sharp knock on the door pulls my attention away. With a mischievous smile, she releases me. She snaps her finger and points at the door.

"Get our coffee, baby."

I leap up and step to the door while Ashley crawls under the covers. David is apparently the man who brought me to this room last night. He brings a cart containing a coffee pot and two cups, hard-boiled eggs, and bacon. He cheerfully rolls the cart in. Ashley pulls the covers up under her arms and waves to him.

"Morning ladies!" he says. "I have coffee and breakfast for you!"

"Thanks," I say.

"Did you ladies have a good night?" he asks. He raises his eyebrows toward Ashley, who nods profusely.

"Yes," I say.

I inspect the coffee and food, my hands on my hips, and avoid Ashley's stare. David rushes out of the room with a dramatic wave. I prepare Ashley's coffee for her, swift and professional.

She cocks her head. "You okay, baby? I felt like we were about to have some fun."

"Yeah I'm fine, I just want to find out what the fuck I'm doing at the White House."

She nods. "It's crazy though, isn't it? Being at the White House."

With disgust, I stomp toward the bathroom, go in, and shower.

*****

Once Ashley and I are showered, coffeed, and fed, we wait silently in the Lincoln sitting room for Josh Winston to enter.

Unsure if I'm equipped to handle this conversation, I fidget, pace, and sip water. Ashley sits in a chair in full makeup, smartly dressed. Her newly obtained perfect posture and poise are an impressive adaptation. I count the days since I last saw her back in San Francisco. Just a week from yesterday. I rest my forearms on the back of a chair and examine her: beautiful, proper, legs crossed. I pace on and stop to look in a mirror. Cora Broussard: tall, subtly attractive, and tough; just like always. I didn't dress up for this.

Eventually, enough time passes that I tire of pacing around the room inspecting things. My nervousness morphs into restlessness, then boredom. I want to get this over with. Ashley and I speak sparingly, which becomes increasingly more awkward.

Across the lawn, the Washington Monument shoots into the sky, dark in front of bright white clouds. I think of my children and wife in San Francisco. Perhaps Jane knows more than I do from Misty and Cheryl. I think of my house in San Francisco and the comfort it brings to me. I smile as I picture my beautiful home, full of love. My wife, children, and of course food and wine. And whiskey. How great it will be to enjoy a drink once this is all over.

The opening door cuts the heavy silence. Josh enters. A smile adorns his sickeningly handsome face. I realize I imagined he would come in wearing a blue suit and a red tie, like a politician at a press conference, but instead he wears pleated khakis with a white shirt.

He approaches me with a wide grin. "Cora," he says.

"Hi," I say.

He correctly senses I don't want to hug him. Instead, he gives me a shoulder squeeze, which I respond to with a glare. He sits down on a chair next to Ashley. I sit on the couch across from them.

"We appreciate you coming out here today to talk."

I regard him with a blank expression. Ashley smiles at him with respect and lets him lead. He appears nervous.

I nod, unsure what to say. "This is all very confusing and strange to me," I start then pause. "Can you just get right to it and let me know what's going on?"

Ashley leans forward in her chair and turns to Josh. He glances at her, and they regard me with tense stares.

Josh clasps his hands and smiles. "I appreciate your bluntness, Cora, that's one of the things I like about you." He leans forward making direct eye contact.

I return his gaze, inscrutable, waiting.

"The president passed away."

"Wait, what? When?" I ask. This is not what I expected. Dread spreads through me as it sinks in that I am learning this at the White House from Josh Winston and not from the media. Then, I realize Josh called him the president and not the Dictator.

"About a week ago." He pauses again and carefully chooses the words he will use next. "Cora, I never approved of the president. I want to make that clear. I was disgusted with him before he became a dictator." He pauses and leans so far forward I am afraid he will fall out of his chair. He purses his lips and closes his eyes.

I stare at him. My heart pounds and my hands go numb.

"But sometimes, Cora, it's necessary to do things you don't want to do in order to get to a greater good. I'm certain you've learned in your own life that behind any achievement is hard work, and often sacrifice. It became impossible for New California to thrive without the United States, and it became impossible for the United States to thrive without those lost to New California. We need to work together and mutually sacrifice. You can't have your cake and eat it too."

"Yes you can," I snap.

Josh smirks at me and takes a deep breath. "Okay, perhaps I shouldn't revert to clichés. Cora, America was faltering without New California. You know that. It wasn't just the policies, it wasn't just that a large portion of educated people left, it was the wealth disparity, it—"

"It was the Dictator," I say.

Josh clasps his hands. "Yes, correct. Partially, yes, it was the Dictator. But, I need to preface this. Cora, I want to rebuild America. I want to restore democracy. I want my country back, the America I loved."

I jump out of my chair and pace as I understand where this is going.

Josh, right behind me, stalks me like a cat. The stupid fucking phallic Washington monument obscenely penetrates the sky. *Our founding fathers.* The phrase slices through me. To my left, Josh, the wholesome narcissist towers over me. I turn and meet his eyes. *American flag-blue.* He puts his soft hand on my shoulder and steps closer.

"I discovered long ago that in order to get to a greater good, morals need to be sacrificed in the short term. Just like the paradox of war, the climb to greatness has an ugly past." He drops his hand and we stand abreast, eyes on the monument. "Many years ago, while negotiating diplomatic ties, I befriended the president."

Disgusted, I step away. My thoughts race and revulsion spreads through every cell of my body. Ashley stares with wide eyes, like this is some sort of sporting match.

"Cora, please hear me out. I have good intentions. I want to make a difference."

He paces his own track around the room and crosses my path. I stop and meet his eyes, many centimeters above my own.

He states: "I'm going to be the president of the United States."

His words hang in the air. Ashley stares at me, completely still. I pace again. I begin to shake. Josh. I steal a glance at him: tall, conventionally handsome, charismatic and instantly likeable. The perfect politician. He was friends with the Dictator. All this time. All those trips to D.C., Ashley probably met the Dictator, shook his hand with the same hand she used to touch me. It feels like the ultimate betrayal. Josh Winston betrayed his country, betrayed his wife, all for his own ambition.

"Why won't the vice president take over?" I ask. Unsure of what to say, I resort to logistics.

"When the government enacted the Presidential Term Act, among the changes included the ability for the president to appoint a new president upon his death," Josh responds calmly.

I recall this now, from all those years ago.

"Why you, Josh? Why did he pick you?"

Anger flashes in his eyes but he extinguishes it so quickly I wonder if I imagined it. "He *believed* in me, Cora."

"Why this? Why collude with a dictator, why not seek the prime ministership in New California?"

"I didn't *collude* with the Dictator, Cora, I'm taking over for him. Colluding would mean supporting him. I never once did that."

A heavy silence befalls the room. I study Ashley's face. She leans forward and pleads with sad, moist eyes.

Josh pierces the silence. "This is the only way to restore democracy. The only way that I saw."

"What about New California? Won't this be considered treason?" I respond.

"Cora, I will attempt to heal the diplomatic relationship. But, as of now, it looks like I can never go back to New California without being charged with treason."

Ashley gasps. Her hands cover her mouth in shock. I roll my eyes at her. *She didn't know that? She didn't think that through?* I turn back to Josh.

"How can you betray your country?" I fire back. "You're an elected official, you took an oath. Do you not love New California? You betrayed me, and you betrayed all of the people of New California."

"It's for the greater good. I've never considered New California my country. I'm an American. I will always be an American. I always knew I would come back here to live one day and I would make it my life's work to serve the American people."

Ashley, poised once again, stares at me intently with her eyebrows raised, her eyes sad. I regard them both, a handsome politician and his... wife now?

"What does this have to do with me?" I blurt out.

Josh approaches me, takes my right hand in his, and squeezes it affectionately. "Cora, I will always give it to you straight. I want you to stay here with us. I will give you an appointment—any job you would like—including vice president. I know you've felt restless, like you need something more, and here is your chance. You can go down in history with me. We will make a great team." He towers over me and grabs my shoulders. "Cora," he says with an urgency that makes me gasp. "I value you so much as a friend, we could be such close friends."

I turn away, shocked, flattered, and horrified. I close my eyes, take a deep breath and collect myself. Ashley stands up and walks to me. Her hands grasp my shoulders and I shrug her away.

"What about your wives?" I ask.

Both their heads cast downwards and shame befalls their faces.

Ashley finally speaks: "Cora, baby, Misty and the kids are coming. They'll stay here with us, I'm not leaving her, not really, baby. Don't worry about her."

Josh's shamed face and silence answer my question for me.

I turn back to Ashley. "So you will be the First Lady of the United States, while Josh's wife is alone in San Francisco?"

Josh cringes.

"Yes," Ashley confirms.

Josh glares at her. I am struck with a pang of jealousy as I realize these people—even Ashley—will be so much more than I ever was. They will go down in history, and I'm just another rich professional class person. A leader of a series of small to medium sized companies. Nothing to show but my net worth, which is so much less than countless others.

"It is the only way to move *forward*," Josh says. His voice shakes with emotion. His tense facial muscles carve deep lines in his handsome face.

I turn away. "Oh, fuck that. At whose expense? What is the point?"

"The point, Cora, is to help America," Josh says.

I roll my eyes and stomp away.

Ashley follows me, grabs my shoulders, and yanks me toward her. "I love you, Cora. I need you."

I spin around and meet her eyes. "Why, Ashley?" I plead. "You're betraying your country."

She shoves me as her hands eject themselves from my shoulders, making me stumble. The poise she possessed only moments ago is gone. I smugly intuit that whatever change occurred in her does not run deep.

"Betraying my country?! Are you fucking kidding me, Cora? Betraying the country where I am a second-class citizen? Come on, Cora. All the people there are fucking awful. Those colonies are awful. I fucking hate it there. Fuck you! Fuck you Cora for not seeing that."

I step back and observe. How did I not see it before? It's so clear now what Ashley was doing. Climbing her way up, her way out. Jane was right.

My compassion ends as soon as I realize she dug her way out by fucking a man. Something women have done for all time, yet we live in a world where I managed to get by just fine on my own wit. I remain calm and still while she unravels before me.

"...There was no way out, nothing I could do. I was miserable. I didn't belong there. I deserve so much better. It's fine for some people, but I just couldn't live my life like that."

She sputters out and Josh approaches her. He attempts to take her in his arms but she squirms out of his grasp and approaches me.

She starts again, taking another tack. "I love you so much, Cora. Please, at least think about it. Your family can come too. You could stay together if you're so happy, but I need you, baby. I think you need me too. You're too complicated for just one woman. You need your drinks and your women, baby. I understand that. But baby, know that I have needs too. I shouldn't be at the colonies, having only my basic needs met. I knew I would be something more, and now I will be the First Lady. I need a powerful man taking care of me. It's a need. I know you wouldn't understand that, but think of your own needs, of me, your career, your women and your drinks. Baby, please—!"

She's talking in circles, but it makes sense and I get it. Josh stands by, waiting for Ashley to calm down. He eyes her and assesses whether he should intervene. All politics.

I let everything register. Ashley approaches me. Her mascara starts to run. She caresses my cheek and I close my eyes.

Josh is the new dictator. Ashley will be his wife. A deep hollowness spreads through me at the realization that this is the end of Ashley and me. I can't be complacent. I don't want any involvement. I want to go back to New California. She's chosen someone much more powerful than me, someone who can give her more than I ever could.

The tension in the room builds as they await my reaction. I

stand still, eyes closed, and savor the tender touch of Ashley's hand. She places her other arm on the small of my back and kisses me gently on the lips.

"I love you Cora." She kisses me again, punctuating her statement. "I really do."

My arms hang limply at my sides, but I let her kiss me. I can tell she thinks she is sealing the deal. Questions scroll through my brain, but I am too numb to ask them. I remove Ashley's arm from my waist and walk to the window. Josh approaches. He places his arm around my shoulders. I feel small and powerless, but calm and resolved.

"I know this is all a shock," he says. Smooth as ever. "I know you love New California, but Cora, there is a lot about the New California government that you don't know. If you knew what I knew, you would be disgusted. We are barely better than the Dictator. I hate that we had to drag you out here to tell you, but you were being surveilled back there. So was I. The Ministry of Catastrophe Anticipation was beginning to piece things together."

He rubs my shoulder while he speaks in a hushed tone, the way someone might speak to a child about a tragedy. I'm disgusted with myself when I realize his tactic is working, that I am comforted. Ashley approaches me, on my other side and places her arm around my waist. A silence befalls us. My mind wanders to my interrogation at the Ministry of Catastrophe Anticipation. They knew, and wanted to make sure I wasn't involved. The questions come back to me. Did Josh know the Dictator? What was Josh doing in D.C.? I picture the coldness of the man's face. His tiny sapphire eyes piercing into mine. I thought he was wasting his time, that nothing was going on, but now I feel sick with the knowledge that maybe I did know something. Maybe, somehow I was complacent in this.

I close my eyes and focus on Ashley's arm around my

waist, of Josh's hand on my shoulder. I inhale deeply and catch
the aroma of Ashley's perfume. Already it brings nostalgia in
place of desire. Some sort of masculine leathery scent that I've
never noticed emanates from Josh. Combined, they smell like
wealth and power. Between them, with their hands on me, I
breathe them in. But somehow I know I am separate, different.
One of these things is not like the other. Ashley kisses my cheek
and rubs my back. I meet her eyes but I have never felt so distant
from her. I glance at Josh and it's like I never knew him, like he's
Josh Winston from the news.

Then—I remember the outages. The outage here. The
outage in New California. I disentangle myself and step back. I
study them: the next president of the United States and his First
Lady. They stand patiently in front of me, the Washington
Monument between them.

"The call I got—about my father having a heart attack, were
you behind that?"

Josh lowers his gaze. "Yes. I didn't want to deceive you,
Cora, but I needed to get you to the U.S. It was much, much safer
that way. We were trying to think of how to get you—"

"The outage. In New California. Are you behind that, Josh?
Did you make that happen?"

"Cora, a lot of people are involved in this transition and due
to the nature of—"

"Did you do it? Are you behind it?"

He steps over to me once again. His eyes, only a few
centimeters from my own, are clear, blue. No emotion, no
politics, just power.

"Yes," he hisses, with such evil, such intention, that Ashley
twists away at the grotesque display before her.

I understand now that his ambition and quest for power is
different from mine. It's all a game to him. He doesn't want to
'help the American people,' he wants credit, he wants power. He

wants to go down in history. A high post in New California is not enough. He wants to lead the western world, with the military and nuclear arsenal ready to fire at his whim.

With that, I whip around to face Ashley. *This is the man you are with,* I think. She lowers her eyes in shame as she gets the message and registers the gravity of the situation.

I storm out, grab my bags and leave the Lincoln Sitting Room. My hands shake. I walk fast. At the bottom of the stairs, a uniformed guard gasps at my sudden presence and approaches me. He blocks my path and holds the barrel of his gun. He's polite in his demeanor, but it's apparent I must stop and obey him.

"I need to leave." I say. "I need to go to the airport. Can someone drive me to the airport, please, or can I get a taxi or something? I need to leave right now."

"Of course. Let me just check on that, Ma'am." He says a code into his walkie-talkie and from down the long corridor, three more armed guards race toward us. I panic, worried I left before Josh informed me I don't have a choice.

CHAPTER 25

I am shaky and relieved when I board the plane. I drink as soon as I can and knock down two glasses of sparkling wine before the airplane door is closed. In five and a half hours, I will be back home in San Francisco with my family. Likely a San Francisco in chaos, but I don't care. Without digital technology and any way to pay for things other than USD, I wonder how I will get home from the airport. If I must walk, I will.

I take a deep breath, unable to relax until we're in the air. I try to rationalize everything in my head and calm myself down. Ashley and Josh's intentions are good. They called me to the White House because of their great affection for me, why would they harm me? They can't force me to do anything. I'm too clever and unpleasant when forced. Ashley is aware my greatest weakness is women, and she certainly tried that angle. They let me leave the White House, but will they let me leave the country?

The last passenger boards the plane. I eye the flight attendants expectantly. One of them moves to close the door, but stops when another flight attendant whispers in her ear. My stomach lurches and I suck in my breath, certain a man with an assault rifle will come in and take me back to the White House. But no, it's a frazzled mother with a young child. The flight attendant expertly uses both hands to pull the door inward. Once it snaps into place, she pulls a handle to lock it.

I exhale, relieved, when the plane pulls away from the gate. The wine and forward motion appease me. Deceived by Ashley and affected by alcohol, I check out the attractive flight attendant and ponder whether I could love her. I tear my gaze away. The thought of a new woman makes me mourn Ashley. I dig through my purse for my screen and browse the video selections. Nothing sounds good, nothing sounds right. I'm too distracted. Finally, I can relax and collect my thoughts.

Josh. I think of him, in front of me, announcing he will become the president of the United States of America. His charm, his charisma—so thick I was almost fooled. I almost saw the situation from his perspective. My attraction to Ashley, and genuine love for her is so strong I am almost powerless. I am usually powerless against my attraction to power itself, but I am outdone. I smile at this thought. The plane is about to take off and the flight attendant approaches to collect my glass. With one big gulp, I finish the drink and hand it to her. Once in the air she refills it with a smile. I love how in first class they act like it's totally normal to consume three glasses of wine by the time the plane reaches its cruising altitude.

My thoughts race. I replay the conversation. Was it just this morning? Yes, it was. I empathize with the concept of sacrifice for the greater good, but who's to say Josh's intentions are good? He left his wife and betrayed his country, leaving it in the chaos he created. Now, he will be a dictator.

The billboards. The blank billboards. They will display Josh's stupid fucking face. In D.C., on the banks of the Potomac, in Michigan—the state where I was born—everywhere. Maybe

Ashley will be on them too. At one point I thought Ashley and I were equally attractive but no, she is much more attractive. I could never appear on a propaganda billboard. If I were Josh's wife, the billboards would just show him. And Cheryl. He had to trade up from skittish little Cheryl to Ashley. Ashley, First Lady of the United States of America. It suits her, she'll love the attention. I'm struck with a now familiar stab of jealousy that these people are going to be internationally known, and perhaps even well-respected.

Josh says he will restore democracy, but will he? Will people really have freedom, like they used to? The kind of freedom of the press in which it will come to light that he and Ashley left their wives and betrayed their country? The kind of freedom they enjoyed in New California? No, of course not.

Everything comes together, everything makes sense now. I'm so glad I left, that I stepped away from those charming sociopaths. I can't believe I let myself be enraptured by them for so long. I look out the window at the tiny forests and homes below, like toys I could stomp out. Outside of the D.C. area, the sky is nearly void of clouds or fog, only crisp blue sky stretching into infinity. The flight attendant comes to refill my wine glass, and I tell her I want bourbon instead. I order it straight—on the rocks—because I can drink it that way. That's how Josh drinks fucking scotch.

"Is Jack Daniels okay?" asks the flight attendant with a soulless smile. She still pretends this rate of drinking is normal and that she is absolutely delighted to serve me. Who knows? Maybe she is. Maybe she wants to see what happens when the middle-aged woman from New California gets wasted. Serving rich assholes on planes sounds pretty lame, she has to find her fun somewhere. Or maybe she can relate because she's a drinker herself and can experience alcohol vicariously through me.

"Yes, fine, thank you," I say. I flash a smile and maintain

long eye contact. She returns the smile, and I wonder if she is flirting with me. I recline my seat and spread out, resting one of my legs on the leg rest. I inspect my long legs in admiration. I'm glad I'm tall—1.75 meters. Tall, but not like man-tall.

"Here you go sweetheart, bourbon on the rocks." She touches my shoulder.

Flight attendants don't accept tips. Maybe she is flirting with me. She appears older than me, mid to late fifties, but beautiful bone structure and good skin.

I picture Ashley last night. Her body pressed against mine while I touched and kissed her everywhere, memorizing every centimeter of her.

The bourbon goes down smoothly. I shake the glass a bit and study the large ice cubes as they change shape and dissolve. My head feels light. I focus on the comforting taste of whiskey, my elixir. Incapable of treason. I take large sips and finish it in a few minutes. My concept of time disappears. I sit up a bit and catch the eye of the flight attendant. She smiles, amused, and rushes over to refill my glass.

Ashley. Always so secretive, so mysterious. Now I understand why. Plotting to leave her wife and betray her country. Maybe she thinks women will be hard to come by now that she's the First fucking Lady in that conservative police-state city she lives in now. Maybe that's all this was, she knew what would happen and she needed a woman, fast. I recall what Misty told me. She targeted me. She knew she had to find a girlfriend because she can't just be with a man.

If I met Ashley before she met Misty and before I met Jane, what would that look like? Could Ashley be what Jane is to me? Would I even want that with her, so many years ago? Would I be enough for her?

No. She said it herself. She needs a powerful man.

I put on headphones and listen to music. I flip through

tracks. Nothing sounds right. I finish my whiskey and request another. Is it the third? Fourth? I can't remember. I get a glass of sparkling water as well. I ask the flight attendant where she's based, but it comes out rushed, slurred, and awkward. Los Angeles, she says with a tight smile. I nod in acknowledgment and settle back into my music.

I reach down to retrieve something from my purse and bump my whiskey, spilling it all over the floor. The passengers nearest me regard me with disgust and morbid curiosity. The flight attendant comes to clean it. I insist I clean it myself. When she turns away, I ask for her to replace it. She stares at me blankly at first, then disgusted, then she smiles and gets the whiskey.

CHAPTER 26

I wake up to bright sunlight pouring through the windows while the plane descends. The man across the aisle detects I'm awake and stares unashamedly, like I'm an animal at the zoo. My head aches and my mouth is dry. The flight attendant wordlessly serves me a water with no smile.

"You can't put your tray table down, we're landing," she snaps.

I nod and drink the entire glass of water in a single gulp. The left side of my pants is wet and smells of whiskey. I must have spilled another glass. I am shaky and weak, devoid of any pride or arrogance. I fix my hair the best I can without a mirror. I'm relieved not all of the alcohol wore off, but it feels gross being simultaneously drunk and hungover. I want to go home and spend time with my family and draw comfort from them, but also don't want to go home such a mess. I sit back and rub my eyes, furious at myself for losing control.

The memories flood back. The outage in New California. Josh will be the new dictator. Ashley's breakdown while she begged me to betray my country. Drinking too much on the plane. Embarrassing myself. I didn't decide to go to sleep, and I don't remember being tired. I guess I blacked out and passed out. I need to figure out how to get home in a de-digitized New California, and the task seems daunting.

I peer out the window. The San Francisco skyline approaches, the bay and the bridges. Why does my house seem so far away? I can practically see it. Everything changed so much—I changed so much—it seems impossible Jane and the kids will still be in the house, unharmed, going about their days. But, of course they will. What else would they do?

*****

I drag myself through the airport. My head aches and I'm mildly nauseous. Where I normally feel young and vigorous, now my age weighs me down like gravity. I smirk at a guy in a suit eating a sandwich out of a plastic bag, until I realize the shops are closed. My nausea increases as a wave of anxiety passes through me. I scan the airport—the only people who aren't passengers are government protection officers. I overhear a loud-talking man say satellite is up, but running slow. He asks why there isn't a plan for bandwidth distribution in case of an outage. I want to tell him the answer, that payments are all so integrated they can't be separated.

I'm relieved to find the line at customs is short. I'm so close to being home and so tired and hungover, that every step seems insurmountably difficult. I notice government protection officers are working the passport booths rather than passport control. The young, bored-looking officer checks the passport of the man in front of me, compares his name to a piece of paper, and asks a few questions. He responds with one-word answers and bureaucratic nods. He is shuffled through and already it's my turn.

"Passport."

I hand it to the officer, opened to the page with my picture. He checks my passport, looks at me, then back at the passport for what seems like an unusually long time with his brow furled. He picks up the piece of paper next to him, holds it next to my passport, and stares at me, frozen with his mouth open.

Fuck. My first instinct is to turn around and run. I consider it, but understand it's already too late. *Fuck. Fuck.* I reach out my hand and smile politely, hoping he will hand me my passport and let me be on my way.

I cock my head and smile. "Is everything okay?" I ask.

He obviously doesn't know what to do. He whips his head around, trying to get the attention of the other officers. They don't notice him. I continue to smile, but inside I panic. It's like claustrophobia, the feeling of imminent doom. The feeling that I would rather be anywhere in the world right now except for right here, right now.

Of course, it's not like claustrophobia, because something is actually wrong. But also, it is like claustrophobia, because I'm claustrophobic, and I get the distinct impression I'm about to be contained in a small space for an undetermined period of time.

The officer gets another officer's attention and he walks over.

I do one last futile survey of the airport and comb through my brain for a solution, but find no way out. I must face this. I try to be strong, but I can't. It's all too much.

I stand and wait, ready to be taken somewhere. My throat tightens like I will choke on my own anxiety. Whatever is about to happen is going to be much worse than the Ministry of Catastrophe Anticipation situation—where they specifically told me I wasn't suspected of any crime. Now, I'm on a list of people who are supposed to be arrested by passport control. This is my penance. This is what I get. Now I will pay for my pleasure.

The young earnest officers motion for me to follow them. They lead me, one in front and one behind me, staying close to ensure I don't flee. The one in front glances back many times with his nervous brown eyes. He chivalrously opens a door marked 'employees only' for me, and then darts back in front of me. Dread shoots through me and poisons me further the deeper we trek into the building. Gone is the open space of the airport terminal. Drop ceilings and florescent lights guide us forward. At each turn, the ceilings get lower, and the hallways narrower.

We approach a windowless office at the end of the hall. Inside, a man sits at a desk cluttered with papers and files. He swivels his chair and his eyes widen when they meet mine. He looks to each officer. The skittish brown-eyed officer takes charge and salutes the man in the office.

"Officer, we have a person here from the list that was distributed—"

The man in the office leans forward. "The Interested Parties List?"

"Yes, sir."

He responds by gaping at me.

I take off my jacket. I'm beginning to sweat.

"Alright…" he says. "I'll contact whoever needs to speak to her." He pauses, then gets up. "Come this way, please."

I breathe fast and my hands shake. He leads me down another narrow hall. At the end of the hall, he unlocks a door and grunts as he pulls it open with both his hands. My eyes dart around the room. I immediately recognize it as a standard New California jail cell with the requisite square meters of space, a bed, a window, a screen mounted on the wall, and a mini fridge. When I step in and scan the room, I calm down a bit. I can spend a few hours in here, no problem. It looks like a dorm room. The twin bed in its built-in wood frame triggers fond memories of girls I knew in college.

Of course they need to talk to me. They must know what
Josh did by now. I didn't do anything wrong, so it shouldn't be a
problem. They'll contact whoever needs to talk to me, they'll
come by, we'll talk, and once everything is cleared up, I will go
home.

"Ms. Broussard," says the man from the office. "I do not
have details, but all I can tell you is that you are currently under
arrest by the government of New California. Per the New
California constitution, we will address this swiftly, and promptly
inform you of your reason for detention. While you are in our
custody, you have the right to humane treatment, including an
unlimited supply of water and a reasonable amount of food."

I know all this, but it never occurred to me it would ever
apply to me. I used to read the prisoner bill of rights with pride
for my country, but it sounds bleak when I am the subject.

"Would I be able to get my suitcase in here?" I ask.

"No, you will not. We will need to take your purse as well."

"But I have medication in there I need to take."

"What medication?" he asks.

The two officers stand at attention to oversee the exchange.

"Xanax," I say.

He laughs. "No."

"Can I make a phone call?"

"Cell networks are down, so no. Was there someone
meeting you at the airport?"

"No, there wasn't," I say.

"Alright Ms. Broussard, we will deliver meal service
shortly. I expect the government agency who needs to speak with
you will come in tonight, despite the late hour. Any questions?"

"No, not at the moment," I say. Panic strikes me. "But what
if I have a question? How do I contact someone?"

He chuckles and places his hands on what must be his hips
beneath his misshapen body. "You'll just have to wait."

A female officer arrives and informs me she will search me. Everyone else leaves. She is young and fit, with taut unblemished skin, fine light brown hair in a tight ponytail, and clear blue eyes. Undressing in front of her, I am hyper-conscious of time's toll on my forty-eight-year-old body, where normally I think I look great for my age. I stare at the floor while she examines me, turns my clothes inside out and back again as she searches them. She returns my clothes and I scurry into them.

The other officers return without my purse and hand me frumpy prison pajamas, made soft by excessive laundering. Satisfied procedure has been followed, all three officers turn to leave. The female officer glances back, and is momentarily jolted when our eyes meet. She smiles faintly, hesitates, and replaces it with a blank, businesslike expression. She closes the heavy door. Fabric rustles before the unnecessarily loud noise of the key in the lock. The metal key slides in, turns, and the deadbolt engages.

All sense of hope drains from me immediately. I pace with my head in my hands. My heart pounds. With desperation, I search for something to soothe myself. I rush to the window and see a parking lot beyond several meters of grass. I open the refrigerator and find it filled with bottled water. Nothing helps. It's the evening. They might not even come tonight to talk to me. *No. No. No. I can't handle this.*

Claustrophobia is more about control than small spaces. I can be in a small space all day long if I have free will to leave any time I want. It's an uncontrollable urge to get out, but I can't, which fuels the fear. It's the worst feeling. The panic mounts. What is it I'm afraid of? Being in this situation for *one. More. Second.* But the second passes, and a new one starts. The dread builds up and spreads through my body like the worst nausea. My brain vomits, sounding all the alarms, uncontrollably, all at once. I lose my peripheral vision and everything is in a pinpoint frame, around which is the bleakest darkness processed through my mind like a kaleidoscope of horror. And then, another second passes and it all happens again.

I place my head in my hands and scream into my pillow. I cry and whimper like a baby. I collapse to the ground. It's the worst kind of pain, but nothing hurts. Just waves and waves of throbbing unpleasantness and no release, no escape. Nothing light, everything dark.

Since I was in my early thirties I kept a Xanax and a small bottle of alcohol in my purse in case I found myself stuck on an elevator, on a stalled train, or locked in a room somewhere. It gave me relief, but I still avoided those situations. So I tried to think of other things I could carry around to help if I were trapped somewhere. One idea was so grim, so dark, I never went through with it: razor blades. I could cut my own throat as my way out. The control, that option, something else to struggle with, would make me more comfortable.

Here, I can't even take Xanax. The alcohol I drank on the plane has definitively worn off and in its place is anxiety deeper than before I took a sip.

The panic rises, and rises, but eventually it plateaus, and I settle into a grim, fragile sort of calm. I lie on the bed and take large slow breaths. The calmness is so thin any thought could bring the panic back. I try to think of nothing and just breathe.

I sit up and scan the room. The screen. I turn it on to check what is available. New California doesn't offer cable, everything is in the cloud. Hopefully they store movies in the network. I turn on the screen and find a menu. So far, so good. I click on movies and then, of course, get a connectivity warning. *Ugh.*

Exhausted, I turn the light off, collapse into the bed, crawl under the covers and drift off to sleep.

*****

It feels like only moments later I awake as the huge metal key penetrates the lock. I sit up and compose myself. The light turns on, and two men in suits recoil in surprise to find me sitting up, awake, smiling faintly. They stride into the room without a word. Immediately upon seeing them, I am certain they normally delegate the task of interrogating people in prison cells to others.

Both sets of eyes study me while they circle me like sharks. I stand and contemplate them. I am slightly taller than the one closest to me and he cranes his neck backward to look down his nose at me. A government protection officer steps in, provides three chairs, and exits.

"Hi," I say. I don't have anything to hide and want to get this over with.

"Hello, Cora Broussard," the shorter guy says. He speaks with a New York accent, which feels both out of place and completely appropriate. "I'm Agent McGuinness, and this is Agent Vickers."

I acknowledge them with a nod.

"What agency do you represent?" I ask.

"We are not obligated to disclose that information," Vickers says.

I nod up at Vickers and a long silence lingers. I stand and hold my ground while both men's cold, beady eyes bore into me, their faces contorted with disgust.

"Can you tell me why I've been arrested?" I am calm, cool, and stoically give away no vulnerability.

McGuinness studies my face and a staring contest commences, which I lose. I realize I am still incredibly tired, so I sit down in one of the chairs. He swoops right in.

"Where are you coming from, Cora?" he asks casually.

He leans on the back of a chair, his knee on the seat of it. I wonder if he is about to sit on it backwards, like this is a nineties sitcom, and I watch in horror. Please don't do that.

"Washington, D.C.," I reply.

"Oh," he says, "cool, what were you doing there?"

I laugh mockingly at him and glance at Agent Vickers, who stares at me with deathly seriousness.

"Josh Winston had me come there. He said he needed to talk to me."

McGuinness cocks his head, barely hiding his genuine surprise at my disclosure. "Josh Winston, huh? So, I guess you guys are friends?"

"We were," I say.

He continues to question me in the same fake casual tone. I tell him about Ashley and how I met Josh, I detail each time I saw Josh and everything Ashley said about him.

McGuinness stands, puts his hands in his pockets, and begins to pace. "So," he says.

The silence lingers in the air. I open my mouth to pierce it, but he beats me to it.

He leans in close. "What did Josh tell you in D.C.?"

I collect my thoughts as I prepare to summarize it. "He told me that the Dictator died and that he's going to be president. He called me there because he wanted to give me a job doing something for the American government, but I told him he was a traitor."

They stare at me, mouths open, surprised by my candidness.

Agent Vickers, mostly silent until now, leans in close. "A man you met recently asks you to enter a foreign country to talk to you about something and you go? Something's not adding up here."

"I was already there, my dad was sick, I just flew to Washington, D.C. It was more for Ashley than Josh, I really cared about her and wanted some type of resolution." I listen to my own words, deflated by how stupid it all sounds.

Vickers shakes his head incredulously while McGuinness

chuckles.

I continue. "By then I knew something big was going on. I just had to know what it was."

Vickers approaches the door and knocks on it. An officer lets him out. McGuinness and I stare at the door in tense silence. A few moments pass before Vickers reappears carrying stacks of USD I recognize from my suitcase.

Vickers approaches me with a bundle in each hand. "Why do you have all this cash in USD, Cora? Do you know using USD in New California is a crime?"

"Yes," I say.

"Though, treason is a much more serious crime," McGuinness interjects.

Both men wait for my reaction.

I shake my head slowly. "How is it treason to have a conversation with Josh Winston before I knew he was betraying his country?"

"Before you knew, huh?" McGuinness says. "Before you knew—and let's assume you didn't know anything at all. You flew to Washington, D.C. to have a conversation with him and somewhere along the way picked up 25,000 in USD?" He shakes his head in disbelief. "Oh, and this is also not the first time you entered the United States and saw Josh Winston. Interesting."

"Sounds like treason to me," Vickers says.

"Can I consult with a lawyer?" I ask. I'm not clear on what the law is in New California because I usually don't commit crimes.

McGuinness laughs. "Not until your trial."

I take a deep breath and try to stay calm. I make eye contact with each of them and attempt to appeal to their humanity, but their cold dead eyes give away nothing. "I got the money because just before I left for D.C., I heard that the internet was down in New California—meaning payments would be down as well."

McGuinness stares at me while Vickers examines the money.

"Honestly," I continue. "25,000 dollars is not all that much money to me."

McGuinness laughs while Vickers smirks. "Not a lot of money to you? Wow, must be nice. Must be nice to be Cora Renée Broussard," McGuinness says.

"Must *have* been nice," Vickers says.

McGuinness raises his hand to silence him. "You know, using USD as currency in this country is a crime regardless of whether or not it's a lot of money to you. Did you know that, Cora?"

"Yes," I say, "but possessing USD is not a crime, and I thought the currency laws might change—or be relaxed—when our actual form of payment is not functional."

"No such thing has happened." Vickers says.

McGuinness shakes his head.

"Okay, fine, but in any case I still have not committed any crime."

"Cora," McGuinness says. He smiles, strolls toward me, and chuckles. When he is close enough to tower over me, he says: "You're not here because of the USD—that's just evidence. You are here, arrested by New California, for treason."

A long silence follows as I glance back and forth between them.

"Listen," I say, "I will answer any of your questions. I will tell you anything you want to know. I'm disgusted with Josh and Ashley. There is nothing I have a problem telling you."

The agents exchange glances for a long while. McGuinness, who appears to be in charge, shrugs at Vickers and then fires off questions. Question, after question, after question. Then, the same question again. Then, questions about events surrounding previously mentioned events and then bam—the same question again. Was I aware Josh knew the Dictator? Did Ashley meet the Dictator? Then back again to: did I know Josh knew the Dictator? Did I know Josh was going to be the president of the United States? Did I know Ashley and Josh planned on fleeing the country? Did I know if Josh was the father of Jimothy Doral? Did I know the Dictator gave Josh a bottle of scotch several months ago? I can't tell if they believe me or if they don't. I begin to lose my sense of time. I become exhausted and the officers begin to ramp down, their questions losing bite, as they likely become exhausted as well. It must be late. I wonder how long they'll keep me here for. Eventually, both men stand and I do as well.

"You're not going anywhere," Agent Vickers says.

"How long am I going to be here?" I ask. A sick feeling washes over me. They already asked every question at least five times. What more could they ask?

"That's none of your business," he sneers. "Your 'friend' betrayed his country and we suspect you of treason. See you tomorrow, Cora." He puts his jacket on and turns to leave, McGuinness follows. Neither of them say goodbye.

I stand in the middle of the room with my arms crossed. A new wave of panic rises. The men exit and do not turn back. The door shuts behind them and the key shifts the metal to trap me inside. I pace to stay calm. I breathe in, and out, and in. I maintain a fragile calm for a moment, then another. I congratulate myself for my calmness, but then there it is, the voice of panic: No, No, No. It revs up, ready to fill every cell of my body. I'm suddenly hot, and I roll up my sleeves, I feel like it's so hot in here that I will die, and then I panic even more when I realize I can't adjust it. I go into the small bathroom to check if it's cooler, it's not but there is a shower. I could take a cold shower if I want to. As soon as the thought occurs to me, I am not hot anymore. I rush to the window and peer out. The base is close to the ground. Right at eye level, I am able to see mowed grass, a half-empty parking lot with a few government vehicles, and not much of anything else. I pace some more. I lie down on the bed, face down, and pull at my hair. I patrol the room once more and try to find anything that will give me comfort, pleasure, amusement, anything.

I turn out the light and I think of Ashley, then—no, not Ashley. She's gone and I can't ever see her again. I think of my ex from years ago, Laura, of her pale hands traced with blue veins. Of her red nails and tight grip. Her hands when they grasp mine, claiming me, and then squeezing, claiming me again. Her adoring, unwavering eyes on mine. Both of our breaths quicken and her hands wander purposefully, always touching me hard, never gently. Her darkest fantasies seeping through her raspy voice in my ear. Then, always a tender touch and an 'I love you.' The thought of her calms me, but then I remember that she doesn't love me anymore, and I feel desperately empty.

I drift toward sleep and think of Jane. I miss her arms around me and her body pressed against mine. It never ceases to be comforting. I think of my kids; Drake with his quick smile and genuine charm, Simone with her silly sense of humor and deep dark thoughts. We will be reunited soon. My exhaustion wins the battle with anxiety, and I fall into a deep sleep.

CHAPTER 27

I wake up refreshed, without a trace of the hangover I had the previous evening. I try not to overthink the fact that I'm contained here, or get my hopes up for the possibility of release. Based on the orange stripes of sunlight peaking in from behind the curtain, and the frequency of planes taking off, it appears to be mid-morning. I decide to take a shower and am oddly excited for something to do. I jump up and start the shower. I find one microfiber towel and one bar of soap labeled 'soap/shampoo/conditioner.'

The shower is scalding hot almost immediately. The water pressure beats down, like a hot sensual fire hose. As soon as it hits any particular part of my body, it nearly goes numb. I sway and move, as the hot water pounds my skin. I make sure to close my eyes extra tight. I'm excited to find something pleasurable to do in this cell, but it occurs to me someone will likely come in soon to interrogate me or bring me breakfast. I reluctantly get out, dry off, and get dressed.

I don't have makeup or hair products, but they let me keep

my hair tie so I utilize it to the extent I can to make myself look presentable. In the harsh flat light of a New California jail cell, my eyes appear smaller and my skin looks worse than usual. The wrinkles around my eyes are more indented. I lean in close to the mirror. The brown in my eyes looks less sharp than when I was young. Still, when I stand back and look at my high cheekbones, my full lips, my figure, I don't look bad for my age. Especially after spending the night in a jail cell.

My thoughts are interrupted by the key in the lock. I desperately hope this means the arrival of breakfast and coffee and not cartoonish interrogators. I am delighted when a uniformed woman wheels in a tray. My eyes dart right to a cup with visible steam, which I pray to be coffee.

She nods at the tray. "Here ya go," she says. I can tell she's from the Midwest.

"Thank you, this looks great," I say.

She rolls her eyes.

"Just curious—where are you from originally?" I ask.

She flashes a tight half smile. "The great state of Indiana," she says. I am desperate for any sort of normal conversation.

"Oh cool, I'm originally from Michigan. Grand Rapids."

She purses her lips and nods. "I'm from a little town about an hour outside Indianapolis."

"Oh, cool, I've never—"

"Sorry to interrupt you, but we're not really supposed to be talkin' to the pris—the people in the cells. Sorry about that, Ma'am."

"Sure, it's cool, I understand." I smile good-naturedly and pick up the steaming cup, which appears to be coffee. It tastes delicious. Much better than I would expect while arrested. I hope I can request a refill.

I expect the interrogators to arrive soon after I am finished with coffee and breakfast, but the time ticks by, and no one comes to the room. I become antsy and pace. At first, I am excited for them to come, just for something to do. Then, I'm bored, and eventually the panic about the uncertainty begins to rise again. I wish I knew how long it would be. I want an itinerary for my incarceration. Like at a long wedding ceremony, where everyone can follow along and know how close they are to their first drink at the reception.

I amuse myself watching planes take off in the tiny strip of sky I can see. The raw power of jet engines stirs something in me every time.

I jump at the sound of the key in the lock. The same woman from this morning wheels in a cart with my lunch. I'm pleased a lot of time passed, but worried they forgot about me.

"Afternoon," the woman says.

Knowing she can't chat with me, I greet her with a friendly smile. I inspect the offering on the plate. "Do you know when they'll be in to question me again? I'm just getting bored sitting and waiting."

She pauses and studies me. "Not sure what I'm supposed to tell ya or not, but don't worry, I think they're coming by soon. Saw some agents arrive and they asked that I bring your lunch now."

"Great, thanks a lot. I won't mention you said anything."

She nods courteously. "That'd be much appreciated," she says. She finishes transferring the plates to a small end table in my cell, and shuffles through her disorganized cart for silverware. I wait patiently while she mumbles to herself. A noise from the hallway pulls her eyes away just long enough to not notice a folded up piece of paper drift to the floor. A conspiratorial thrill courses through me at the thought that I may get to find out what that paper says. The woman finds the silverware, meets my eyes, and hands it to me.

"Good day, Ms. Broussard," she says.

"Thank you so much," I respond.

While she pulls the cart backwards out of the room, I maintain eye contact and wave to pull her attention away from the paper on the floor. Once the door closes and the lock is engaged, the paper remains on the stark white tile of the floor. White on white. Invisible, besides disrupting the pattern of the tile grout. The room falls silent and I grab the paper, casually, like it was a napkin and place it under the bedsheets. The question of *if* I am being surveilled sails through my mind and crashes against the question of, why would they stop now? When they have every right. When, my 'friend' betrayed his country. When, barely a day ago I was on foreign soil colluding with a dictator. I lay on the bed, my head on the pillow, and sigh.

The sad plate of food on the tiny table beguiles my rumbling stomach. I reluctantly make my way over to it and scoop spoonful's of the salty organic mush into my hungry mouth. It's not bad. I think about the paper under my pillow. It's probably nothing, I tell myself. It's probably everything, I counter.

I think of the woman who served the food and the moment of eye contact before she left. Was she trying to tell me something? I realize that I treat her in the same kind but professional manner I treat servers in restaurants and, surprisingly, she treats me like someone she serves and not a prisoner.

The paper beats like a heart under the pillow. Maybe it's just some sort of list of food or something inane like that. I formulate a plan. I will slip the paper into my pants and unfold it slowly in the bathroom while the toilet flushes. The surveillance is likely automated audio-based, with a list of sounds they expect, a list of sounds that require review, and a list of sounds that trigger an alarm. I know the asshole who invented the technology.

I jump at the sound of the key in the door and stand. Two

officers armed with tranq guns on slings enter the room.

"Cora Broussard?"

"Yes."

"Come with me."

The armed guards flank me and we walk down the long, narrow corridor. Their boots echo with each step. We enter a room in which McGuinness and Vickers sit at a table.

I sit on the molded plastic chair allocated for me. Vickers scrolls through a government tablet and McGuinness studies me. Vickers wears the same suit that he wore last night. I wonder if men frequently wear the same suit two days in a row. McGuinness is wearing a black suit and the one from last night was charcoal. I almost wish he had on the same suit as well, it would add to the cartoonish effect.

McGuinness clears his throat. "Cora Broussard. Nice to see you again."

I nod, unsure if I am supposed to say it's nice to see him too. He doesn't wait for an answer.

"We have some follow-up questions for you," he says.

"Okay, I'm happy to answer them," I respond.

McGuinness pauses and glances at the door. He and Vickers exchange a look. As if in response, the door opens and a government protection officer enters with a glass of water. He sets it down in front of me, carefully, to minimize the glassy thud, and rushes out. McGuinness and Vickers eye me expectantly and I sip the water to appease them.

Apparently sated, McGuinness scrolls through a list on his screen and leans back in his seat. "The sixth of April, 2032, when you and Josh Winston had lunch. It was just the two of you?"

"Yes," I respond.

He nods slowly. "Was it business or pleasure?"

"What do you mean?" I ask.

He shrugs. "Just—was it business or pleasure, that's all,

why did the two of you get together?"

"It wasn't business, we talked about personal matters mostly. He asked about my son's basketball game, we talked about where we grew up, things like that."

"Sounds like you two went on a date."

"No. It wasn't like that at all, it was just two friends having lunch and talking."

"Well, Josh is a nice looking guy, you already knew he had stepped out on his wife with Ashley, and then he asks you for lunch. Did you think it would be a date?"

"No. I definitely did not think it was going to be a date and it definitely wasn't. I did not want it to be a date."

McGuinness nods. Vickers stares at me, unblinking. So still I wonder if he is breathing.

"Did Josh smile at you while you were talking?" McGuinness asks.

"Yeah, Josh smiles all the time."

"Did Josh, at any point, place his hand over yours across the table?"

This throws me off. I realize they must have talked to someone who was at the restaurant. I think back and recall he did. I remember the softness and warmth of his hand.

"Yeah, I think he did, but I interpreted it as being a friendly gesture." I say. I glance at Vickers and discern he is in fact breathing.

"Have you ever had a sexual encounter with Josh Winston?" McGuinness asks.

"No, absolutely not," I respond.

"Not in New York?"

"No, not in New York, nowhere. I have never had any kind of sexual encounter with Josh Winston."

"Did either Josh Winston or Ashley Doral ever invite you to engage in a sexual encounter with the two of them?" McGuinness asks.

"With both of them? Never."

Another long pause. Vickers stares at my water glass, of which I've only consumed about a quarter. Reminded of it, I gulp down the rest to offset my salty lunch.

"Would you say that Josh Winston was your friend?" Vickers asks.

I turn to Vickers. "Yes, kind of. I mean, yes, but only through Ashley. That time when we went out for lunch was the only time we were alone together."

"When you had lunch with Josh Winston, did he ask you if you were interested in going into politics?" Vickers asks.

I search my memory. "Not specifically. He casually asked if I ever considered running for office and I said that no, I had not."

"Did Josh try to convince you to run for office?" McGuinness asks.

"Not really. He just said that I would be good at it."

The two men exchange glances. McGuinness flips to a different page on his screen. A buzz in the air makes me gasp with delight. But—it's not a buzz. It's a glow. A tiny streak of light that I can hear and feel like a tingle in my spine. A giggle bubbles up my throat but I suppress it. I search for the feeling, for the source, but it eludes me. I study the room, the cinderblocks, the wood grain of the table, nothing looks different, but it's as if everything is in crystal clear focus and I can *feel* it. On the floor, a thin sheet of dust separates the shiny marble exquisiteness from the air resting above it. An urge to clean the floor and break down that dimension makes me twitch, but I resist. My mouth tingles and I lean forward, excited and ready to speak.

McGuinness eyes me and smiles wide, exposing his teeth like a crocodile. He rubs his hands together and leans forward. "Has Ashley Doral ever expressed ill will toward the country of New California?"

I scan my brain for an answer. Surprisingly, all knowledge, all facts, all words, are waiting at the ledge between my brain, my mouth, and the rest of the world. "No, not specifically. At least, not until she was trying to persuade me to stay in D.C. In New California, she made some comments, minor ones, which led me to believe she was less patriotic than I am."

Both men lean in, interested.

"What kinds of comments?" Vickers asks.

"Just—a few things here and there, she asked me my opinion, how I felt about the country. I said that I love it here and that I'm proud to be here. I don't remember what she said. Nothing even outwardly negative, just that 'it's not all that it seems to be' or something like that."

Both men nod and urge me to continue.

"Oh—there was something, actually. It wasn't that long ago. She was upset. She said there is a lot we don't know about, as citizens. I asked if Josh had told her something, if she knew something I didn't know, and she said no and dismissed the topic."

This interests them. They exchange a glance and McGuinness enters something into his screen. I melt into a state of relaxed stimulation. I speak coherently, but my usual constant tedious calculation evades me. My words flow like they're coming from someone else, like I have no control.

The questioning goes on, and on. They ask again about everything I told them last night, except now—for everything I say—they ask if someone can corroborate my story. What did the server at the restaurant look like? Who saw Ashley and I at the hotel in New York?

They ask for my Uber account credentials and I comply. The upper corner of the screen shows a satellite connection on a network called "NC EMERGENCY." They scroll through the rides and screenshot the ones to Ashley's colony. McGuinness and

Vickers hover over the screen. While they're distracted, I scan the room. My eyes dart between the cinderblock walls, the drop-ceiling, the door and its shiny metal lock. I breathe and savor the clean oxygen in my lungs. The mild euphoria begins to contract. I can see it, round like a balloon, slowly leaking out. I try my hardest to remain calm and strong. Wanting to prolong and enhance the feeling, I request another glass of water. Vickers jumps up and knocks on the door. A tall handsome officer opens the door, and Vickers brusquely requests a glass of water, pointing at me. The officer looks at me, meets Vickers eyes, and nods knowingly. The water arrives and I gulp it, savoring the sweet taste on my tongue.

Vickers meets my eyes. Starting with the most recent Uber ride, he asks what the purpose of each one was and whether it involved Ashley. A part of me floats away, while a part of me keeps talking. Cataloging my encounters with Ashley in great detail. What we said, what we did. I glance at the clock on the wall, but there is no clock and never was. I cock my head and stare at the space where a clock should be. Words flow from my mouth but I can't understand them. The questions stop and silence hangs in the air. The grain of the wood table commands my full attention until the opening door stirs the air. A different government protection officer enters the room, annihilating the fragile rapport I had with Vickers and McGuinness. His malleable hot dog fingers leach onto a small glass of water, which he hands me. The liquid shakes, stirred with his energy.

"Drink this," he says. His deep voice resonates like it's amplified. This is your captain speaking. I meet his eyes and he appeases me with a moment of focus and a pleasant smile, before retreating back into himself.

I sip the water. McGuinness and Vickers watch me do it. I study their faces and wonder if straight women find them attractive. Maybe Vickers because he's tall? Straight women like tall. His eyes are blue. Pastel, like Easter. He would look adorable in a bunny suit. At this thought I laugh and nearly spit out the water.

"Something funny, Cora?" McGuinness.

"No," I say. I meet his serious brown eyes. He raises his eyebrows, scolding me.

"Drink the water," McGuinness says.

I nod and finish the water. The aftertaste is distinctly different than the last glass. The energy slowly leaks from the room. Suddenly, the thought of Vickers in a bunny suit is not funny at all. My limbs are numb and heavy. I stretch my legs and relax. My normally overactive brain is practically blank. Almost like I can't think of anything at all.

"Cora," McGuinness says. He allows for a dramatic pause. "We need to verify everything you're telling us—and I mean everything. Then, we'll likely have some follow-up questions. Most of what you told us last night has been verified."

I nod, rapt with attention at any possibly update on the status of my incarceration.

"You're going to spend another night here—that much I can tell you. Beyond that, who knows. We're not promising to not press charges, but it's in your best interest to continue to cooperate with us."

I nod again, surprised by the change of tone, but depressed that despite it all, I won't be released.

I realize this is my one and only chance to make requests. "Is there any way I can be given something to do in my cell?"

"Something to do?"

"Yeah," I say. I hesitate, unsure why this is such an odd question. "The screen in there doesn't work, I have nothing to do." I trail off.

"The screen doesn't work?" McGuinness asks.

"Yeah, I assume it's because of the outage."

He shakes his head. "No, it shouldn't be. Jail screens are on a local network—too many people hacked into the internet before they did that. We'll have someone take a look."

*****

To my delight, they are able to fix the screen. I settle into bed with a mediocre meal and a bottled water to watch a New California propaganda video, a documentary about elephants, and then a romantic comedy. Whatever they put in my water changes with each passing hour, leaving me with a stiff emotionless exhaustion. At some point, time passes with nothing to mark it, and I fall into a deep sleep.

CHAPTER 28

The first time I wake up, the faint glow of the sun has just begun to peak around the window shade. I wish Jane was with me, or Ashley, but then I feel a stab of pain when I think of Ashley. I can't reconcile what happened. I can't think it through rationally—I miss her, then I crave her, and then I am angry, jealous, and confused. It overwhelms me so I switch to thoughts of Jane.

I am awoken again by the key in the lock. The sun is at full brightness. I sit and attempt to fix myself up. The door creaks open and the woman from Indiana enters.

"Morning," she says.

She wheels in a tray of food and a cup of coffee. I rush and grab the coffee first.

"Good morning," I say. "Thank you." I sip the coffee, which burns my tongue but tastes good.

She gives me a tight insincere smile.

"Do you happen to know anything about my schedule for today? Are they going to need to talk to me again?"

She shrugs. "Can't be sure. The only time they tell me anything is when it affects your meals. As of now, your next meal is supposed to be delivered right in here, but that can change."

I nod and watch her exit. Her presence reminds me of something. I sit up in bed and sip my coffee. In my head, I scroll through what it could be. Despite all of my hours of sleep, my thoughts come slow and fuzzy. I study the room to trigger my memory. The white tile floor brings it back all at once. *The paper.* It's right here, under the sheet. I quietly grab it. In the bathroom, I turn on the shower to conceal the noise, and unfurl it with shaky delicate hands.

The first words I see make me gasp. It's not a food service schedule, or a memo, or a shipping label. No—It's a dossier about *me*.

I hungrily ingest the information. It's just one page, a print out, of what is likely a lengthy catalog of information. In the right corner is a picture of me. Not my passport photo, not my New California driver's license photo, but a photo from social media. Everything is there from the basic, to the secretive, to the information that I don't even know.

Cora Broussard (ACTIVE INVESTIGATION)

Full Name:	Cora Renée Broussard	**Alias:**	None
Preferred Name:	Cora	**Citizenship:**	New California: 2022 – Present USA: 1984 (Birth) –2022
Date of Birth:	14 May, 1984	**Current Age:**	48

Appearance:

Ethnicity:	White	**Language(s):**	English
Place of Birth:	Grand Rapids, Michigan. USA.	**Residence:**	San Francisco
Height:	1.75 Meters	**Hair Color:**	Brown
Weight:	70 Kilograms	**Build:**	Medium
Eye Color:	Brown	**Tattoos/ Scars:**	None

Affiliations:

Marital Status:	Married	**Parents:**	Robert Michael Broussard (b. 1951) Carol Schneider Broussard (b. 1955)
Current Spouse:	Jane McCullough Broussard	**Children:**	Simone Dagny Broussard (b. 2020) Drake Rearden Broussard (b. 2016)
Other Close Relationships:	Ashley Doral (ACTIVE WARRANT - **ENEMY OF THE STATE**), Laura Fitzpatrick (past)	**Siblings:**	Samantha Broussard Rollins (b. 1983) Tessa Broussard Hammer (b. 1987)
Religion:	Catholic (family), Atheist/ Agnostic (current)	**Political/ Social Movement:**	None
Political Affiliation:	None	**Political Tags:**	Liberal, Libertarian, Capitalist, Compassionate, Free Market, Idealist

Financial:

Class:	Professional, No Gov. Assistance	**Net Worth:**	$5-10 Million NCD (estimated)
Profession(s):	CEO (current), Digital Technology, Product Manager	**Current Salary:**	$200,000 NCD + Significant Stock Share

Health:

Addiction(s):	Alcohol (undiagnosed), Opiates (past) (undiagnosed), Nicotine (past)	**Mental Illness:**	Anxiety (current), ADHD (current), Addiction (undiagnosed), Narcissistic Personality Disorder (undiagnosed), Overindulgent Love Disorder (undiagnosed), Severe Depression (past)
Chronic Diseases:	None	**Medications:**	Xanax (Alprazolam) - Situational, Adderall (Amphetamine Salts) – Daily
Diet:	Grain-avoidant, Organic, Gluten Free (non allergy)	**Truth Serum:**	Mescaline (micro), LSD (micro), Cocaine (micro), Alprazolam (0.5 mg), Pentothal (0.5 g)
Exploitable Weaknesses:	Women, Alcohol (whiskey, wine), Family (spouse, children, parents, sisters)	**Calming Serum:**	Alprazolam, Ketamine

I read through the whole thing, then my eyes dart around the page, in shock of what they know, and what they assume. All the demographic info is easy to find, even that of my U.S. citizen parents. But how do they know I was severely depressed as a teenager? And why do they think I have overindulgent love disorder? And what the fuck—they gave me cocaine and hallucinogens?

After one more read, I tear up the sheet and flush it down the toilet. In the shower, I try to let the warm pressurized stream of water massage away my unease, but it settles in. A deep disappointment spreads through me like a dull pain and I nearly collapse to the floor. I grimace and hold my face in my hands. In desperate need of a solution, of some comfort, my thoughts flail. Do I want some more truth serum? No. Cocaine and hallucinogens will amplify this feeling. What I want is a strong drink and love from a woman. But Ashley's gone, and I can't drink in here. I'm forty-eight years old, how will I even find a replacement? Sure, I could seduce some brainless young woman who barely knew America. Who never voted in a U.S. election. Who wasn't born yet when the planes hit the towers.

Tears sting my eyes and I sob. The hot water cleanses my face. I mourn Ashley yet again. Picture her smell, the taste of her mouth. The way her hands held me tight, clutching me like she was afraid I would leave. The way she felt under me when I held her hands above her head. Ashley on top of me, in my arms, and me in hers. I dismiss my thoughts of Ashley, but only find emptiness.

Cleansed and dressed in prison pajamas once again, I search for a distraction. I browse the selections on the screen. They offer documentaries about koalas, cows, horses—but no cool and aggressive animals, like wolves, that violent criminals could learn from.

*****

After animal documentaries and lunch, I jump as the key slides in the lock again. I'm escorted to an interrogation room where McGuinness and Vickers sit. Their suits are both wrinkled, hinting their day started much earlier.

"Good afternoon, Cora," McGuinness says.

I sit down in the familiar plastic chair. "Good afternoon," I respond.

McGuinness leans forward and places his hands on the table. "First of all, the country of New California thanks you for your candidness during this investigation. We had our office extensively investigate all information you gave us and we were able to verify most of what you told us."

Pleased at this news, I nod and urge him to continue.

"We have a few follow-up questions," he continues.

"Sure," I respond.

"Laura Fitzpatrick," he says.

My stomach drops. My ex's name from McGuinness' mouth feels like a violation. I take a deep breath. "Yes?" I ask.

"Your relationship with her was of a sexual nature, correct?"

"Yes. It was. But I am no longer involved with her. We've been apart for quite some time."

"How long?"

I contemplate this. Has it really been so long? "A year and a half."

"How long were you and her involved in a relationship?"

"It was on and off for almost twenty years."

He cocks his head and opens his mouth as if to ask another question. After a short pause he moves on to the next scripted question. "She is a citizen of the United States of America, is that correct?"

"Yes, that is correct."

"Was she a supporter of the Dictator?"

"No, absolutely not." I respond. "She never was—even before he got elected. She didn't vote for him."

McGuinness nods. His eyes bore into mine. "Are you sure about that?"

"Yes, absolutely."

"Are you aware of Laura Fitzpatrick attending a fundraiser for the Dictator, during the time that you two were together?"

"No, I am not."

"Are you aware of Laura Fitzpatrick maintaining relationships with friends who are supporters of the Dictator?"

"Well, actually, yes—I mean, she lived in Houston. There are a lot of supporters there. She lived out in the suburbs, in Houston. She's not very political herself and she doesn't judge people for what they believe. So, yes, I do recall her telling me that she had friends who were supporters of the Dictator."

I pause, but they stare at me blankly like they want more.

I continue: "I should mention—that I only ever met three people that Laura knows. One was her sister, and that was before the Dictator was president. Another was a former girlfriend, around that same time, and a third was a woman we ran into in San Francisco. She was someone that Laura described to me as being very liberal and very anti-dictator. Laura has all sorts of friends."

The questions about Laura continue interminably. Her political affiliations, when she entered New California, and so on.

The questions move on to my dad, is he a supporter of the Dictator? Then, my mom. Then, they start on my sisters. If they start asking about my seventeen cousins, I will laugh. But to my surprise, they ask about Jane and my children. What are Drake's political opinions? How about Simone's?

Finally, we wrap up, and I am escorted to my cell. I am told we will reconvene later this evening.

Back in my cell, I come to terms with the very real

possibility that I will be here longer than expected. I put a documentary about koalas on the screen. I want to zone out to a show about cute animals, but their noses bother me and something about the way they move is annoying. Like they're performing actors. Still, I watch, disappointed I'm not as entertained as I would like to be. Nothing else sounds good to watch and I despair, worried I will be forced to stay another night in here.

The familiar sound of the key in the lock fills me with hope. I get out of bed and stand. My dinner rolls in on the jail food cart. My hope at release becomes smaller. The woman from Indiana moves quickly and efficiently with an air of excitement. Feeding me is probably the last thing she needs to do today before she goes home. I try to eat slowly and savor the mediocre food. Once sated, I turn off the screen and lay in silence, watching planes take off and land.

Finally, the door opens once again, and I'm escorted back to the interrogation room where McGuinness and Vickers wait with their suits further crumpled and their eyes bleary. I sit down and they don't waste any time.

"Cora Broussard. You're going home tonight," McGuinness says. Both men sit sprawled out, their eyes relaxed, much less serious than they were previously.

Relief floods through me. "Thank you!" I respond.

"We're not charging you with any crime. However—we cannot let you go with USD. We are seizing the cash."

He gauges my reaction and his muscles relax when I nod.

He talks quickly. "Additionally, due to the uncertain political situation, and your personal relationship with two former citizens assumed guilty of treason, your New California passport will be revoked for at least one year. After that time period expires, you can apply for a new passport. Do you understand?"

"Wait, but, so that means I can't leave New California for at least a year?" I stare at them incredulously. "I can't even go to Mexico?"

"That's correct." He sits up in his chair and tenses up. "Any questions?"

I decide to accept it for now. "No," I respond.

Vickers stands up and calls out the door to someone, an officer comes with my purse and suitcase.

All of my things except for my passport and $25,000.

CHAPTER 29

A government protection officer drives me home. I settle into the back seat of the government car—identical to the one I took to lunch with Josh—and numbly stare out the window with the airport in the rear view mirror. My eyes trace the outline of a palm tree, still a novelty each time I return from the Midwest. The realization that I returned days ago but have not gone outside inflames a new burst of anxiety. My shaky hands retrieve my sunglasses from my purse. I put them on, lean against the window, and wring my hands.

The car barrels down the highway at 180 kilometers per hour through the dusty brown hills of South San Francisco, and onto the shores of Brisbane. We shoot past the expansive bay, with trees bent over like they are about to jump in. A thick fog cloaks the industrial area on the other side.

It hits me that I am going home. I am not a prisoner. I am not a criminal. I am going to my house, which features a view of this beautiful bay. I close my eyes and ponder if I am still the same person. I feel vulnerable, skittish, and changed irrevocably. I place my sunglasses on my lap and run my hands over the length of my face. I need a drink to put myself back together.

When we arrive at my house, it appears simultaneously smaller and more imposing. Filled with exhaustion, I check the address and pause. Familiar curtains and furniture shapes reinforce what the number above the door tells me.

Drake's silhouette appears in the upstairs window. I find the energy to drag myself and my suitcase up the steps to the front door. I check my purse for my keys, but change my mind and decide to ring the doorbell. I wait nervously, feeling changed and unequipped. I'm a parent, a wife, and—Jesus fucking Christ—a CEO to a small organization. Standing here, I feel weak and it seems impossible I ever did any of those things. I worry momentarily what will be behind the door, like some sort of sick dystopian game show. I hear Drake's footsteps and my heart swells with love. The door opens, and he smiles like he did as a baby: instantaneous and with pure joy. He holds out his arms.

I hug him and bury my face in his shoulder. "Drake."

He hugs me tight. I pull back and look at him. His steel gray eyes well up and his wide thin lips form a tight smile. His face contorts back to his natural smile.

He shakes his head. "Mom," he says. "What—where—we missed you so much!" He carries my suitcase into the house.

Simone runs up the stairs from the den. She emerges, wide-eyed with her thick curly hair unkempt and wild, like she just snapped back to reality. Her cheeks form a smile. She runs to me and we hug. I never know if my baby Simone will be affectionate, but when she is it can be overwhelming. She hugs me hard. She stands back and both kids stare at me with their mouths open.

"Where's your other mother?" I ask.

"She's with Misty," Drake says. "There's a situation with Cheryl."

"What? Cheryl, Josh Winston's wife?"

"Yeah," Drake says.

Simone leans forward. "They weren't able to get a hold of her."

"Right, because the phones and everything are still down, right?" I say.

"They think there might be some kind of emergency," Simone says.

Suddenly weighed down by gravity, I walk over to the couch and sit down. The kids follow me and sit on either side. I don't know what to say or where to start. I think about the past few days. I was suspected of treason and jailed by the country I love. I think of Josh and Ashley over in their fucking palace. A five-hour flight away. I feel sick thinking about Cheryl and Misty and what they must be going through with Ashley and Josh gone.

My children regard me with tender eyes. They wait for me to speak, to tell the story of my trip, but the thought of it overwhelms me.

"Hey, did your mom get a package in the mail?" I ask.

"Yes, she got the money you sent, thank you," Drake says. He speaks softly, like he matured in the short time I was gone.

I nod, pleased they got the package. They wait expectantly, but I don't know what to say to them, or where to start.

"I'll be right back," I say.

Three days have passed since I landed in New California. Three days without a drink. I pause when I grasp the familiar whiskey bottle. I look at it closely, that familiar shade of brown. I trace my hand over the bottle, uncap it, smell the familiar scent. I pictured having this drink for the last three days, thinking of how good it would feel. But this doesn't feel good, this feels awful. The alternative, however, isn't much better. Cold, stiff, sobriety; my overactive mind paralyzing me. I take a deep breath, push the thoughts away, and make my bourbon Manhattan quickly. The first sip snakes down my throat like drain cleaner, dissolving all the impurities in its wake. Almost instantly, my mind relaxes.

I close my eyes and savor the feeling before returning to the living room. Drake and Simone wait for me silently. I sit down and Simone slides toward me on the couch and leans her head against my arm. Unsure what to say or do, I choke back tears.

"They think Cheryl might be dead," Simone announces.

Drake jerks his neck to glare at her.

"What?" I say.

Drake throws his hands up angrily. "What the hell, Simone? No one said that," he scolds.

"Why do you say that, Simone?" I ask.

"Misty said she went into Cheryl's house and found a note. That's when mom looked worried."

"You don't know anything about that note," Drake says.

I hug Simone because I agree with her suspicion.

We sit in silence. I hold Simone in my arms and sip my cocktail. Drake typically does not worry or read into anything until the facts are absolutely known. I'm not sure if it's a Drake thing, or a male thing.

"So Grandpa's completely okay?" Drake asks.

"Yes. Completely fine. It wasn't even a heart attack. All the tests came back saying he's very healthy."

Drake smiles. "Do you know who it was who called you?"

I pause, unsure of where to go with the question. "No, not specifically."

"Whoever they were, they lied," Simone states factually.

"That's right, Simone," I respond.

So many questions loom over us, so much to be said, but we don't say any of it. The events that occurred and the political turmoil is so much bigger than all of us.

"Is Josh Winston going to be the president? In the U.S.?" Drake asks.

"Yes," I say. I glance up, both of their eyes are on me. "Yeah, the Dictator died and Josh is going to be the president." I turn away and sip my drink. A rush of comfort washes over me as it flows through my bloodstream, its flammable tentacles brushing away the grit of anxiety.

"The Dictator died?" Drake asks.

"Yeah, well, that's what Josh said anyway."

"Do you think Josh will bring back freedom in the U.S.?" Drake asks.

"No," I respond. "No, probably not. I don't think Josh is a good man. I think he'll be much better than the Dictator, but I don't think he'll restore freedom."

Drake nods slowly with his brow furled. "I thought he was your friend."

"He was."

"Why isn't he your friend anymore?" Simone asks.

I pause and contemplate what to tell them. "I thought he was my friend, but he betrayed his country and his wife. All just for power. He could be the prime minister of New California, but instead, that whole time he was friends with the Dictator." I shake my head in disbelief.

I get up to fix myself another drink. The alcohol soothes and puts me back together. Everything begins to fall back into its right place. I look out the window in the kitchen. The fog from earlier lifted and the rust color of the Golden Gate Bridge is clear and crisp. Cheryl. I never met her but somehow I feel connected to her, like I could have done something. I think of the conversation I had with Josh. Something about how he described her stayed with me. Her shyness and clinginess to her husband suggested vulnerability. Of course she can't be the First Lady of the United States, or New California for that matter. It would break someone like her. I hope Simone's wrong. I hope she's okay.

I hear the unusual purr of a gas-powered car outside. I peer out the window at what must be a 2010 Toyota in front of my house. The car gives one final gassy spurt before the driver cuts the ignition. I watch, hypnotized by the mundanity of observing a person park their vehicle and exit. The car is significantly older than my children. Both doors unlatch and I'm shocked when Jane emerges from the passenger side door. Her expression is severe, but she otherwise appears beautiful and youthful. I can't recall the last time I noticed how attractive my wife is. Misty exits from the driver's side door. Jane waits for her on the curb. Misty is dressed in a flattering pair of jeans and a sweater. Her dark brown hair accented with untreated gray blows in the wind and she runs her hand through it. Her face is slashed with deep lines, like she grimaced for twenty years and it finally stuck. Despite all this, I realize she is actually somewhat attractive. She's taller than Jane—though not as tall as me—and slim. She meets Jane on the sidewalk and puts her hand lightly on Jane's shoulder. They hug, which strikes intense curiosity in me. I wonder what they've been up to these past few days. I intuit something between them. They pull apart and walk side by side. Jane opens the door with a key because her screen is not working. I run to greet them right as the door opens. At the sight of me, Jane gasps and her head jolts back. Misty scowls.

I smile at Jane. "Hi," I say.

Jane hugs me, then pulls back and meets my eyes. I realize I don't look into her eyes very often. They are greener than usual, the creases around them deeper.

"Hi," she says. "Wow, I'm glad you're home." She steps away and takes off her shoes.

I glance toward Misty, she crosses her arms and eyes me suspiciously.

Jane regards me with sad contempt. "We have a lot to talk about," she says.

I nod and she responds with a side-eyed glare.

I wonder if she's referring to the general series of events or if there is more. Misty continues to stand completely still with her arms crossed. I notice Simone peek around the corner. I flash her a mischievous smile.

Jane turns to Misty and touches her arm. "Let's all talk," she says.

Misty nods dutifully and proceeds to take off her shoes.

"Can I get either of you a drink?" I ask.

"Yes, there's cider in the fridge," Jane says.

I nod. "Anything for you, Misty?"

She tilts her head and half smiles. "Yes, um, do I want a drink... yes. Can you make me a whiskey sour?"

"Yes, ma'am," I say. I scurry off to make her a complicated drink while she relaxes with my wife.

Simone follows me and watches with arms crossed while I make the cocktail. I place ice cubes in the shaker, add unmeasured pours from the ornate bottles, and stir. Her love of the pageantry of alcohol strikes fear and anxiety in me.

I hand Misty her drink with a gracious smile. Misty takes the drink and thanks me. Now that I'm waiting on her, her manner is less rude. I sit down and observe her sip the drink. Her movements are swift. She has an energy to her, like she is ready to pounce. Beneath her bitterness appears a strength I was unable to see before.

Misty and Jane sit on the couch quite close to one another. Misty sits with her legs spread apart and her arms over the back of the couch. I'm surprised I never noticed how masculine she is. When I met her before, I detected a meekness, but now, free of Ashley, she has regained some swagger.

Jane has had a few relationships with people throughout our marriage. Always men—nice, but effeminate ones—and always casual. Friends with benefits, really. She met them on the internet and everything always played out exactly like it was supposed to.

I occasionally snoop through her messages and emails, to see if she flirts with anyone and I'm always a little disappointed that nothing is going on. This situation with Misty, however, intrigues me. I sip my whiskey and examine them together. Misty remains splayed out. Jane crosses her legs, either comfortable with or oblivious to Misty's arm above her on the back of the couch, only inches away.

Jane inhales. "We all need to talk. Why don't we go up to our room?"

"Sure," I say. "Let me just refresh my drink."

After I leave the room, I glance around the corner and Misty is rubbing Jane's arm. When I return, they jump up and follow me upstairs. We enter the bedroom. I sit down on the chair across from the loveseat, forcing them to sit together.

Misty leans forward and rests her elbows on her knees. "Cheryl killed herself," she says, "Cheryl, Josh's wife."

I inhale deeply. "Oh no, that's awful."

"Yep," Misty responds. "We had spent quite a bit of time with her, Jane and I, over the past week or so. We just got back from the police station and they confirmed she went over the bridge yesterday."

"The bridge," I say. "I'm sorry. That's just so awful. Has anyone told Josh?"

"Nope," Misty says. "Not yet, but I'm sure those two will get a hold of me soon. Ashley needs her children."

She says this matter-of-factly. I listen and nod slowly. Everything is so out of sorts, no one knows what to say.

"I'm really sorry for what you're going through," I say.

She eyes me, unsure if she can trust me. I try to display sincerity, but I can't quite do it.

Misty's voice pierces the silence. "So what was it?" she asks. "What was the plan? What did they want from you?"

I shake my head in disbelief. "I still am not sure I

understand. So—I assume you know that Josh is taking over for the Dictator, right? And that the Dictator is dead now?"

They nod.

"Okay," I continue. "Well, Josh offered me any government position I wanted, including vice president."

Misty nods and cocks her head, apparently surprised.

"And," I continue, unsure if this will be a sensitive subject, "I guess Ashley just liked me being around."

"Huh," Misty says matter-of-factly. She leans back and places her arms across the back of the couch. She nods and scowls at me through dark, narrowed eyes.

Jane leans back and eyes me up and down. I sigh. I don't have the strength for this. After three days of interrogation, I am drained. I always felt like I was strong, like I could handle anything, but now I am defeated and deflated. My country suspecting me of treason is one thing, but my wife doubting me is more than I can handle.

Jane breaks the silence. "Why did you go?" she says. "Why did you even go to D.C.? That was *after* we called you with Cheryl."

I shake my head. "I don't know why I went. I just wanted answers. That's so sad about Cheryl, I can't believe that happened."

"I really liked her," Jane says. "I thought we would become good friends."

I nod solemnly and study their untrusting faces. Jane's stare pierces through me. I take a deep breath and fight back tears.

"None of this makes sense to me," Jane says.

I avert my gaze and shrug.

Misty leans forward. "So. Let me get this straight. You flew to D.C. on Wednesday? And then you spent four days with them?"

I vehemently shake my head. "No."

Misty crosses her arms. "And you expect us to believe that you're not involved in this? Smells like bullshit to me."

"I—" I start. I'm about to fall apart. I breathe in and gather my strength. "I didn't spend four days with them. I flew to D.C. late Wednesday night, talked to Ashley and Josh Thursday morning, and flew back to San Francisco on Thursday—"

"You've been back since Thursday?" Jane asks.

Misty shakes her head in disgust and falls into a bitter sarcastic laugh at my expense.

"I was arrested!" I shout.

Shocked into silence, Jane inhales sharply. Misty regards me blankly.

"I was arrested at the airport and interrogated for days, for three days, and they just let me out today."

I can't hold it together anymore. I bury my face in my hands and despite straining my face to stop them, deep wracking sobs ooze out of me. I double over and cry. Jane's arms encircle me. I burn with shame falling apart in front of Misty. Just as I think this, she places her hand on my shoulder. Her hand is gentle, tender, and decidedly different than Ashley's.

"I'm sorry," she says.

I stop and Misty hands me a tissue. I lean back in the chair.

"Why were you arrested?" she asks.

Jane rubs my back, soothing me.

I try several times to form the word, but my lips betray me. "Treason," I finally say. I cover my face and sob once again.

They both gasp.

"Ashley and Josh can never come back."

I watch Misty comprehend this. *Of course*, I bet she thinks.

Misty says, "I wonder how long it will be until the CIA kidnaps my children."

I reign in a reflexive urge to interject, to tell her she's paranoid. But then it strikes me that perhaps she is not.

"How long have Ashley and Josh been seeing each other?" I ask Misty.

She swats away the question. "Who knows. I first found out shortly before Jimothy was born, but I think they were together for a while before that."

"Wow," I say. "That's much longer than I thought."

Misty and Jane return to the couch. We sip our drinks in silence. I am ashamed of my emotional outburst, but also soothed by it.

"So," I say to Misty, "when I was in D.C., Ashley said that she talked to you and that you and the kids would be moving out there. Is there any truth to that?"

She laughs. "Well, isn't that the million-dollar question?" she asks. "I just don't know. I wasn't kidding when I said I wonder when the CIA will kidnap my children. Last time I spoke with Ashley, she refused to come up with any sort of international joint custody agreement. John's seventeen, so he can do what he wants soon, but the other two, well, she was very insistent."

"I think you should go to D.C.," I say.

Jane shoots me an angry look.

"Oh yeah, why's that?" Misty asks. She spreads out her arms on the couch, taking up space aggressively.

"It just seems like Ashley is going to get what she wants either way, so this is the one way where you can also still be with your children."

She loosens up and appears disappointed I didn't say anything classist and awful. "It's just that, Ashley and I, we held onto this relationship for so long when we shouldn't have. It's really my fault. I refused to let her go. Thought I would go crazy if she left me, and don't even get me started about what I thought that it would do to the kids. But, now that it happened, I feel so much better." She sighs. "I just hate the thought of being a participant in all of this."

I nod. "Well, something to consider," I say, "is that unless Josh can do something diplomatically to change things, Ashley and Josh can never come back here. They will be imprisoned for treason. I also don't think the government of New California will be cool with you guys, or even just your kids, travelling back and forth to go see people they view as traitors. They may revoke your passports. They took mine, even though they let me come home. If you stay, it basically means your kids may never see their other mother again—or that they may only see her once they turn eighteen—which may involve committing treason. And, that's assuming they can even keep their passports."

Misty nods as she begins to grasp the corner she is backed into.

I continue: "You need to think of every possibility and then think of how Ashley might react. And it's not just Ashley—it's also Josh—who is apparently now the president of the United States. You are up against a powerful force." I pause and think the situation through. I turn back to Misty. "My suggestion is that you go to D.C., but that you use your kids as a bargaining tool in order to find the best possible outcome. So, like, if you want to live in the White House—"

She vehemently shakes her head.

"Okay, well, if you *don't* want to live in the White House, then factor that in. You just need to think of the most palatable option considering the circumstances and negotiate that."

She nods. "But what if they don't hold up their end of the deal?"

"Assuming you go to D.C. and that your requests are reasonable, there is no reason for them not to. Getting you a house or something in D.C. isn't anything to them. Also—we're talking about children here, not a tangible asset. She doesn't want you to speak ill of her to them, and I'm sure she also doesn't want to take them away from you. You are also their mother."

"Hmm, yeah, you're right. But if I go I can never come back. I will be charged with treason, too."

"Yeah," I say, "and I know that sounds really dramatic and awful, but is it really so bad? You're from Pittsburgh, right? So I'm guessing you don't have family here? And is life really so great in the colonies?"

"No," she says, "you're right."

Jane leans forward and places her hands on her knees. "That all makes sense logically," she says, "but we're talking about colluding with the U.S. government. It just doesn't seem right."

"Yeah," I say, "but Misty just needs to understand her options. She does need to think about this logically. Also, Josh is not the old dictator, he says he wants to restore democracy, so, who knows? Maybe he will actually do something good."

Misty places her hands on her knees, "Well," she says, "I sure have a lot to think about. I appreciate the perspective, Cora, you've provided a lot of great thoughts. I understand now why you've been so successful in business."

I smile and thank her.

"I should go. What I really need now is some sleep. It's been a long day."

"Yes it has," Jane says. "I still can't believe it about Cheryl."

"Just my luck," Misty says. "I thought I had a classy new friend and then she tosses herself off the Golden Gate Bridge!"

"It's just awful," Jane says. "I really liked her too."

"I never met her," I say, "but Josh told me about her. When we were still friends."

They glare, annoyed at my participation in their grief.

"Let me walk you out," Jane says to Misty.

They stand and begin to shuffle out. I say goodbye to Misty. She barely acknowledges me and follows Jane. I climb into the bed, giving me access to our window where I can watch them. I have gained empathy and a new respect for Misty. As scandalized as I am about the series of events that took place, I emerged largely unscathed. Misty's future contains nothing but uncertainty, and the possibility she could lose her children, or be forced to leave the country.

Jane and Misty emerge from the front door. They're deep in conversation. They stand on the stoop and hug, definitely platonic. I'm almost disappointed. Jane re-enters the house. I dash off the bed and down the stairs to be together with my whole family at once. Jane walks in the front door and I take her in my arms. She holds me and leans her head on my shoulder. We stay like this for a long time and listen to each other breathe.

She leans back and meets my eyes. "I'm so glad you're back," she says.

"Me too."

"I'm sorry you got arrested."

"Me too," I say. "Where are the kids?"

"They should be downstairs. You'll be impressed when you find out how they've been entertaining themselves since the internet has been down."

"Oh? I thought they must be reading all those books strewn all over the place."

"Well, that too. I'm so glad we kept those books."

"Me too," I say.

She pulls my hand and leads me to the basement. I follow her, excited to see my kids' sweet faces again. We trot down the stairs. Drake sits at our large screen and Simone sits near him with a laptop. They're so deep in concentration, they don't look up when we come down.

"What are you guys doing?" I ask.

Simone smiles shyly. "We're coding. We're making our own internet."

I gasp with excitement.

"It only runs on our internal network," Drake says, "because the router still works, it just isn't connected to anything outside of the network. I setup the laptop as a server where everything is hosted, and then anyone connected to our network can visit the sites we set up."

"The neighbors are connected!" Simone announces.

"Yeah, you can see here that twenty-two devices are connected," Drake says.

I lean over his shoulder and twenty-two device icons are shown.

"I think only about nine of them our ours," he continues.

"Let me show you the site," Simone says.

I step to where she sits at her laptop. She alt-tabs from a page full of code to an html page. She clicks a link called "Send a message," and a drop-down appears with a list of names. She selects "Jane Broussard," types "THIS IS ONLY A TEST," and clicks send. Jane's screen dings.

Jane reads "This is only a test," with a grin.

"That's amazing Simone! I'm so proud of you guys!"

"I did most of the coding," Simone announces, "but Drake setup the network and the host server and stuff."

Drake rolls his eyes. "And I also did the QA, Simone is a sloppy coder," he says.

I laugh. This sloppiness and lack of attention to detail is something she's inherited from me, and is exactly the reason why I never bothered to learn to code.

"Check this out," Simone says.

She clicks on a tab called "News." A message board appears with a series of rumors and updates from us and the neighbors. While she demonstrates this with child-like enthusiasm, I maintain a tight smile to keep from crying. This—the two of them working together in a positive way to entertain themselves—is exactly what I need right now. Fuck you, Josh Winston. If you shut down the internet, my fucking kids will rebuild it.

CHAPTER 30

Drake becomes our family internet-checker. He frequently attempts to reload a few websites. I secretly do it too, and it becomes a sort of compulsion.

A few days after my release from jail, I stop into work already knowing it will be empty. What would we all do? I wonder how it went down and what it was like when it first happened. Did people still dutifully report to work despite it being impossible to work without the internet? I would have. If for no other reason than to connect with other people, exchange rumors and gossip. Only one full week passed since I was last at work, but it seems like a lifetime ago.

When I arrive at the building, the door is locked and my key fob doesn't work. I dig out my physical keys. The elevator displays a hand-written sign that reads "out of order." The handwriting is childish, likely written by someone so young they never learned penmanship. I trudge up the stairs and am surprised to find I'm out of breath. When I arrive at the office, I peer through the glass door. No lights are on, making the wooden beams and floors appear gray, as if all color were sucked out of the office. I unlock the door with the key and enter. I stroll around the various desks and think of the people who occupy them.

At Kim's desk, I pause and examine the items on it. Lotions, chapsticks, lipsticks, and a tiny makeup mirror. An almost-gone pouch of sugar-free gum. Pictures of her with groups of friends—tipsy overdone straight women in near identical apparel. Kim on a male stripper's lap. Kim hiking. It's all so boring, so basic. Even Kim herself has only ever been a thoroughly mediocre employee, making up for her lack of intellect and vision with charm and flirtation. I could never love *Kim*.

I find myself at my desk, which appears small and depressing. Maybe because I gave up a chance for so much power, or because I never liked it here. I admire the pictures of Drake and Simone, which I suddenly realize are outdated. How could that be, I've only been with this company for two years. Or is it three now?

I touch the shiny mahogany, gently running my fingers over its surface. Careful, as if it could wake up. I study my hand, old and ugly, despite my recent silver manicure. I'm not fooling anyone.

I sit in my chair and close my eyes, savoring the scent of the oiled leather, the clean wood. I relax, but am overcome with a deep sadness. I lost a relationship that gave me joy, someone I considered a true friend and, most of all—passed up an opportunity to be a truly powerful person. I could change history. I could be the vice president of the United States of America. I could repair the damage the Dictator created.

But, my wife and my kids would lose a part of me. They would think my ambition is truly bottomless and more important than my love for them. Maybe that is the truth, but I couldn't do it. The thought of colluding with Josh, of letting him hold his power while I claim my tiny slice of it, wasn't worth it. Besides, I can't imagine talking to Jane about it. I would lose her. She would never be able to come back to New California and this is where her sister, niece, nephew, and father live. Where her mother is buried.

If I went, I would have to go without her. I would lose her and the children. I leap from my chair and touch my hand to the window. I gaze at my city: San Francisco. Most of the lights in the offices are off. The streets are emptier than normal. I can't believe it didn't occur to me until now that if I took Josh's offer, I would lose Jane and the kids. The melancholy that plagued me since I returned begins to drift away. Taking Josh up on his offer wasn't an option. While my ambition is perhaps bottomless, I am nothing without Jane and the kids. Besides, I don't even like D.C. I will not be Josh Winston's puppet. I have my own dreams.

*****

At home I relax on my rooftop deck while a slow-moving, drone-less San Francisco drags itself through another disconnected day. I attempt to read a paper book that I can't remember if I read before. It doesn't matter anyway because the book is awful. Once used to it, I realized it was kind of relaxing not to have the internet and hang out with my kids all day.

A car honks, and then another. Not an angry honk, but the rhythm of a celebratory honk. I wonder what day it is. Is it a holiday? Drake sprints up the stairs, the way he does, like gravity doesn't affect him as much as other people. He bursts out the door, his screen in hand, pointed toward me.

"It's back! The internet is back!" he says.

I jump up, excited. He shows me a site he pulled up and clicks around. I run down the stairs and grab one of my screens.

The din of honking and cheering continues. I run back up to

293

the roof to bask in the excitement of the end of this nightmare. Someone puts on cheesy dance music and I laugh. I'm so surprised and delighted I can't decide what to check first. Messages start to roll in. My message icon scrolls, counting messages like a slot machine adding up winnings. I excitedly click on the icon. Several messages are from Ashley and the excitement is washed away.

Ashley is going to be the First Lady of the United States. I can't get it through my head without the desire to pick up the information and smash it. With a sick feeling in my stomach I pull up her messages.

I thought you loved me, Cora. When I say I love someone, it's for real, but apparently it's not like that for you. Have you ever made sacrifices for anyone? For anything? This should be the happiest time of my life, but it's not. I thought I could count on you. I need you, Cora. I love you. One last chance, baby.

I could smash my screen. It's so transparent that even if I wanted to come back to her, I would reconsider after reading the message. Did she think this would be effective?

I write:

I didn't lie to you, I just—

I delete it.

I've made lots of sacrifices. I can't believe you even thought that I would be okay with you and—

Delete. I take a deep breath and reread her message. I let it go for now. The cacophony of car horns, streamed music, and cheering grows louder. A drone flies overhead and I smile.

I check the headlines. There it is: *Josh Winston Takes Over for U.S. Dictator.* The news is out. I scroll for more. *Josh Winston Wanted for Treason in New California.* Nothing new to me. I pause and scan the foggy San Francisco sky. The dark blue bay in the distance peaks out between tufts of fog. As if on cue, someone on the street shouts "Death to Josh Winston." I surprise myself by cheering.

I glance back at the headlines, *All U.S./New California Travel Prohibited by New California Government.* I almost choke. I click on the article. I read it through as my dread builds. No one in, no one out. Forty-eight hours given for New California residents to return. I am overcome with strong déjà vu as memories of this from over ten years ago in the U.S. come back into focus. Growing up in the eighties and nineties, I never would have guessed I would go through so much political instability in my lifetime. I wonder if the pendulum will swing and the U.S. will become the free country, while New California becomes paranoid.

I become mesmerized by the swirling drones. I hear Jane's footsteps on the stairs. She approaches, a severe expression on her face.

"Did you read about the travel restrictions?" she asks.

"Yes," I state.

Jane shakes her head.

"I don't think it will last very long. We just had a major political leader betray our country, and knock down the internet while he was at it," I say.

She turns to me. "Josh was behind that?" she asks.

I was able to skirt the topic of the details of my conversation with Ashley and Josh in D.C., but here it is.

"Yes," I say.

"And you knew?" she asks.

I roll my eyes at her. "He told me when I was in D.C."

She brings her knees to her chest and contemplates this. "What did you say when he told you?" she asks.

"I don't know. I don't think I said anything. I think that's when I left."

She moves closer to me and puts her arm around me. I slouch and let her hold me. We admire the sunset, the dark gray bay with a streak of shimmery silver, the drones. I pick up my screen and check the headlines. Jane reads them over my shoulder. Just more of the same while the news media pieces together what Josh did. I set the screen aside.

"I'm pretty sure Misty went to D.C.," Jane says.

"Oh yeah? Did she tell you she was going?"

"Not specifically, but she was leaning toward it. She was planning what she would say and what she would ask for when she talked to Ashley. Also, knowing now that Josh was behind the outage, it makes sense that they would wait until the situation with Misty and the kids was resolved before restoring it." Jane says.

I nod slowly. "Yeah, I guess. It just seems so weird and petty and drastic to knock out the internet for an entire country in order to resolve a personal situation," I say.

"Well, you actually know Ashley and Josh. Does it seem like something they would do?"

I take a deep breath and contemplate this, watching the shadows grow longer from the setting sun. "Actually, yes, it does."

She shakes her head in disgust. "And this is a woman that you've had a relationship with these past several months."

"Yeah, I know, it was a bad choice. It's just so bizarre because when I first met Ashley, she was a jobber, but then somehow I ended up embroiled in a political scandal." I shake my head in disbelief. "And now, she's the First Lady of the United States."

Jane turns and meets my eyes with a weathered look of bitterness. "Yeah, sure she was a jobber, and she lived at the colonies, but the first time you ever went out with her, Josh Winston showed up. It was a bizarre situation right from the start." She shakes her head angrily. "I wish I would have said something, or asked more questions, or… something. I know you were idiotically blinded by her attractiveness, but I feel like I should have known."

"It's easy to say that now," I say, "but no one could have possibly predicted that those people were on their way to be the president and First Lady of the United States. We thought Josh was just a politician, having an affair."

"Yeah," Jane says. "I guess you're right. We couldn't have predicted what exactly was going to happen, but I feel like we should have been able to foresee that the whole situation should be avoided."

I shrug, which frustrates Jane. We sit in silence. Do I wish I never met Ashley, or that I broke things off before they became what they were? It seems like a silly question. Not only is it impossible, it's all so big. So irreversible and historic. I don't know if I would do things differently. A part of me wants to be in a life situation in which I could say yes to Josh and claim my little slice of history. A part of me is excited to be so close to a historic event. I don't wish that I cut things off with Ashley. This new chapter in history is no fault of mine and it would play out the same way regardless of my involvement with those people.

"You're right," I say. "I should have seen that something was off sooner and ended the situation."

She smiles and kisses me. "Thank you," she says.

On my screen, I find an official statement released by the Government of New California. I am delighted to see much of the information is directly from me. They announce that Josh was behind the outage, that the Dictator is dead, and that Josh's wife

Cheryl committed suicide. They even mention Ashley—though not by name—just that she is a woman he has had a long-time affair with. I feel a twinge of jealousy at that part. The sting of loss has not subsided. The logical part of me is glad to be rid of her, but the emotional and sexual sides of me want her back.

I navigate to one of the five U.S. news sources to find out how they spin the news about Josh. The page loads and loads, but nothing comes up. I try the other sites. They're all down. The internet is back up in the U.S. This can only mean the sites are blocked by New California.

A notification comes across my screen that I have a new message from my dad. He wants to video chat with our whole family. Jane and I head down the stairs and wrangle the children. Drake is excited to talk to them and Simone displays a trace of childlike excitement. We gather in the living room and send the call. My parents appear on screen, big Midwestern smiles and waves.

"Hi Grandma and Grandpa!" Drake says.

"Hi Drake, hi Simone! Hi Cora and Jane," my dad says.

"Hi everyone!" my mom says.

"We just wanted to say hello because we heard the internet was back up, and our internet is back up too," my dad says.

"It just came up today," Simone says. "Everyone outside is cheering and honking."

"I'll bet," my dad responds.

"So is everyone doing okay?" my mom asks. "It's been hard for us not being able to get a hold of you."

Jane and I glance at each other. "We're fine," we say in unison. My parents are completely still as they await more.

My dad breaks the silence. "Cora, when you went to Washington, D.C. to see Josh Winston, did you go to the White House? Did you get to hear the news before everyone else?"

"Yes," I say meekly.

"Wow," my dad says.

They look at me expectantly.

"Goll, that must have been fascinating," my mom says.

I change the subject: "I was curious how the U.S. news sources are portraying Josh Winston's presidency, but none of the U.S. sites are loading. Are they working for you?"

"Yes," my mom says. "We just read the latest article a few minutes ago. Everyone is so excited about Josh Winston."

The now familiar unsettled feeling resurfaces.

"What do the articles say?" I ask.

"Do you want me to read you one?" My dad asks.

"Yes," I respond.

"Okay—here it is."

...After the tragic and untimely death of our nation's most beloved president we have a new leader. Josh Winston, formerly of New California, has been appointed president of the United States of America. A true moderate, Josh Winston has been in politics for ten years and most recently served as New California's Minister of Technology. Despite having lived in New California since the beginning, President Winston always planned to return and serve the American people. "I love the United States of America. If anything, being away for so long just cemented my patriotism deeper and deeper."

President Winston hopes to unite the American people and provide even more opportunities for democratic participation and freedom of expression, all while leading us away from the dark road of our past in which democracy and freedom of speech were abused, leading to confusion and mass chaos. "Of course we will maintain the Truth Laws, it's preposterous to even consider legalizing published lies. We will, however, provide opportunities for all Americans to express their opinions, no matter how unpopular."

President Winston has moved into the White House along with his wife, Ashley, and their seven-year-old son, James.

Jane and I gasp at the last part. My mom cocks her head in confusion.

"His name is Jimothy," Jane says.

My mom laughs. "What, really? Jimothy?" she says.

"Yes, and Josh is not his—" I think this through, what Misty said about how long they'd been together. The Ministry of Catastrophe Anticipation interrogation. *Jesus fucking Christ.* "Never mind." This is all too much to explain over a video call between six people.

"Josh sure moves on quickly," Simone says.

I laugh, surprised at her cattiness.

She rolls her eyes and shakes her head. "Cheryl just jumped off the bridge like a week ago!" she continues.

My parents cock their heads like confused dogs, not wanting to pry into a situation involving a suicide.

"Well," my mom says, "we'd like to come visit you guys as soon as the travel ban is lifted. I'm so interested in hearing more about your experiences with the outage, and Cora! Your visit to the White House, wow!"

"Yeah, we definitely want to hear about that," my dad says.

I nod, relieved there is time to come up with a parent-appropriate version of events.

He continues: "Just one question—did you spend the night there, at the White House?"

"Yes," I say.

"What room did you stay in? Do you know?"

"The Lincoln Bedroom."

"Wow," my dad says. "I can't wait to hear about it. We will buy tickets as soon as the ban is lifted."

We cheerfully say our goodbyes and end the call, after which we sit in perplexed silence.

"Why would Josh marry someone else so soon after his wife died?" Simone asks. "And who is Ashley?"

Jane raises her eyebrows at me. I always handle the difficult conversations.

"Well—so, remember when we met that jobber family at Drake's basketball game?"

Simone nods.

"The woman that I knew, the nice, pretty one with blonde hair? That was Ashley."

She shakes her head, truly shocked and scandalized. "*That* Ashley is the one married to Josh Winston now?"

"Yes. Also, so, Josh and Ashley were together before Cheryl passed away. For a lot of the time that Josh was married to Cheryl, Ashley was his secret girlfriend on the side."

She starts to comprehend this and nods. "Like, an affair?" she asks.

"Yes, like an affair. But, sometimes when people have affairs, they get confused by all of the intense feelings and then they end up ignoring the commitment they made to the person they are married to, so they end up getting a divorce and getting married to the person they were having an affair with."

Her face changes shape as she registers this. "Is that why Cheryl killed herself?" Simone asks.

"I don't know, Simone. I don't know what was going through her head. When people kill themselves they're usually mentally ill or very depressed, it's rarely because of one thing that happened."

She nods, her eyes cast downward. I glance at Drake who is silent, calm, and stoic. Jane approaches Simone and puts her arm around her.

"Cheryl was really funny!" Simone says.

"Oh yeah?" I say. "I didn't know you met her. Did she come over here?"

"Yes, it was while you were gone," she says.

"Yeah," Jane says, "remember when we called you? Misty

and Cheryl and I?"

"Oh yeah. So how was she funny? What did she say?" I ask Simone.

Simone's childlike belly laugh fills the room and even Drake cracks a smile. Simone cycles between shyness and hysterical laughter, and then back to shyness again.

"She said—she was like— 'I—' then—"

She erupts into another fit of uncontrollable laughter, which soothes me to a surprising extent.

She takes a deep breath and manages to calm herself. She continues: "She was like, she was talking about someone Josh works with, and his wife, and she said that she said 'I didn't know that jobbers were real!' like maybe they were made up." She stops laughing. "Maybe you had to be there, but it was just funny the way she told the story, right?" She glances at Jane and Drake.

"It was funny," Jane confirms.

Drake nods in confirmation and smiles at his sister.

Simone lets Jane hold her. Her mouth quivers and tears start to build up in her sad brown eyes. She cries, and before I can get to her, Drake rushes over and holds her.

He rubs her back and hugs her. "It's okay, Simone," he says.

I run and grab Simone something to blow her nose with. I sit back down, across the room, and watch them. I wish I could do something to protect my kids from this kind of pain and from the current political uncertainty. Simone stops crying, blows her nose, and smiles. Like me, she holds a lot of strength between those emotions. I return her smile.

"I love you, Simone," I say.

"I love you too," she says.

Her curly hair is wild, her brown eyes sadder than a puppy's, but she smiles. Drake and Jane comfort her. I am absolutely content and relaxed watching the three people I love the most—my family—hug and comfort one another, while I sip my whiskey.

EPILOGUE

Sometimes life is consumed by the enormous question of whether or not you will ever hear from a particular person again. All of the times in a day that you check a screen for their name. Knowing the shape of it—what to look for, so you know if it's from them sooner than the time it takes to read their name. The importance of needing to know that nanosecond sooner is vital, yet irrational in every possible way. There are those moments of yearning, but so rarely does the message come at that time. Sometimes, the years tick by and the likelihood of hearing from them becomes less, and less, and less.

Then, sometimes, when you least expect it—and invariably when most inconvenient—their name shows up on your screen. You recognize it instantly, but need to read it again, to make sure your brain isn't playing tricks on you. Then: should you open the message now? You're unequipped. You feel your heart beat—you hear it. That noise, the rumble in your chest, the sensation that can't be reproduced by anything but your own heart. The waves of emotion almost make you nauseous.

It wasn't like that with Ashley. Sure, I thought about her, and I often missed her. I largely ignored the news coverage because it made me angry and a bit jealous. Of what, I don't know. Just vaguely, and definitively, jealous. When I drank quite a bit, sometimes a certain mood would strike where I would lunge at my screen with an urgent need to see pictures of her and Josh. I was delighted when they included the painfully awkward and shell-shocked 'James.'

Almost half a year after I last saw her, my screen rings. It is a D.C. area code. I am walking to work feeling strong, sober and energized. Like the bit of me that suffered from this situation has re-blossomed into something that resembles an inner peace and calm that I never felt previously. In the mood for some amusement, I answer.

"Hello, this is Cora," I say as professionally as possible.

"Baby." She sounds surprised I picked up. "Baby, it's Ash."

I never called her that, and the manipulative forced casualness pushes my smirk over the edge into a scathing sneer.

"Hi." I give nothing away.

She sighs. "I didn't think you'd answer. Cora! Baby, it feels so good to be talking with you." She giggles in her seductive way and sighs.

A piece of me is sucked back in. I slow my pace and head towards a park nearby.

I laugh mischievously. "I didn't think it would be, but it's nice to hear from you too."

She laughs much louder. "You didn't think it would be?"

I find I'm smiling. I laugh. "No, I didn't. But, it is, so here we are."

"Yes, here we are my baby, Cora."

"Here we are."

"Where are you?" she asks. Her tone, genuinely curious and chatty. Her voice irresistibly sexy.

"I don't know."

"You don't know?"

I giggle and she does too, charmed by me.

"Yeah, I don't know," I say defiantly, flirting.

"Are you in San Francisco?" she asks.

My face is plastered with a smile. I run my hand through my hair. "Yeah, I just walked to a park bench."

"You're so cute. Are you on your way to work?"

"Yeah."

"Yeah?"

"Yeah."

She breathes deeply. "I miss you, Cora," she says.

I lean my head back and take this in. It feels so right talking to her. Her voice shoots through my whole body like a drug.

"Yeah..." I remain noncommittal.

"Please tell me you miss me, baby. You can't not, baby, I know you miss me."

I sit silently for several moments, unaware of what the truth is, and reply, "Sometimes I do and sometimes I don't."

"Yeah?"

"Yeah."

She bursts into laughter at this. "What are you feeling, baby? Talk to me about it."

I lean my elbows on my knees and run my hands through my hair once again. "I don't know, Ashley, I just feel manipulated, I guess. Like I was part of your game."

"I didn't manipulate you. My feelings were genuine— always, baby. You've got to believe that."

"Did you target me in some way before we met?"

"What?" She skips a breath, surprised by the question. "Honey, Cora baby, no—of course not, not really."

"Not really?"

"No! Not at all. What do you mean by that, that I targeted you? Targeted you for what, baby?"

"That you knew in advance you would seduce me because

you knew you wanted to find a woman quickly that you could bring to D.C. with you." I blurt it all out sloppily and my words hang in the air, for so long I glance at the screen to make sure we're still connected.

"Is that what you thought?"

"Yeah, well—yeah, sort of. I know you went to my first talk at the school—"

"How did you know that?" she asks.

"Misty told me."

"Ugh! Misty!"

"Yes, she said you came like, disguised and then New California government cars followed my car."

She laughs. "What!"

"Yeah," I say.

"Honey, if New California government cars followed your Lone, it had nothing to do with me or Josh. Maybe they were just escorting the nice professional class lady out of the scary colonies. And baby, ugh! Yeah, I went to your first talk at the school. I hadn't told Josh about you, or anything. There was no government conspiracy and it had nothing to do with the plans in D.C. It was just you, baby, I ran a search on you and I had a crush on you. Like, a big, nerdy crush. I thought that I wouldn't like you in person because—that happens to me all the time, but then when I went and I saw you, I just liked you even more, and I decided after that I would have you."

We sit in silence, listening to each other's breath. It makes sense now.

"Josh didn't even want me to find a girlfriend before we left. You were a liability as far as he was concerned," she continues. "But, then of course, he really fell for you too."

"Why did you like me more in person?" I ask.

"Oh, I don't know, you were sweet. You had a sweetness to you that most people don't have. Something nurturing, yet you were also brash, and just a little bit—I don't know, disconnected.

Like your feet were planted on the ground while you smiled and paced loudly, but your head was in the clouds—and not because you were distracted, but because you were dreaming. I wanted to be in your world, Cora. I really can't love a lot of people. Most people aren't worth it. But you, Cora, with your sweetness, with your cuteness, your swagger, your intensity and sense of humor— baby, I knew I could love you. And, I truly did. So much. The more I got to know you, the more I loved you…" She stops. Sputters out as she runs out of insight.

This blows my mind. All this time maybe she did love me. Of course it wouldn't make sense for Ashley to begin a relationship when their escape to the U.S. was imminent, how did I miss that?

"I love you, Cora," she says.

I lean back on the park bench, run my hand through my hair and look up at the sky, as if for answers. Unsure what will come out of my mouth, I begin: "Ashley, I don't know what to say. It's over now. There was no way I could go to D.C. unless I was willing to lose Jane and the kids."

"I know," she says. "I understand that now."

"You didn't think it through when you invited me to D.C.?"

"Honestly, no, I didn't. I mean, I—I went to D.C. with Josh sometimes before all of this and we went back and forth, no problem. I didn't realize that once Josh was the president that we couldn't go back to New California."

"You didn't realize that? Did Josh say anything?" I ask.

"Nope."

"Wow." I say. She probably didn't know until it was too late she could lose her children. "I'm guessing Misty came with the kids?"

"Yes, she's in D.C. Josh got her a house. Johnald and Misty Jr. are with her and we have Jimothy—because—yeah, as I'm sure you figured out, Josh is his father."

"Yeah, I actually had wondered that."

"Why would you wonder that?"

"Misty said you'd been seeing each other since about a year before he was born, and also when I was interrogated at the Ministry of Catastrophe Anticipation, they asked about it."

"You were interrogated?"

"Yes."

"Why didn't you tell me?"

"I wasn't allowed to tell anyone. Were you ever interrogated?"

"All the time! I must have been pulled in about ten times!" she responds.

We laugh. Of course Ashley was interrogated; she was actually up to something.

"I would just act all sexy and try to get them to crack a smile," she says.

I laugh harder. "Did they?"

"Yes! Usually. They just thought I was Josh's sexy little toy."

I smile ear to ear as I picture this. "Ah, I see, very strategic."

"I'm smarter than I seem, baby."

"I always thought you were smart."

She sighs and a comfortable silence befalls us. I close my eyes and savor this feeling, this easy conversation.

"So how is it? Your new life? How are you?" I ask.

She chuckles at the enormity of the question. "It's fine. It's better than my old life anyway."

"Have you found a new girlfriend?"

"No. Though I've had some offers."

"Yeah? Why did you turn them down?"

"I don't know, baby. They were women Josh found and I could tell they were there just for him and just, like, wanted a threesome or something. Threesomes with men do nothing for me, so there's that, and then—I don't know. I just don't like the idea of being with a woman that he finds, I don't know why, but I don't like it."

"You want a woman all to yourself?" I ask.

"Yeah, maybe, I don't know. Who knows. Honestly, baby, I just don't like a lot of people to that extent. I like people liking me—it never bothers me or creeps me out, I always like it—but I just rarely meet someone I'm attracted to."

"I'm pretty picky myself," I say.

"And besides, I don't want a new woman right now, baby, I'm not ready."

"Why not?"

She laughs shyly, which jolts me. I sit up and my heart drums through my chest in anticipation.

"Because I'm in love with Cora Broussard." She says this softly, deeply.

So often I was suspicious of her words, even right from the beginning, but these words cut right through and melt my heart. The silence hangs in the air, like something tangible we built that spans 2400 miles. We listen to each other breathe. I close my eyes.

"Ashley—" I start, then sputter out. "I can't come to D.C., it's just not possible. Especially in the near future. They took away my passport. Maybe we will see each other again someday, but in the near future, it just can't—I can't—I don't know, Ashley, I don't know what to say. It just can't be."

Her breath quickens and becomes shaky. "I know, baby," she whimpers. "Just know," she says, her voice stronger. "Just know, my baby Cora. Just know that I love you. It was for real. There's no one like you Cora. I don't want to compare—well, my baby, you are certainly unique, and I never felt this way towards anyone before. I won't stop thinking about you. I will always love you. I know that, somehow. If things change in any way, please come find me, okay baby?"

"Okay. If things change, I will remember that." I take a deep breath. "I'm glad we talked. I feel so much better. I felt so confused and angry but now I feel better—except that I miss you more now."

"Good, I'm glad you feel better. I miss you more now too."

We both sigh. I listen to her breath, and the distinctive ruffling sound of sheets through a headset.

"You must really love New California," she says.

"Yeah," I say.

"Yeah?"

"Yeah." I survey the increasingly crowded sidewalks full of a diverse selection of tech workers. The beauty of the bay, the bridge enveloped in fog. The drones fly their coordinated dance above the steep street. The crisp air. "I guess I do."

ABOUT THE AUTHOR

Lisa Renée Julien grew up in Grand Rapids, Michigan but moved to Chicago for college in 2003, and has lived there ever since. She lives with her wife, Caitlin, three-year-old son, Lars, and newborn daughter, Violet. She is currently writing a prequel to Midnight in New California.

When not writing, she works full-time as a product manager in the payments industry. She earned a BFA in photography in 2007, after which she pursued a career in business, and then earned an MBA in 2017, after which she wrote a novel and pursued a career as a writer.

ACKNOWLEDGMENTS

First and foremost, I would like to thank my wife, Caitlin Julien, who provided incredible support and encouragement during the writing process. She helped edit, contribute ideas, provide feedback, and most importantly—continued to encourage me despite the fact that in addition to working full time, finishing up my MBA, and caring for our newborn son, I decided to devote significant amounts of time to this book. Thank you so much. You're much more amazing than any book character I could come up with.

Lars, my son. Somehow, being responsible for, and having great influence over a vulnerable new human life, contributed to the flurry of circumstances that inspired me to finally write a novel, something I had wanted to do for over fifteen years. I already know that you'll turn out to be much more interesting, smart, and intense than Drake and I can't wait to continue to watch you evolve.

Violet, my daughter. It was while writing this book, that I realized the idea of having a biological child filled me with great anxiety. Watching your brother grow up into the sweetest boy possible made me want to make another one like him. You are the happiest most adorable baby I've ever met in my life. I can't wait to watch you grow up and to see what you have to say and what you are interested in.

Mom, Dad, Katie, and Michelle, thank you so much for being a wonderful, supportive, non-dramatic family. Extra thanks to my Mom, who was one of the first people to beta read my first finished draft. I'm incredibly thankful to be from such a great family.

Special thanks to all of the people in online writing forums who helped me with my book. Dave Owens, thanks for your harsh but necessary feedback and encouragement which really helped me bring my book to the next level. Special thanks to all of the people on Fiverr I hired for beta reader feedback and editing. Special thanks to Jacki Dee for doing a great job on the audiobook.

A – You were the first person after my wife to read my very rough unfinished drafts of this book, and I greatly appreciated your support and feedback. Your encouragement of all things in my life during the years that we were close had a profound impact on the trajectory of my life. Thank you.

D – Thank you for your encouragement of my writing career, my other career, and every aspect of my life. Your sweetness, humor, intelligence, strength, and vulnerability, make being close to you an honor.

Lastly, to anyone who reads my book, thank you. I hope you enjoyed it.